THE DON JUANES

THE DON JUANES

BY

MARCEL PREVOST

TRANSLATED BY

JENNY COVAN

NEW YORK
BRENTANO'S
PUBLISHERS

TO
MISS GERALDINE FARRAR
J. C.

FIRST PART

THE DON JUANES

I

WHEN the steel of the cannons and the bronze of the church bells boomed forth the stupendous news of the armistice, sure forerunner of peace, the relief after all these years of war, of ruin and famine and misery, was too great. There came a moment of stupor.

Bowed during fifty-two long months beneath destiny's grim burden, the peoples of the earth had finally become used to its merciless shackles; they traveled into the dark as if drugged or perhaps suffering from hallucinations; nor did they ask where they were going nor how long the journey would last, since they were past the point where they counted its perils and its sorrows. One lived, one died: one day was bearable, the next a nightmare. Why then worry beforehand or remember afterwards, since after all nothing could be changed or helped?

Still here and there a mere gesture of joy would jerk out woodenly, because stronger than everything else is man's will to live life and enjoy life: but these gestures sought the mysterious, the unknown, or perhaps only an excuse to cheer the dying. Pleasure, unless it masqueraded beneath a domino of stark hypocrisy, was almost considered a crime, thus making its thrill both more bitter and more sensuous. Cut away from all the ordinary social rules, mingling races, castes, age and youth in a grim and sadistic saraband, lust used the cloak of pity. At the front blood spotted the hands that were still warm with caresses, and kisses were poisoned by iodoform; behind the lines those who kissed did not dare look each other in the eye, for there adultery seemed almost sacrilege.

Suddenly the heavy ordnance shattered the air, this time to bring a message not of death, but one of life and the joy of life.

Up in the belfries the round maws of the bells clanked their deep notes, not to ring the tocsin or toll for the dead, but to sing the paean of the living. The frightful machine which had dragged the peoples into war stopped all at once; its sudden jolting tremor echoed amidst the tumult. Then all movement stopped; and momentarily the world remained stupefied.

War, a rhythmic flail, an organized, continuous, lasting catastrophe. It killed people. Yet, for five years, it gave them cause and reason for living. It gave to each and every one his place and his pittance. It swept away that hoary turmoil of debts and glory and love, replacing it all with one single thought: the wish not to die. And this war, this supreme moratorium of human will and human liberty, had ceased to function, existed no longer. Once more men were free, responsible; after years of frenzy, once more man remembered his own Self. His individuality, his personality of yesterday which he had either forgotten or denied, returned. It seized him again. Man had been all the world; now man was once more only himself. And after that first reaction of stupor came anguish; the anguish of slaves too suddenly freed, of night-birds winging too suddenly aslant the brazen light of day.

Everybody was free; too free, without that guardianship to which he had become accustomed. Furthermore, this freedom was a freedom amidst ruins. Ruins of

houses, of factories and workshops; ruins of enterprises
and ancient patrimonies; ruins, too, of what, in one's
home, could not be repaired with brick and stone. Relationship, friendship, love—the war had destroyed it
all with the blindness of its fury; or had soldered together
incongruous elements. And now, the war over, these
elements *remained put, joined,* just as, during the war,
after a bombardment, one had seen some precious art
object deeply embedded in clay and muck.

Suddenly freed, they were appalled by the enormous
work of reparation and reorganization. How were they
going to set about doing it—with their mutilated hands,
their weary, tired arms, their brains that still echoed the
sound and sorrow of bursting shells? And then—
this campaign of peace—who was going to command it? Which general-in-chief was going to draw
up the plans and organize the staff? Where were
the generals in charge of brigades, of army corps,
of divisions, of all those formations tapering down
to the squadron? Where was the sergeant who would
say: "Hey—you there—get busy with that trowel!
And you over there—the stones!" And would there
be a civilian commissariat and supply column to
furnish quarters and tools, to serve you wherever you
worked, as if by wizardry, with hot soup at the proper
hour? Yesterday's generals commanded no longer, but
yesterday's soldiers had not yet forgotten to obey blindly,
without responsibility of their own. The old formula
was still on their lips: "I should worry!" But yesterday the phrase had been heroic; to-day it was cowardly.
They had turned the trick during their long agony.
Now, the storm over, they would carry on. Doubtless.
After all, could the future be worse than the past? Of
course not! All right then. . . .

And with all constructive resolve thrown to the dogs,

without sustained or organized effort, carelessly, the people adventured into peace with the fatalism and the irresponsibility of war. Only the one element which had coördinated the various efforts of war had disappeared: the discipline in the face of danger. They were like schoolboys who, the lesson over, run out into the yard, not, at once, to play some organized game, but just to jump about and shout and laugh. So, free once more, the people jumped about and shouted and laughed. Since the beginning of time man has celebrated liberty with the same gestures: noise, riot, caresses. And the greater, the more all-embracing this freedom, the greater the hysteria of joy. In spite of the war-bred hate which still fermented in the back-cells of half-maddened brains, the alcohol of victory intoxicated the victors. Came a paroxysm of reaction. Incredible excitement seized the crowds, almost bodily. On the strength of an obscure, half-digested peace treaty, they dreamt of the spoils of victory, the looting of the vanquished foe; in fact, everybody's pockets were crammed with paper money that had not yet commenced to depreciate. Therefore: no shackles, no restraint—soldiers on furlough—spending recklessly! The frenzy of spending grew bloated; it became tainted with the sheer frenzy of free motion, of eating and drinking, of physical passion. And if anywhere there were places where one could give way to that triple obsession and where, furthermore, one could spend money like water, cynically, madly, with a gesture of bravado, these were the places to rush to.

And there were such places. *"Les dancings."* Everybody rushed there.

"Les dancings." The very name was exotic. It was not French in the slightest degree. Dance, like music and poetry, is essentially national, part of a people's racial inheritance. Our dances are thoroughly French; they

have come down to us from the days of the Kings of
France. The provinces, conservative, old-fashioned,
have preserved them. They are soundly national in
measure and step. They are orderly and decent,
rhythmical without over-accentuation. Bodies seldom
touch, and then but briefly. The steps and attitudes
express politeness rather than desire. Our dances are
square, not round, from the pavane of the courtiers to
the quadrille of the country people. Even the mazurkas
and waltzes which Vienna and Warsaw sent us during
the Nineteenth Century had to adapt themselves to the
French taste, lost some of their sensuality and gained in
modesty; and yet, even after they were changed, they
never became really popular. Our provinces kept the old
square dances; and, on Sundays, from the gorse-covered
countryside of the Bretagne to the vine-clad hills of the
South, boys and girls danced more in groups than by
couples and more often held each other by the hand than
around the waist.

The war changed everything, leveled everything, and
mingling khaki uniforms and blue capes in life as well
as in death, it now transformed all these people into a
single instrument for pleasure. The soft thrill of new
dances was revealed to the French who congenitally did
not care for dancing, but who in these new dances tasted,
even more than the foreigners, a poignant sensuality. It
was no longer the discreet embrace of the waltz where
the thighs hardly touch, but that of a man and a woman
whom desire throws into each other's arms. The woman,
conquered, offers herself with body tense and head thrown
back, while the man, victorious and thrilling to his
victory, drags her along with short steps, his feverish
lips seeking the little white ear half-hidden by moist
locks. Imported from North or South America, fox-
trot or tango, shimmy or paso-doble, rhythm of sighs or

rhythm of thrills, it was after all the same thing; it pictured only an episode in the battle of the sexes, framed between the first steps side by side and the moment of possession. And it was the very thing needed by these people whom the war had decimated and crushed and enervated, by the two sexes who for five long years had been separated by a wall of earth and iron and fire, and who now once more found each other, eager to meet, to embrace, to kiss. They needed a public symbol of their new freedom, their joy, their passions once more achieved. It was to them both a challenge into the teeth of fate and a clarion call of revenge.

"*Le dancing*" became this symbol, with its dry champagne and its spiced food, with its orchestra of frenzied negroes, with its arrogant luxury of furs, pearls and diamonds, with its cynical mingling of courtezans and decent women, both half-naked, of famous men of the world and young ruffians dressed in the same style; "*le dancing*" with all that it meant, openly advertised and brazen, in triumphant licentiousness, in money thrown out of windows, in excessive and discordant noises, in crude frankness, in a very orgy of public neurosis: the revenge of love over death.

Towards the middle of December 1919, *Celtic's* was the most fashionable "dancing" in Paris. Such fashions, like all the other fads of a delirious world, never last long. On a sudden whim a place would become the rage, be the center of all that bizarre Paris night life where real society mingled with war profiteers, artists, professional dancers and chorus girls. Night after night this motley band would foregather there to dine and dance and flirt. Foreigners would follow suit; too, the parvenus and idle rich and couples whom dance had thrown together in their hunt after extravagant pleasures. For a fortnight it was all the rage. One had to book one's table ten days in advance. The owner could charge tenfold for admission fee and food, sell champagne at 150 francs a bottle and grapes at 500 francs a small basket; could turn away each night enough people to fill another restaurant. Then, suddenly, the people would become bored with the decorations, the room, the cooking, the music, the location. A new "dancing"—different from the other or exactly alike, it did not matter—would become the fashion. The first would sink into neglect and bankruptcy, while, in its turn, the new place would be invaded by the festive throng, would be showered with gold. A mere caprice, hysterical, feverish. . . .

Thus, toward the middle of December 1919, *Celtic's* was the fad of the moment.

Celtic's was a cellar, tucked away in an ordinary business block, next to the great boulevards. One reached it from the outside through a narrow vestibule, level with the street, whence a long staircase curved down twistingly. There were brazen white and gold lights; balconies surrounding a sort of patio on stucco pillars; tables framing the central dance space which was sunk into the floor so that it resembled a dry swimming-pool. This time the crowd had not made a bad choice. Besides the fact that it was a cellar, reminiscent of old drinking-bouts, the arrangement was ingenious. The diners could see everything that was going on. At one glance they could take in everything: the frenzied musicians in full evening dress, the dancing couples contorting their bodies in the dry pool, the tables with the women's breasts rising above them like waxen bouquets, and chiefly the winding staircase with its continuous succession of new arrivals, men in black and white, glimpses of women throwing back chinchilla and sable wraps from scented bodies that seemed undressed rather than dressed. Yes, it was a spectacle even to the cold-blooded observer who did not

care to mix with the crowd. No beauty. Not even
luxury, unless a Pullman car, a palace, or painted props
of the theater are considered luxuries. But there was
something of "class"—the sort of class which the mere
fact of what it costs gives to even worthless objects.
The smallest table for four people represented a supper
at fifty louis d'or. Most of the women who came down
the stairs, walking slowly, wisely, had spent five thousand
francs for the sheathlike dresses that molded their breasts
and legs. People caught a glimpse of jewels, pearl necklaces and diamond sunbursts, speculated as to their price.
"Those jewels cost her a cold million. . . ." "Yes—and
Pergolet charged her 300,000 francs for that fur wrap."
And, like the response in a litany: "So-and-so won three
millions the other day on Galicia. . . ." "So-and-so is
going to be prosecuted—tax fraud—neglected to declare
seven million francs war profits. . . ." The fantastic
figures, of millions and again millions, flew through an
atmosphere blue with cigarette smoke, thick with human
breath and over-sweet, musty scent, torn by the thump of
the drums, the high yells of the brass instruments, the
guttural cries of the musicians, mostly negroes, whose
duty it was to lead this hectic symphony. Yes: a
spectacle, profoundly significant, never to be forgotten
by the keen-eyed spectators, chiefly by those who still
kept in the back cells of their brains a vision of recent
battlefields scarlet with the blood of the attack, of squat,
crumbling villages, of hospitals ensanguined and yelling
with pain, of fallen horses, stark and stiffened in death,
of hecatombs of fighting men, the war-blue of the French
mingling with the war-gray of the Germans, sleeping their
last sleep in moldy moss graves. . . .

.   .   .   .

It was Saturday, the chic evening at *Celtic's*. It was

about half past ten, and amidst the mad riot of bugles and trumpets, of violins and wooden drums and the negroes' jungly yells, late diners smoked and sipped their liquors; the early supper crowd was beginning to file in, eagerly watching the tables and ready to pounce upon them as soon as the diners would get up to go. But the latter did not budge, paying ransom by buying bottles of champagne, often hardly troubling to have them opened.

They seemed young, those women, when they came, but young with the artificial bloom of paint and powder whitening cheeks and breasts. Yet after a few hours in that atmosphere surcharged with the fumes of tobacco and wine and food, the painted bloom of youth drooped and died. Eyes became haggard, necks wilted, grew flabby, loose; the real complexion, pimply, blotched, appeared beneath the coating of rose and ivory. Early in the evening, for instance, one would see at the next table a beautiful creature overflowing with gayety. Dinner over, one turned to take another look—and saw a grim caricature of the same woman. And these women, these sorry flowers, painted and glued, repainted and reglued, were everywhere. The men hardly looked at them—they were only the figurantes, the dumb mummers of a tragicomedy nightly re-acted. Still, here and there, one saw a young girl, a fresh, dewy bud, defying the miasmic atmosphere of the place, the odor of over-spiced food and stale alcohol, even more charming when she regained her table after a dance, little pearls of perspiration jeweling her forehead, her arms, her graceful back, facing insolently the older women's spiteful glances and the cynical lust in the men's eyes.

Too, there were women of that poignant type and age whose beauty had been kept intact by a strong soul, supervised and rigorously disciplined without an orgy of paint and powder, but with the help of sobriety, hygiene, atten-

tion and vigil that never relaxed day or night, disputing
the implacable pin pricks of every minute and every
second, disputing each tiniest flaw and wrinkle, disputing,
finally, the crass and pitiless truth which age writes with
the hardening of arteries, the dimming of bright eyes,
the dull graying of locks. They were like tough-thewed
wrestlers who did not lie, each morning, to their mirrors
nor tried to seek refuge in an illusion of drugs and
carmine and oxygene; who, provident, had commenced
their fight with age before their twenty-first birthday;
who, twenty years later, having spent in this fight more
energy and intelligence than in endeavoring to achieve
riches and glory, showed unwrinkled complexions, bright
eyes, an abundance of hair, faultless teeth, and also that
certain deep emanation of coördinated body and soul, an
ardent promise that did not deign to compete with
brazen, careless youth—glowing with the slightly pathetic
appeal of a beautiful thing that is still untouched, though
already threatened. Like those glorious, deep-red June
roses that are more sumptuous, more charged with
perfume than a tiny bud, but that have already outlived
their rose life and, suddenly, in the first southern wind
or light morning shower, will crumple into shapeless,
nameless things. . . .

It was the hour when dancing began. More than ever
the central space seemed like a dry pool packed with
swimmers. The people, those who danced as well as
those who did not, could be easily divided into two
categories.

There were numbers of curious, of passers-by, of all
those men and women, who do not really belong to Paris
but, come to Paris and the "dancings" of Paris as though
to a spectacle, understand about as much of what it all
means as the average foreigner at a French theater.

There were others: foreigners, the sort who are neither accepted by their native society, nor will, by the same token, ever be accepted by that of other lands; newly rich, too rich as well as too new; cousins from the provinces; solid French bourgeois who have dropped in just to see once and for all what such a place is like, rather frightened and cross, already pronouncing definite and draconic judgments that will give them food for conversation for months to come; young couples eager for adventure, newly-fledged in the life of business or pleasure; sharp-featured, weasel-eyed couples who watch the psychological moment, who will grasp their chance as soon as they see it, and, perhaps to-morrow, perhaps, to-night, will cease being mere spectators and join the ranks of the active participants in this nightly show.

There are many of these actors. Not only the young professionals, rather too young, too handsome, too elegant, who, paid by the week, mix with the dancers and bring a certain amount of rhythm and discipline into the crowd's mad, incongruous riot. Not only the mannequins with their perfect figures, their audacious dresses, tripping tango after tango, employees of the restaurant fully as much as the headwaiter and the jazz band. There are also the star performers: Whip, the cartoonist who resembles a genial jockey; his chum, the editor-in-chief of the greatest literary daily; his other chum, the proprietor of a huge department store on the left side of the Seine and main stockholder in half a dozen periodicals. There are the three "chickens" whom they are entertaining—"larding" as they put it in the slang of the boulevards—one a scout for modern plays, the second a dancer in the Russian ballet, the third a simple debutante, but already labeled as a comer by the gay world. There is at a larger table which fills a whole corner, that African prince whose enormous and majestic paunch is ludicrously out of keeping with his European trousers and dinner jacket, and whose bronzed face, topped by kinky hair, rises incongruously above white collar and shirt and black necktie. His three sons are with him, going and coming between their table and the dry pool. They are lean, brown, good-looking, exciting the curiosity of the women who are brazen in their advances. At the prince's right sits the Grand-Duchess Hilda von Finsburg, a German by birth. But peace made her a Dane as it did her husband, Grand-Duke Otto, who, by the way, was always francophile and who at the time of the war preferred voluntary exile to fighting against France. Hilda is tall and lean, with arms and legs that are too long and too powerfully muscled, a narrow, hatchet-like face that shows no age, blue, rather dimmed eyes, a coarse mane of an exquisite shade of russet. Hilda, for all her German birth, is Parisian, just like the African potentate, and her predilection for artists, chiefly musicians, made her famous long before the war. Peace signed, she returned at once to Paris for which she longed with all her heart—*"Ich schwäre für Paris,"* as she put it—and the "dancings" drew her immediately into their mad vortex. There she is, held close in the arms of her dance partner, Ramon Genaz, who is vaguely suspected by all the world yet receives the best society in his small villa at Passy. The African potentate's other guests are also Parisians, even this middle-aged Norman gentleman who earns a precarious livelihood by supervising the renting and decorating of apartments for prominent half-breeds and by supplying the newspapers with social items about the latter; even Madame de Verzieux, an authentic countess, of ancient Angevin nobility; even that aviator who is so conceited that he refuses to wear the ribbon of his war cross; even Mercueil, that modern "Tallemant des Réaux," that professional chronicler and teller of anecdotes, here, as he says, to "get documentary evidence," and who, in his very eyes that slowly take in everything, in the deep wrinkle across the forehead and his negligent habit of forgetting the others and leaning across the table regardless of his neighbors' comfort, shows indeed that he is here for professional reasons only, to observe.

At a table, diagonally across from the prince's, are other star performers in Paris' human comedy: those four women, superbly gowned, with no male chaperon except a second lieutenant in sky-blue uniform, very evidently the son of one of them, a young-looking, gray-haired woman whom he resembles strikingly. Two of the other women have the beauty of roses too fully blown, afraid of the mid-day sun as well as of morning rain; they are different in figure and coloring, the one a tall brunette, the other small and red-haired. The fourth woman is of a pronounced Semitic type of countenance, with beautiful neck and shoulders that are marvelously young, a skin dead-white beneath her paint, a black, extravagantly large head-dress coming deep down over her eyes that are like those of an Ouled-Nail, a Saharan desert dancer. The headwaiters flit about the table, even more subservient and attentive than they are to the prince, and presently, according to the latest custom, a number of younger men join the party: friends, dancing-men, who have been invited to drop in toward the end of dinner. They dance in turn with Camille Englemann, the woman with the black head-dress, daughter of a former president of the Crédit Général who died during the war, now a shrewd business woman who for years has been the real manager of the bank; and with Madame de Trévoux, mother of the young lieutenant who dances nearly exclusively with the tiny, exquisite red-haired doll. "She looks rather like the knight on a chess board," Whip, the cartoonist, had said about her a moment earlier. All eyes follow the dancing couple, while her name is being whispered by everybody, Parisians as well as strangers. She is Berthe Lorande, famous not only for her gracefulness, her wit, her extraordinary eloquence and the mystery that surrounds her intimate life, but also because of her writings which, published at long intervals in four tiny volumes, a man's Christian name the title of each, have put her on a level with the greatest living French novelists.

The fourth woman has not moved. She is the most beautiful of them all. She observes with a distracted air the crowded restaurant that gradually, dinner over, is losing all semblance of orderliness and beginning to look like a casino or the promenoir of a music-hall. Tables, wrecked and spotted, broken glasses, napkins thrown pell-mell; intimate whisperings in the aisles and on the stairs; dancing couples in the dry pool. The air grows heavy, thick, feverish; voices are raised to compete with the strident clamor of the jazz band; it seems like some methodical orgy of sound, like the blaring riot of a dozen country-fair orchestras. Motionless, paying hardly any attention to the young men who flutter about, the tall woman is now alone at table, the cynosure of all eyes. But it does not embarrass her, nor does it please or amuse her. One of her beautiful arms, the wrist encircled by a pearl bracelet, rests on the table cloth, while the other arm trails languorously, a half-smoked cigarette held between the exquisite patrician fingers. But for the modern note expressed in the cigarette, Countess Anderny reminds you of the Ladies Waldgrave, and Mrs. Bradyl, whose noble characters, calm attitudes, and classic, dignified features have been immortalized by Reynolds' brush. Only, the English painter's models radiate a profound peace of soul, a serene contentment with life, while Countess Anderny's eyes flash like the points of a dagger beneath her chiseled, hooded brows; her breast rises and falls to her heart's quickening rhythm; her ardent, hectic soul shows occasionally in the expression of her face and the attitude of her body. Mercueil has left the African potentate's table without a word of apology. He half hides behind one of the stucco pillars; stares fixedly at Countess Anderny. He records in his algebraic, chronicling brain the curve of her arms, the fullness of her breast, the corsage of black tulle ornamented with midnight-blue jet, the pure and generous face, fully rounded, but not coarse or heavy, the clear depth of her eyes. "Reynolds," he thinks at once—and this quick comparison, too, will lodge in his retentive brain until he will have need of it. Attentively, he watches her. She looks at the spectacle with a sort of disdainful curiosity; smiles a casual greeting to some acquaintance in the crowd; exchanges a few polite banalities with men who bow over her hand and kiss it; then, rather hesitatingly, her glance centers on a table, on a level with her own and not far distant, occupied by four people, three men and one woman.

Mercueil knows three of the four, precisely those three whom Countess Anderny can see, full face or profile. Each in a different way these three, too, are star performers in Paris' tragi-comedy. There are Mr. and Mrs. Saulnois. The woman is good-looking and graceful, with a certain childlike appeal beneath her growing maturity, dressed with faultless elegance in black crêpe without jewels, depending for sole ornament on her glorious, ash-blond mane of hair. The man is tall and lean, dark-blond and slightly bald, very small gold-framed glasses accentuating his pale, intellectual face. His manners are charming, his tailor excellent. Instinctively Mercueil runs over his list of Parisian types:

"Saulnois, professor at the College of France, philosopher dancing attendance to the rich and the upper middle-classes, gifted writer and speaker, rather too facile, rather spoiled by success.   Very popular in society, thanks to his charming wife, *née* Jeanne de Gueyse, who has introduced him everywhere.   She knows how to do it, the clever little minx, and he really should burn a nice, fat candle before this Madonna of his—as beautiful as Corysandre and as faithful as Penelope in spite of the husband's escapades.   After all—perhaps she doesn't know about them.   But who is that keen, elegant young chap who sits between them?   I know his silhouette, his pointed profile—ah,—it's Guilloux.   Maurice de Guilloux, attached to our Vienna embassy before the war, honorable conduct during the war, and now a big-wig in the Reparation Commission or the League of Nations—I forget which—at all events busy with one of those profitable substitutes that thrive on a nation's ruins.   No doubt—he is trying to have an affair with our little Jeanne Saulnois . . . nothing doing, my boy!   Few of the girls here are what you might call of cast-iron virtue—perhaps Madame Saulnois is the only one—just your bad luck that you had to fall for her!   And the other young fellow, dressed in a prehistoric dinner jacket—with that ravaged face beneath a mop of hair that looks like a cap of astrakhan fur?   Rotten barber—rotten tailor!   Rotten bad form, too . . . half thoroughbred, half Bohemian without gayety!   Wonder who it can be?   Still, Countess Anderny seems fascinated by his back—stares at him—sees nobody else.   Too, all the 'chickens' who pass rather ogle him—seems to give them a thrill.   Funny—I can see nothing attractive in him with his astrakhan head, his badly tied necktie, his poorly laundered collar . . . perhaps some provincial professor, one of Saulnois' friends—?   Still—he seems very thick with Guilloux. . . ."

At the table occupied by the Saulnois, Guilloux and the strange young man with the astrakhan hair, Countess Anderny's persistent eagerness had not passed without comment.

"Guilloux, it's you she is after," jested Jeanne Saulnois.

"Oh no! She hardly acknowledged my discreet bow when I came in. Better watch your husband—that eminent professor who once taught my young mind. Albine Anderny is just the sort to fall for a philosopher. This type must be missing from her collection."

"Oh, I know her," said Saulnois. "I met her several times at Berthe Lorande's house."

"You allow your husband to visit Berthe Lorande?" asked Guilloux, looking meaningly at Jeanne Saulnois.

Jeanne did not seem to notice the words' slurring suggestion. She looked tenderly at her husband. "I let him see whomever he pleases, especially a woman of genius like Mme. Lorande. Anyway," she added, "they say she's harmless."

"It's a rumor that she herself has spread," grumbled Guilloux. "Mme. Récamier in a modern edition. Very clever! I once knew a lady in London who, in league with a handsome gynecologist, persuaded her husband that a quarter of an hour of passion would kill her."

The guest with the ravaged face, old-fashioned clothes and the too bushy hair, who had listened silently to the conversation, stopped scratching the tablecloth with his silver knife and looked up.

"Is Countess Anderny inclined to be gay?"

Guilloux pretended to be shocked.

"Oh! my poor Vaugrenier, what a way of putting it! Gay? The lawful wife of the late Count Anderny, a Moldavian magnate, and formerly a diplomat, like myself! The daughter of Pierre de Mestrot, of an excellent

Périgord family, almost from the same part of France as
Mme. Saulnois here!"

"Yes, and even a relation," interrupted Jeanne.   "Our
grandmothers were first cousins."

"Oh!   I didn't know that. . . ."

"Briefly, a well-born woman, once happily married, to-
day a widow, clever, an artist—she has painted some
charming landscapes—and who is received by nearly all
classes of society."

"Nearly," interrupted Saulnois, "is right."

"Well," replied the diplomat, "nearly is the thing that
really counts. As for the group that keeps itself apart,
nobody cares to join it. When twenty people place five
hundred in quarantine, it's they who are really
quarantined."

"Even in this vast, easy-going group which constitutes
the social world of Paris," concluded Saulnois, this time
addressing Roger Vaugrenier in the peremptory tone
which even mundane professors acquire through habit
of speaking without being contradicted, "Countess
Anderny is not considered exactly gay. Why—she isn't
mercenary, and has only discreet affairs. But she is outside the pale of everyday morality. There is a number
of women like that in Paris, and we have a few specimens
here to-night: the Grand-Duchess Hilda, this Camille
Englemann who is a sort of Catherine the Second or a
Queen Elizabeth of finance, endowed with a man's brain,
energy, temperament; . . ."

"Berthe Lorande," cut in Guilloux, half-affirmatively,
half-questioningly.

Saulnois protested dryly. "The people who say so
know it's slander. Let them name one single man who
has been Berthe Lorande's lover."

"All right, all right!" from Guilloux. "You are better
informed than I."

And he looked again at Jeanne Saulnois in a correct but bitingly ironic way. The latter laughed, with a flash of her fine teeth.

"What have you against Mme. Lorande? I find her very sympathetic, because she admires Albert sincerely and sings his praises eloquently everywhere. Anyway, enough of this. We are exasperating Roger Vaugrenier. He has a Bolshevik-Puritan soul! In two minutes he's going to explode!"

The young man with the astrakhan hair raised his fine, ravaged head. His eyebrows, like his hair, were too thick and under their bushy curve his brown eyes shone like agate. These beautiful, sparkling eyes gave a youthful appearance to the entire face, as did the tender mouth with the clean-shaven lips, contrasting sharply with the premature wrinkles of the forehead and especially with the long, deep furrows across his cheeks. The complexion was sallow and bilious, the teeth strong and healthy beneath the thick lips which looked as though they had been rouged. Was he good looking? All men answered "no" with sincerity. But this strange face did not fail to attract the attention of every woman.

He replied to Mme. Saulnois in a quiet, slightly constrained voice:

"I—explode? Because of these old hens? They can cackle and preen their feathers to their hearts' content. It does not disturb me in the least. On the contrary, I like it! Everything I see here, all you tell me—orgies, recklessness, the crashing down of conventional morals! Why—what else have people fought for? Guilloux can tell you that I foresaw all this when he and I were studying philosophy in trench 307. Isn't that right, Guilloux? When that dunce of a lieutenant Septier who died, would assure us that heroism, self-sacrifice, brotherhood and decency would reign as soon as peace was declared, and

that our humble lives were none too dear a price to pay
for this golden era—what did I tell him? I would say:
'Fool! You, I, we all fight so that to-morrow's generation may be slightly more rotten, closer to the dung
heap than yesterday's. The survivors of every catastrophe invariably go insane!' And it's happened. Just
look!"

With a simultaneous 'movement of chin and hand, he
indicated the hectic scene in the basement of the *"Celtic."*
Under the stimulus of wine and music, little by little the
veneer of good-breeding which still persisted after the
first few dances, was beginning to crack and peel. An
intimate disorder hovered about the tables. Half empty
champagne bottles thrown into ice pails, withered flowers,
scarfs flung aside, newspapers, forgotten meshbags, cigar
butts smoldering in ash-trays. The people who did not
dance crowded the stairway to watch those who did.
Women sat on the steps, heedless of the provocative
appeal of their silk clad, crossed legs. The dry pool was
so crowded with couples that the stamping could no
longer be called dancing. With the growing frenzy of
the orchestra, this tornado of clasped humans took on
more and more the aspect of a frantic mob.

And what an incongruous mob! Couples, the men in
business suits, the women in shirtwaists and skirts, danced
side by side with others dressed by Poiret and Bender.
A fat, bald-headed, mustached man towed about a little
shop girl whose hair brushed against his chin. Jean
de Trévoux, his arms encircling Berthe Lorande's elfin
figure, rubbed elbows with a suspicious-looking boy, too
young, too good-looking, who clasped a tall, emaciated
woman with the face of a ghoul and hysterical eyes.
Coarse male hands with stubby nails kneaded fat women's
spines. Instinctively all heads were raised in search of
purer air. Some couples fled this inferno of foul breaths

and sweat and made towards the less crowded balconies
or the empty tables.

There, chairs drawn close together, bending towards
each other, one guessed they were continuing in a breathless tête-à-tête, the conversation conceived in the tango's
sultry sway. Thus Camille Englemann and her partner.
He was well-bred, elegant. His attitude betrayed both
contentment and voluntary respect. She held him spellbound with her golden stare, and seemed to fathom his
soul. Thus were the Grand-Duchess Hilda and Ramon
Genaz. More familiar and less concerned with appearances, these two had deserted of their own accord the
prince's table for one on the balcony, where they were
being pointed out, she brushing his tuxedo-clad shoulder
with her firm, bare flesh, and from time to time, caressing
with her beautiful fingers the Spaniard's small, chubby
dark hands.

The head waiters kept on popping bottles, pouring out
the amber froth, receiving disdainfully sheafs of 100
franc notes which paid for the simplest meal. The
negroes beat their drums, blew staccato brasses, banged
the piano keys like a jockey whipping his horse forward
the winning post; the acid fumes of champagne mingled
with the honeyed odor of Egyptian cigarettes and perfume
clinging to hair, fans, scarfs, also with the smell from
women's arm-pits where occasionally a stubborn growth
of hair would stipple the shaven skin.

"This," concluded Vaugrenier, "is why lieutenant
Septier had his guts blown out one night in shelter No.
21. This is why I had a tendon split in two at Louvain.
And you, Guilloux, lucky devil, this is why you were
gassed at Montdidier, thereby being forever deprived of
the beautiful baritone voice which was your pride. All's
well!"

His words dropped into silence. The orchestra had

suddenly stopped playing; the dancing floor was being cleared by orders of the professionals who directed the entertainment. Grand-Duchess Hilda, followed by Ramon Genaz, returned to the prince's table. She greeted in passing the Countess Anderny in the polyglot jargon which she affected:

"Chère! You look ravishing! Don't bother about watching the performance this, oh—how shall I put it?—brace of whirling Tanagrettes! Mr. Ramon Genaz, a great artist, *ach! Wunderbar!*" she made a gesture of introduction, "assures me that they are mere puppets, paid like these jazzing negroes. You will soon see Mr. Genaz dance with La Vitzina at his home, his garden in Passy, for a chosen few. . . . Ramon, you must invite the Countess!"

"Madame may rest assured. I would be delighted," said Genaz, bowing.

Albine did not thank him.

"That dear Mme. Lelievre isn't with your Highness to-night," she said. "Is she ill?"

"Yes. A touch of the flu, *la pauvre!* Besides, she is bored stiff with dancing. Ramon! They've started. *Komm schnell!*"

And without taking leave of Albine, with the impertinence of a queen, she dragged her Spaniard towards the performance which "wasn't worth seeing."

An usher was exhibiting at the end of a stick a poster with the word "Attraction" across it in big red capitals. Obediently, the dancers returned to their seats. The head waiters used the opportunity to solicit imperiously more orders for champagne. While the orchestra was beginning to strum, a couple appeared on the dancing floor; both professional dancers and in addition to that, both models for tailor and dressmaker, respectively. With the nervous suppleness of tame panthers, they

offered to the curious gaze of the onlookers the spectacle
of their voluptuous art, the woman undulating like a
scarf in the man's arms, and, in turn, coiling, clinging,
whirling, gliding, flashing like a flame.

They were applauded, watched for a time. Then the
crowd grew indifferent and, while they continued their
performance, conversation was again resumed around the
tables where fresh bottles were being opened.

Countess Anderny's table had retrieved all its guests,
first Camille Engelmann who had introduced her dancing partner: "Mr. Max Dutrier, chief of the bond
department at my bank." Sitting slightly apart, she continued her conversation with him, her eyes prodding him
ceaselessly. Jean de Trévoux had resumed his seat
between his mother and Berthe Lorande. Suddenly
grown pale and without trying to hide his misery, he
watched the novelist smile across the floor at Albert
Saulnois who bowed to her. Berthe became aware of it.
She stopped smiling abruptly, and flashed a look of such
ardent tenderness and such utter abandon to the blue
officer, that a wiser man would have felt less jealous.
She held him under this glance just long enough to make
certain that he was once more docile and enslaved. Then
she addressed Countess Anderny who had hardly shifted
her position since the table had become crowded once
more. She had lit another cigarette. Apparently indifferent to what was going on around her, she was still
watching Jeanne Saulnois' table. Berthe Lorande seized
this opportunity to dispel entirely the blue lieutenant's
doubts.

"Albine darling," she said in her beautiful, filmy contralto, "I implore you, do not disturb the peace of my
friend Saulnois's household. His wife is exquisite. She
is faithful, and he, they say, is not without his
weaknesses—"

"I am not looking at him," answered Albine, her face glowing so radiantly that for a second she seemed to grow young. "Imagine," she added turning to Trévoux and Berthe, "for more than fifteen minutes I've been exercising vainly this influence of the distant stare which so many physicians proclaim infallible. I've fervently wished to make this badly dressed young man sitting opposite Mme. Saulnois turn around my way. . . ."

"The man with the astrakhan hair?" questioned Mme. de Trévoux. And having scrutinized him through her lorgnette, she murmured:

"His profile seems interesting."

"Very interesting," echoed Albine. "It is energetic. The constant change from immobility to gesticulation shows a harassed temperament. But this isn't the only reason I've wanted to hypnotize him. Berthe, you know the maddening feeling of having already seen a man or a woman, somewhere, and being unable to remember where. Well, then, this crop of woolly hair, these square shoulders and chest tapering down to the waist, this rapid switching from immobility to exaltation—I've already seen it all. But where? And when?"

Again the orchestra stopped playing. The professional couple bowed to the plaudits of the crowd. The bushy-haired young man with the broad shoulders and narrow waist rose and bent forward to see the dancers. Before resuming his seat he turned around, and in spite of his professed contempt for the crowd, he glanced curiously at the row of tables back of him.

"Oh!" murmured the Countess. "I remember. . . ."

"Some one you know?" asked Mme de Trévoux.

"Very slightly. A hospital acquaintance, when I was at the Flanders front."

"When you were Mrs. Sanders?" said Berthe smiling.

"When I was Mrs. Sanders."

The jazz band struck up again. Berthe whirled away with Trévoux. Mme. de Trévoux was whisked off by Dutrier, while Camille Englemann glided on the arm of the latter's friend, a well-dressed young man whose youthful face contrasted strangely with his grayish hair, lending it an appearance of being powdered. Dutrier had presented him as "Mr. Laurent Sixte, of the Banque des Vosges." There was vivid curiosity as the prince was finally dragged into the dry pool by Mme de Verzieux, and, shown off as by a miniature impresario, was stamping out of time with the music while he jostled the amused couples about him.

"You aren't going to refuse me this shimmy?" asked Guilloux of Mme. Saulnois.

The latter glanced inquiringly at her husband who nodded his approval. Roger Vaugrenier remained alone at the table with Saulnois. The latter's eyes followed his wife and the diplomat gliding across the floor.

"Nice chap, don't you think?" he asked Guilloux, looking at Vaugrenier.

The clamor of the jazz band, sustained by the deep notes of a sinister bugle, became so violent for a moment that Vaugrenier was compelled to wait before answering.

"There are many things in him that I don't like," he replied in his usual tone of hostile contradiction. "He is a snob; he is ambitious, and an opportunist. But he is intelligent, and he has nerve. Also, war friendships, I believe, are even stronger than college friendships. Several months in succession he and I were constant companions."

"You were assistant physician, Guilloux told me."

"Yes. War called me out just when I had completed my first year of hospital service."

"But how did you happen to live with Guilloux who was lieutenant in the artillery?"

"Our first-aid quarters were next door to his battery. So we messed together."

A head waiter interrupted their conversation. Somewhat hesitatingly and mispronouncing the name, he murmured:

"Mr. Vandrenier?"

"Yes."

"There's a lady asking Mr. Vandrenier to please come and speak to her. The lady over there—sitting alone at the table in back of you, sir."

"Countess Anderny?" asked Saulnois.

"Yes, sir. She begs Mr. Vandrenier to come to her table. She says she knows you, sir."

The army doctor's swarthy, bilious complexion turned brick red, and beneath the quivering lids the eyes seemed like glowing embers that had suddenly been stirred into flame.

"Tell the lady that I do not know her and that . . ."

Saulnois interrupted him by putting his hand on his arm.

"All right," he said to the head waiter, "the gentleman will come. "Pardon me," he added, turning to Vaugrenier while the head waiter left. "You will of course do as you wish. But Mme. Anderny is a society woman personally known to us all. There is no reason whatsoever why after having met her previously you should insult her by ignoring her request."

"I've never met her before."

"So much more reason," said Saulnois, his eyes gleaming amusedly behind their gold rimmed glasses. "The Countess Anderny sends Doctor Vaugrenier a message through a head waiter saying she would like to speak to him," he said to his wife and Guilloux who were coming back, their dance finished. "He ought to go, eh?"

"Why, of course!" exclaimed Guilloux, "Go on, Roger,

don't make a fool of either yourself or ourselves. Hurry up. It's going to be very amusing."

"Guilloux is right," added Jeanne Saulnois in answer to Vaugrenier's questioning look.

He went reluctantly. The Saulnois and Guilloux watched him approach with awkward impertinence the table where the countess had remained alone, bow coldly, exchange a few words standing, and finally, obeying her gesture, sit down hesitatingly. She was speaking, relating something; and, little by little, Roger's strained resistance appeared to relax, and he seemed to become interested.

"Funny chap," whispered Guilloux. "He isn't handsome nor elegant, he's barely polite, yet all the women fall for him. He'd have adventures galore, if he weren't so unbearable and full of scruples into the bargain."

"Well, I like your friend very much," said Jeanne Saulnois. "He seems a little moody, rather mad, but intelligent and high-strung. We adore this type."

"There you are!" said Guilloux, affecting a comic resignation. "He's got you too, with his Solomon-like airs and his lofty words. He annoys me. I'll entertain that bird in male company only, from now on!"

Again the three watched the scene at the other table. The countess was no longer monopolizing the conversation. Roger, less taut, more at ease, made lengthy replies and at times grew animated. Berthe Lorande and the Trévoux discreetly did not go back to their table and instead, joined Camille Englemann, framed between Duttrier and his friend Sixte. The room was beginning to empty, because all night permits at that time were seldom granted to dance halls.

"Is she going to keep him till the place closes?" grumbled Guilloux, whose lungs had become delicate since he had been gassed, and who, concerned about his health, always tried to be home before midnight. "What the devil can they be saying to each other?"

"Yes," repeated Jeanne thoughtfully. "What can they be saying to each other, and why did that clever friend of yours pretend he did not know her?"

And here is what they actually did say to each other.

Countess Anderny looked straight into Roger's blue eyes and, extending her right hand which was bare and ringless, said:

"You do not want to recognize me, doctor?"

He recognized her at once and, since he had steeled himself to meet a stranger he now felt lost. He murmured:

"Mrs. Sanders?"

"Yes, Mrs. Sanders, your head nurse at the Jellicoe Hospital, the one who put the first-aid bandages about your split tendon. The first ones only, for I left the hospital shortly afterwards."

"But I was told a moment ago—"

"You were told that my name is Countess Anderny? It's true, indeed. Acting on the suggestion of my British chief, I called myself Mrs. Sanders at the hospital. I found it very convenient. There's nothing romantic about it, and many British society women did the same. Sanders was simply—well—my 'nom de guerre.'"

She interrupted herself, laughed. Her laughter was youthful, as were her eyes.

"Ah! I recognize once more the wicked air you used to affect at Jellicoe. Why are you wrinkling those black eyebrows of yours? I happened to see you, I called you over to say hello and find out how you are, that's all. If it annoys you, I release you. . . ."

She grew a bit more serious, more formal. Vaugrenier saw the ridiculousness of his position. He protested.

"Why, Madame, I am on the contrary extremely happy. . . ."

"Then sit down and tell me what has happened to you. I lost track of you completely since I left Jellicoe, three days after your arrival."

"Yes, I remember," replied Roger whose features relaxed and who, childlike, jumped from constraint to confidence in one breath. "I even asked why our nurse had been replaced."

"That's very nice, and even more so since I had a charming substitute, Miss Ada Briggs."

Roger hesitated to say what was on the tip of his tongue, decided not to, and made a wry face instead.

Albine's clear laughter rang out again.

"Miss Ada Briggs wasn't pretty, but she was devotion personified. As for me, I was obliged to take a few months' rest at the home of my friend Mme. de Trévoux in the South. My strength had given out."

"You aren't looking the same as you did, it's true," said Vaugrenier naïvely.

His face expressed an admiration which did not escape the countess' attention.

"When youth is gone," she replied, "a woman can't overtax herself without paying a penalty for it."

Roger thought: "Youth gone? How old is she, then? Thirty, thirty-five perhaps. She is very beautiful." And something within him was growing impatient with this beauty which was being talked of by everybody, which he had vowed to resist, and which had already subtly encroached upon his freedom.

"And you," resumed Albine, "how did you finish the war?"

Usually so silent and listless except when engaged in a discussion, he was amazed at his pleasure in replying to her and at the ease with which he spoke.

"I was discharged from the hospital at the end of seventeen days," he said. "I was still limping and thought I'd go on limping all my life."

"But you're absolutely well now?"

"Absolutely. Both my legs are equally fit. I got permission to spend my month's furlough at Cornwall, where my tutor lives. I think I mentioned him to you."

"Indeed, I remember. Have you any relatives in England?"

"No, I've no blood relations left since my mother's death. Only this tutor who is my godfather and who brought me up—Doctor Hobson."

"I remember. You speak English perfectly, exactly like an Englishman. And then what?"

"And then I re-enlisted with the third army, at the beginning of 1918. I was in both retreats following Ludendorff's offensives, then in the final drive."

"You weren't wounded again?"

"No. Then I was stationed at Mayence. I've just returned to Paris on a year's leave of absence. I intend to resign from the army and become a simple civilian doctor."

"In Paris?"

"Probably. I don't know."

He looked down, repeated: "I don't know," but immediately looked up again, annoyed with himself.

Albine's reddish-brown eyes gazed at him intently; and her glance instead of troubling, soothed him.

"You haven't changed in the least," she said. "You used to be a little paler. But I'd have recognized you in a thousand, if only by your hair, your eyebrows, your slender waist and those athletic shoulders. You know the Saulnois?" she added after a brief pause, abruptly changing the conversation.

"Only since this evening. Maurice de Guilloux in-

vited me to meet them. We were together in the trenches
in 1915 and 1916."

While he spoke the words his eyes, as though disobey-
ing him, were taking possession of Albine's face, her hair,
her ears, and also of her bare shoulders and arms, and the
décolletage cut so low that it barely covered the rounded
curve of her breasts.

"Oh! well," he thought, "of course she is very beautiful.
But what is it to me?"

"You haven't danced?"

"I never dance," he replied rather brusquely.

Around them was the hubbub of departure. Camille
Englemann, Mme. de Trévoux and Berthe asked for their
cloaks. A soloist played his violin in front of the orchestra. The dance floor was deserted. The head
waiters began to straighten the room.

"Will you drive me home, dear?" Berthe turned to the
Countess.

"Gladly. Let me present Doctor Vaugrenier. I knew
him at the front."

Berthe's blue-green eyes glanced quickly at the doctor's
face and figure, then, for a moment, crossed Albine's
eyes: the interchange of looks lasted no longer than
an electric spark, but it held a question and an answer.
Berthe joined Mme. de Trévoux. Albine, rising, said
to Vaugrenier:

"Now that you've settled down in Paris, come to see
me. I live at 40 rue Raynouard."

"I don't go about much socially," objected Roger,
sulky once more, and very glad at heart to have retrieved
his sulkiness.

"There is no question of social functions. Come
early. Around four o'clock. Not to-morrow. I'll be
away. The day after to-morrow, will you? You'll find
me alone. Good-bye!"

She offered her hand which he shook rather awkwardly, exasperated by this very awkwardness of which he was fully aware. Suddenly, he found himself alone, standing stiffly erect. Escorted by the blue lieutenant and the two financiers, the sealskin, mole and ermine cloaks were disappearing.

"Well! The beautiful Anderny has changed you into a pillar of salt!"

Guilloux tapped him on the shoulder. He added:

"If you feel inclined to spend the night here, go ahead! We are going home."

Already the clustering lights flickered out. Impudent waiters jostled late guests as they piled up the chairs and pushed the tables out of the way. The nauseating atmosphere was saturated with wine, sweat, stale food, and everything was cloaked with smoky dust. The place seemed immense, lonely.

"Let's go!" said Roger.

They joined Saulnois and his wife who were already downstairs waiting for them. Without a word—for the deserted place commanded silence—they all started toward the door. Passing by the orchestra, they saw these black and white demons who a short while ago had led the dance, busily putting away their instruments with a meticulous, bureaucratic care. The violinist slid his instrument into its case, almost tenderly, like a nurse putting a child to sleep. The cornet player emptied the nickeled coils of his brass. Discreetly and repeatedly the pianist struck a key which needed tuning, then dropped the cover with a sound like a plaintive echo reverberating sonorously through the room.

The mob had scattered. The passage between street and lobby was empty. The Saulnois, Roger and Guil-

loux, reaching the winding stairway were greeted by a
gust of wintry gale.

II

In Countess Anderny's oblong dining-room that resembled a Chinese red lacquer box decorated with figures
of burnished gold, hidden radiators kept up an even tem-
perature. The leaping flames of a light wood fire
brightened this December Monday, which in spite of the
absence of snow or rain, was so foggy that its dullish
sheen melted in the ruddy reflection of the log fire on
the walls, the furniture, the faces.

Albine's guests, Berthe Lorande, Guilloux and Jean de
Trévoux, were finishing a rather English luncheon:
poached eggs, tender lamb chops with sauté potatoes, and
vegetables. All this was deftly served by the butler.
A pale-green cloth was spread on the table. The plates
rested on finely hemstitched doilies. There was an excellent white wine and fresh, sparkling water in beautiful
crystal glasses. The house, medium-sized, located in the
rue Raynouard not far from Auteuil, gave an impression
of costly simplicity. No blatant luxury, nothing con-
spicuous; choice pieces of furniture and trinkets, a few
paintings by old masters, a rigid style in appointments
and service.

While peeling apples, bananas, pears and tangerines, the
guests were discussing Camille Englemann. Guilloux,
his fine, vulpine face glowing with the warmth of the
meal, was chattering away as usual:

"Do you remember that first chap she tangoed with,
Dutrier—you know—coarse, rather husky, about forty
years old? Well—she recruited him from the, let us
say, masculine reserves of her own bank. Quick pro-

motion of course; raised from twelve to thirty-eight thousand within seven months. I've had several dealings with him. I've some money deposited at the bank. Intelligent, shrewd. Her other dancing partner, the younger man, better bred, is a certain Laurent Sixte of the Banque des Vosges, a friend of Dutrier's. It's funny, just the same, that a sly fox like Dutrier should be so careless as to introduce a possible rival."

"Are you through discussing my friend Camille?" interrupted Berthe Lorande, putting her gold fork on a plate of Indian porcelain.

"But I'm only saying what everybody already knows . . . even you madame, who are her friend. . . ."

"Precisely because I am her friend I protest against the right which people assume to take inventory of her life and criticise her actions. She danced with one of the department heads of her bank, then with a friend of the latter. What's so extraordinary about it? They were not society men, but their manners were perfectly correct, and she danced with them in an absolutely proper fashion. We know nothing of what happened between them before and after the evening at *Celtic's* and it doesn't concern us."

"Bravo, madame," exclaimed Jean de Trévoux, who was gazing at her with fervent adoration.

He was dressed to-day in civilian clothes, and they endowed his movements with that almost feminine grace which most men no matter how elegant, lack by the time they are thirty.

Albine took no part in the conversation. Guilloux was irritated.

"You may love Camille Englemann," he protested. "Sing her praises. Defend her. But you'll not change the world's opinion about her. Oh! she has splendid qualities! The brain, the energy of a man! I've seen her at work, a young girl of twenty-three, when she had received her diploma of bachelor of sciences and began to help her father, finally supplanting him after his first stroke. She can claim in all fairness that the bank is her creation. And what a creation!"

"And what about her conduct during the war?" insisted Berthe Lorande.

"She was brave, courageous! There too she acted just like a man. In fact, many a man wouldn't have had the spunk that she displayed at Souilly, when she moved her wounded right under the fire of the airplanes and got those two horrible wounds, one in the stomach, the other in the head."

"Well, then?"

"All this doesn't alter the fact that being endowed with the genius, will-power, conscience and courage of a man she also possesses a man's nature. A Messalina? No! But an Elizabeth or a Catherine II. She inspires me with the same mingled feelings of regard, admiration and naïve fear as do those historical man-eaters. When I meet her I bow and make my getaway as quickly as I can."

"Don't be afraid," said Berthe. "You aren't her type."

"I know it and am glad of it. But it's humiliating just the same. That's why I avoid her."

Albine still remained aloof. She dipped her finger tips in the fragrant water of a bowl, wiped them, and rose. With her three guests she passed into a small drawing-room library which was her favorite room. Conversation languished over coffee and amber-colored cigarettes. Guilloux, a bookworm and lover of rare editions and old bindings, was inspecting through the gold wire lattice a charming collection of tiny XVIIIth Century books, all of uniform size but bound differently, in calfskin, parchment and morocco.

"Seems to me this little red Crébillon is new?" he asked the countess.

"Yes. Genaz picked it up for me. He's a marvel. No professional dealer can touch him. All I did was to say to him: 'I am looking for the small Crébillon, 1773 edition.' Four days later I received it."

"Expensive?"

"Of course!"

"That gentleman is a shrewd customer. He has just laid his hands for his own account on a bibelot less charming to look upon and handle than your Crébillon, but which he'll try to keep for himself. Did you notice him Saturday at *Celtic's* while Links and Tanagrette were kicking their legs about in the midst of the crowd's indifference? Notice how cynically he exhibited that grand-duchess of his?"

Berthe and Trévoux had drawn closer together. All four sat down. Purple ashes were smoldering in the grate; outside the day was so bleak that it seemed almost like twilight. This semi-darkness intensified the close intimacy of the little room. Jean de Trévoux, his body touching Berthe's on a narrow settee, asked:

"Who is this Grand-Duchess Hilda?"

"A Schwerin who married the Duke Otto von Finsburg. Isn't that so, Guilloux?" said the Countess.

"Yes," replied Guilloux, "she married him at the age of nineteen. He was then twenty-eight."

And, glad to show off his perfect familiarity with the noble families of Europe, he continued:

"I knew her at the time. She was then a tall, lanky girl with the same horsey nose and the same coarse golden hair, in short, a big, clumsy gawk. But very fine ankles and wrists, a fairly aristocratic carriage and also the witchery of youth. I assure you that she was not bad to look upon. They say that Otto was very much in love with her."

"Oh!" protested Trévoux.

"Yes, young innocent, very much in love. You know nothing about it yet." Trévoux smiled; Berthe Lorande's hand touched his. "Otto was mad about her and, although since then her looks have not exactly improved, she has caused many a heart to skip a beat. By the way, I've been assured that she is at her best when in the correct attire for her favorite athletic sports, a sort of tall adolescent with almost no breasts, flat stomach, and well proportioned muscles. She belongs to that category of women of whom Franklin said that they'd be desirable on condition that you cover their heads with a basket."

"Did Franklin say such horrible things?" asked Berthe, astonished.

"Yes, just about. But let me revert to the grand-duchess' life history for Trévoux's benefit. After the marriage, mutual love. To her, marriage was the revelation of life itself. She adored her Otto so vehemently that, towards the end of the first year, he took advantage of her first pregnancy in order to take up his quarters in the wing of the castle remotest from their bedroom. Motherhood having in no way appeased Hilda's fleshly appetites and the Duke having made her understand that hereafter he would look upon her chiefly as the mother of his children, the thing which every one foresaw happened. . . ."

"Divorce?" asked Trévoux.

"Why no, innocent warrior! She sought a new object for her affections and found him at the duke's own court in the person of the lieutenant in chief of the stables, a bachelor of about thirty. She was brutally faithful to him, and the over-happy officer in turn had no other

means of escaping this excess happiness but to go to
Berlin and marry. The grand-duchess' conviction that
all men are worthless and have no appreciation of
women's hearts dates back to that episode."

"And she calls it her heart!" murmured Berthe.

"She is sincere," replied Guilloux. "It's by far the
most curious side of her nature. She calls herself a senti-
mentalist and, really, she is. She adored her Otto, and
she adored her succeeding—ah—husbands as well. In
every one of them she sought her ideal. She sought it
with her Teutonic sentimentality, with words of dream
and moonlight, with an exchange of lyric love notes, trysts
kept in old ruins, stars to be gazed upon at the same hour
when you're separated. Her sensual emotion harmonizes
perfectly with her poetic emotion. To her the subtle dis-
tinction, so dear to all women, between esoteric love and
physical passion means nothing. After all, she may be
right."

In the shadows Berthe Lorande's and Trévoux' clasped
fingers fell apart, moved by an instinctive embarrassment.
Berthe, her voice somewhat tremulous, questioned the
diplomat who was enjoying the effect of his words.

"What about Duke Otto? What were his feelings in
the matter?"

"He formed a pleasant attachment with a lady of Finsburg society, who had a more moderate appetite than the
duchess. Thanks to this mutual tolerance, peace reigned
in the household, so much so that within ten years' time
four little duchesses were born at the Finsburg palace.
Only one of them has the impudence of not resembling
the duke, but the duchess. Rich, leisured, the couple
travel about a great deal, often together, occasionally
alone. When they come to Paris, the duke leads the traditional life of royalty, while his better half devotes her-

self especially to artists, chiefly musicians. She herself is *musikalish* and plays the harp like a virtuoso. If she can't get musicians, she takes on painters, lastly writers. Literature bores her, she reads little and gets her information on French authors and books through her Luxemburg lady-in-waiting, Mme. Lelièvre, who is said to be her illegitimate half-sister. By the way, Mme. Lelièvre wasn't at *Celtic's* the other evening. But she muddles everything, and with the impertinence of the great, she congratulates this one on the work of that one, and knocks a book to its own author."

The countess, who had seemed listless during Guilloux's speech as well as during luncheon, made an effort to join the conversation.

"I can't understand how this German woman can show her face in Paris these days?"

"I'm being told she isn't the only one," said Trévoux.

"Madame," rejoined Guilloux, "the treaty of Versailles made peaceful Danes out of the citizens of Finsburg, and consequently they're our friends. Furthermore, let's be fair: Hilda has always preferred France, and we are indebted to her husband, the duke, for having categorically refused to take up arms against our country. They made it very hot for him, and for a time he was obliged to seek refuge in Switzerland."

Without realizing exactly why, Trévoux felt embarrassed at this calm dissection of a woman's soul, as precise as a medical report. Brought up by a wordly-wise, irreproachable mother, he had enlisted at the age of sixteen, stepping straight from college into war, where he had been an enthusiastic officer as formerly he had been an enthusiastic student. Still pious and religious, love to him was not only a crisis of the senses, but also a crisis of conscience. He knew nothing of life. But intelligent, and an artist, he realized this ignorance. And he knew the importance of knowing. Guilloux's chatter aroused in him a disdainful curiosity.

"And who," he asked, "are the Parisians whom this lady has honored with her favors?"

"They aren't legion, although she has often favored military men. But they could be summed up in the Comédie Française, the Ecole des Beaux-Arts, the Conservatoire, and the Institut. Age is no obstacle, although she prefers the thirty years of a Genaz. In Paris, she has numbered among her subjects a great surgeon like Decanet, a profligate like Mercueil who made love to her just long enough to get documentary evidence for one of those privately circulated books wherein he excels, and very recently this young composer whom you know, madame," he addressed the countess; "Frédéric Dugor, whose charming household she disrupted, and who, after contemplating suicide, was obliged to spend two years in a sanitarium in order to regain his mental equilibrium. . . ."

"Is she so wicked?" asked Trévoux.

It was Albine who answered:

"Oh! not in the least!"

"The countess is right. Hilda wouldn't harm a fly. But just imagine the havoc wrought in an artistic household by the love of such a woman! Ignorant of all practical realities, like most royal personages, she never considers her favorites' financial resources. She thinks it perfectly natural that a man like Frédéric Dugor should offer her a pearl costing thirty thousand francs, which they both happened to admire in the rue de la Paix, or rent for her a palace in Venice. It's ruin that drove the poor boy crazy. She learned it later. It made her very unhappy. And since then I'm told that Mme. Lelièvre is instructed, during the usual preliminaries, to ascertain as nearly as possible the chosen one's financial standing. It's both comic and touching."

"If she has succeeded to find out about Ramon Genaz's source of income," said Berthe Lorande laughingly, "she must be very clever."

"No one's duller, more stupid than Mme. Lelièvre," said Guilloux. "Besides, who in Paris to-day doubts the wealth of this brilliant exotic, whose very birthplace is known to no one? He has a villa at Passy, where he entertains sumptuously, an automobile costing one hundred thousand francs, a wealth of black hair tossed back from his forehead, the mask and complexion of a hidalgo, and he dances . . . Oh! no one can deny it; he dances as no one has danced since the days of Vestris."

"In short," said the countess, "he's a dancing teacher, no more no less."

"He denies it. In fact, he has no dancing classes, he gives no private lessons by appointment, and no one knows what his fees are. When they beg and implore him to teach others a little of his craft, he consents at times to do so provided the applicant is worthwhile. But there is never any question of money."

"Only," said Berthe, "he proposes afterwards a little business deal, a trinket costing a thousand francs for which he charges ten thousand, thereby gaining his point."

"I see you're well informed," said Trévoux.

"My friend, Mlle. Courtessin, had just such an experience with him. That's how I get my information. But don't you think we've been talking long enough about this young couple?"

"No, madame," said Guilloux in the somewhat offensive tone which he assumed whenever a friendly, trifling criticism cast a reflection on his abilities as a conversationalist. We haven't as yet come to the moral of this fable, or rather this piquant short story entitled 'The Grand-Duchess and the Dancer.' "

Berthe and Albine who knew Guilloux thoroughly, exchanged one of those glances which constituted to them a secret telegraphic code.

"Is there a moral to it?" asked Trévoux.

"Here it is," said the diplomat. "Hilda is what Mercueil calls a Don Juane, and he knows very well that this word, having sprung up like a mushroom, and being wrong etymologically, is corking just the same because it fully conveys its meaning and stings like a whip. Hilda is a Don Juane: she has ignored the moral laws of both sexes, she has satisfied her flesh's craving ingenuously as well as cynically, just as people eat and drink— eat and drink too much, in fact. She calls it love. Well and good! But, of a sudden, having reached the sunny side of forty, she has made the discovery that love is a different story altogether."

He rose in order to make himself better heard and, his right hand on the mantelpiece, he continued:

"Ramon Genaz is no longer for her a mere physical pleasant diversion of body and brain like Mercueil, Ducharge of the stables and so many others. Not even a pleasant diversion of body and brain like Mercueil, Dugor, Decanet, a mixture of intellectual snobbishness and sensuous thrill. She really loves her dancer with the black hair and the olive skin. Oh! I've first-hand information from witnesses—at his house, not hers. That's why I'm so certain. That foxy dancer calls her 'my sovereign lady' and simulates ecstatic fits before her horse-like face with the golden mane. He showers her with attentions and presents, but—and this is the tragedy's comic relief—he is shy with her like a timid young girl, in the name of respect and love. A Minos, respectful and bashful: imagine the effect on this Pasiphaë!

In short, she loves him; she feels at last the imperious need of his presence, obsession, jealousy, anxiety. She's upset; she suffers, and suffering holds out to her a dream of tremendous happiness. For his sake she wishes she were again a virgin. She senses the blessedness of devoting her life to one human being only, of sacrificing all for him. . . ."

"That sort of thing has happened to princesses before," said Trévoux.

"It'll happen again. In short, real love reveals itself to Hilda von Finsburg for the first time, shortly after she has reached her forties. And hand in hand with love, loom up the good old moral platitudes which she thought she'd abolished twenty years ago, and bar the way. The moral law is the old idol of stone, it's like the commander's statue in the operatic version of Don Juan. It always falls on him and crushes him. Read the libretto. . . . But I'm becoming a bore, I feel it. Forgive me. Listening to my own discourse made me forget the time. I have kept my chief waiting at the Quai d'Orsay for over twenty minutes by now."

It was his way of scoffing at himself, a preventive measure against the irony of others. Frankly speaking, since switching from anecdotes into almost philosophical theories, he had felt a slight hostility in his audience. In the midst of a chilly silence he kissed the hand of the countess and that of Mme. Lorande.

"I'm taking you with me as we arranged, Trévoux," he said. "You told me you had business at the colonial ministry."

"Yes," replied the officer, reading permission in Berthe's eyes. "Drop me at the Quai d'Orsay, since you're in a hurry."

They left the drawing-room together. The two women looked after them.

"Really," said the countess after a short silence, "he's delightful."

"Guilloux?"

"That chatterbox? That fake ironist? Oh, no! There are one or two like him in every embassy and in every European capital. I am speaking of Trévoux."

"Isn't he charming, though?" replied Berthe.

With a quick motion, like the flight of a sparrow from branch to branch, she rose, ran toward Albine's arm-chair and dropped down beside her on a low, upholstered stool. She took the long, slender hands between her own and, clasping them on the countess' knees, leaned her chin on them, her eyes lifted, looking up with a radiant, impish smile.

"Oh!" she said. "How I suffered while listening to this babbler's careful improvisations. I suffered because I knew that Jean did. He's so clean-minded. So up-right! So sincere! . . . He felt vaguely that Guilloux wanted to slight us a bit, you and me, and he has so much respect for me!"

"Why, little Berthe," said Albine smiling, "you deserve all the respect in the world."

"I should think so," she replied with exquisite ingen-uousness. "I was married six months to a husband who . . . never mind! Since our separation I've been as chaste as a nun. And yet my reputation is open to ques-tion! What do they want, good Heaven?"

"They want less beauty, less genius, less success. . . . Good God! How beautiful you are to-day!" added the countess, placing her hands on the other's shoulders and holding Berthe's fragile body at a slight distance, the better to see her features, as one examines at length a charming miniature, a priceless bit of enamel. "There's an appealing radiance about you that was not there a month ago, while that boy was still at the Rhine and you only remembered him as a child."

Berthe sighed deeply and lowered her eyes. She was embarrassed.

"Ah!" continued the countess, "just now I did Guilloux an injustice. How horribly shrewd he is! It wasn't by accident that he commented on the late advent of true love in the life of a woman who has been emancipated for years. He wanted to terrify us both."

Berthe's wide-open eyes showed genuine amazement.

"That he spoke for my benefit is certain. He sees very well that Jean and I . . . But you?"

"He meant me too. Did you notice how all through luncheon and afterwards in here, while he spoke of *Celtic's* and Saturday night, he gossiped about everybody except one, namely, the man who was with him that night, his invited guest, his old war comrade?"

". . . What's his name—? Valgrenier?"

"Roger Vaugrenier. Guilloux expected me to mention him first, to ask questions about him, in short to show my curiosity. But I held back as well as he."

"He doesn't imagine that you'll take this bird of passage for your lover?"

"No. But doubtless the bird of passage spoke of me to him, questioned him. He knows that I'm going to see him to-day."

"Oh! Are you . . . ?"

"Yes. At four o'clock."

Berthe Lorande jumped to her feet with the easy grace of an acrobat. She consulted the hexagon of diamonds fixed to her tiny wrist by a platinum ribbon, then the Louis XVI clock on the mantelpiece, an alabaster dial between two gilded cupids.

"It's nearly four," she said. "I'm going."

Albine got up too. She was so much the taller of the two that standing beside her friend, she felt the rich odor of the red hair rise to her nostrils.

"Come to the Opera to-night," she said. "I don't like going alone."

"Gladly!"

They left silently, crossed a large, dimly-lit drawing-room, and stopped at the double door which led to the stairway.

"Yes," murmured Berthe Lorande as though speaking to herself. "To see the birth of passion in the human heart, to penetrate thus little by little to its deepest recesses, since all pretense is cast aside when one loves . . . it is such a glorious voyage of adventure, and you're going to make it once more. Life is only worth living because of such journeys. Happy those who embark upon it. . . . I . . . Never . . ."

"Never?"

"You know it! I'm desperately in love with love, and I've pined away because I never found love's human incarnation. People say I'm a coquette and a barbarian. No one is more sincere than I; all I ask is an equation of passion. But it seems as though I were banished from the sphere of my mates, the men who complement the sort of woman I am. Appearances deceive me for a moment; then the evidence looms up. I can find men for other women, none for myself. Saulnois, for instance."

"Is it all over?"

"It's all over on my part. He still tries."

They said nothing and stood facing each other for a long time. Berthe broke the silence.

"Do you remember," she said almost in a whisper, her bluish eyes staring, as though following down through her memory the arabesque of a far recollection—"do you remember the convent at Maorta?"

"In Corsica, on our way back from our cruise through the Mediterranean?"

"The chapel?"

"Yes. . . . The two nuns praying in front of the Holy Sacrament? One had covered her face with her hands. The other's beautiful young face reflected the luminous whiteness of the Host."

"When we came out, you said to me: 'I've felt the faint rustle of angel wings! Some day, I'll return here.'"

Albine smiled.

"One says such things on leaving a hushed chapel or a picturesque landscape. Just at present I admit I have no desire to enter a convent. How about you? What reminded you of Maorta? Is your old nurse Clarisse about to convert you?"

"No. Clarisse's piety is discreet. She is satisfied to pray for me. But Trévoux was piously brought up. He still has a father confessor."

"You'll be the stronger, if you really love him. Only, *do* you love him?"

"I tremble lest I discover that he too isn't of my sphere," she replied, recovering her childish gayety. "Although this time there's something novel in me."

"What?"

"The sudden eclipse of everything that isn't he."

"What else?" Albine went on, grave and attentive:

"The longing not to leave him, not to be free of him for a single moment, ever."

"And what else?"

"The torture of not being his age," she whispered very low: "the inability of giving up my whole life. The past years seem wasted. Why do you ask me all this?"

Albine did not answer. She bent over Berthe, took
her into her arms, kissed her twice.

"Until to-night," she said.

"Until to-night."

III

"What's become of you since Saturday? Did you keep
on rushing to *dancings?*"

"Heavens—no! I only let Guilloux drag me along."

Albine had resumed her place in the arm-chair by the
fire. Vaugrenier sat opposite her: a low stool was between them, the very one on which a little while ago
Berthe had sat at Albine's feet. Vaugrenier wore a blue
serge suit evidently cut by a military tailor, dark brown
gloves, stout brogues carefully shined, a department store
necktie. Yet the nobility of his face, the quiet strength
of his whole body, imbued him with a peculiar elegance
that any sensitive woman would recognize at once. It
was not he who was wrong, but his clothes. Ulysses
rising from the marsh-reeds in his leafy garb did not seem
ridiculous to Nausicaa.

Between the gilded arms of the two cupids the alabaster
dial marked ten minutes past four.

"I only let Guilloux drag me along," Vaugrenier said,
and became silent. The Countess whose eyes never left
his face guessed that he had swallowed words of scathing
criticism which burned his lips. She changed the
conversation.

"Besides, you must be a very busy man. Have you already a clientele here in Paris?"

"No. Some old friends, a few strangers brought by
Guilloux who is really clever and most obliging. I am
also looking into some offers from an agency, to become

a local physician. One of them is fairly tempting because the retiring physician would surrender his apartment as well. . . . It's in the rue Montparnasse, in the XIVth precinct."

"Why do I tell her all this?" he thought: "It's idiotic. And why did I come?"

Almost none of his rambling thoughts escaped Albine. She decided not to rescue him from his embarrassment for some time yet, and merely replied by interested nods. Scolding himself inwardly for not daring to keep silent Vaugrenier went on:

"And so, having few patients and caring little about the pleasures Paris has to offer, I devote all the spare time these annoying matters leave me, to work which interests me tremendously."

"Laboratory work?"

"Not just now. A book."

"Oh!" said the countess with genuine interest, "a book on what?"

He was on the point of telling her, but a sudden bashfulness choked the words on his lips. No . . . impossible in this Eighteenth Century boudoir, alone with this woman of the world, to even mention the title of the manuscript at which he worked every day with a sort of furious ardor.

"A purely medical subject which will only be of interest to specialists."

In spite of her broad-mindedness Albine was a woman, thus curious. What could be the unavowable title of this mysterious book? She almost insisted, but refrained from such a blunder and affected indifference.

"I spoke a great deal of you last night," she continued, "to some one who knows and respects you. It was at the Artaud de Léons. Not the ones of the Faubourg

Saint-Honoré . . . those of the rue Saint-Dominique."

"I know no Artaud de Léons in either Faubourg or street," cut the doctor in sharply.

And he himself thought: "Why am I so disagreeable? She's charming and kindly."

Albine went on unheeding:

"It was general Helgot Desmarais, your chief; our chief in Flanders. . . ."

Roger's face became animated.

"A real chief," he said. "Brains and a heart! If only there had been more like him! . . ."

He did not say how it might have changed things.

"I learned from him," continued Albine, "many things about you that I didn't know. The Moulin Corbin affair, the fire at the first-aid post No. 203, the rescue of the sergeant-major in the Caméléon trench. The general —and he means what he says—uttered the word heroism."

"Madame," interrupted Vaugrenier, brusquely, and suddenly his timidity dropped like a wind-torn cloak, and he resumed ease and authority together with some intangible, rather savage charm, "I beg you, drop this subject. I've never been a hero. I've never wanted to be one. I made war like any stupid peasant of ours, simply because I was drafted. I was told: Go there! I went. Do this! I did it. Had I refused I would have been shot. A few who did met with such fate, and I consider them far superior heroes. Now then, I may have been carried away at certain moments by the collective enthusiasm of war. It may be that, while in action, I ceased to reason, and my instinct of self-preservation grew numb. All this is possible! A battle is as intoxicating as alcohol. But is one brave because one is drunk? This sort of heroism is common to all humans and most animals. I had a very heroic horse at Vauquois. It doesn't in the least, however, alter the fact that during

my quiet moments, before, during and after the war I
haven't deviated the slightest bit from my hatred and
horror against bloodshed. I find it detestable, infamous.
There's only one campaign I'd gladly take part in; the one
whose objective would be to kill the monsters who make
war possible, who prepare it, who dream of it yet!"

Albine watched the young man who now spoke oblivious of her presence, moved by a passionate impulse.
This is why he failed to see a sort of complacency, both
admiring and ironic, which curled her beautiful lips in
a faint smile. As he stopped for breath, she only
murmured:

"Yes, war is dreadful."

"Less so than what follows in its wake," grumbled
Vaugrenier, more and more bitter. "I much prefer our
war to what they call our peace. The horrors of peace!
There's a title for a pamphlet à la Paul Louis Courier!
I saw them last Saturday, at *Celtic's,* these horrors of
peace; I filled my eyes with them. That mixture of
revelers, intellectuals, aristocrats, ruffians and prostitutes!
That rain of gold poured out for barbarous pleasures
and canteen food, while in the meantime French families
are crashing into ruins and whole nations are starving.
That grotesque cult for pinchbeck souvenirs, for acrobats
like Links, for so-called society women who are nothing
but courtezans, worse than the professional ones, and
who haven't even the excuse of youth and poverty. . . ."

His mouth was dry, and he was out of breath. He
stopped short. Albine, who had grown serious, thought:
"Guilloux certainly did his customary work well, but
why am I so hurt by what this hot-headed child is saying?" Grief was weighing on her free, strong heart.
During the ensuing silence, they looked at each other.
Vaugrenier could not mistake the expression of suffering
that veiled the motionless face. And of a sudden his ve-

hement anger left him; he despised himself for having caused pain to a human being who had nursed him with her own hands; who, having met him again, was once more kind to him, and with whom he could find no fault except that she was attractive.

"Your viewpoint," said Albine simply, "is harsh and uncompromising."

She had entirely too much control over her emotions to break into tears. But those tears, held back, altered the expression of her eyes and though hardly perceptibly, their very shape. However, the impetuous theoretician who had offended her was one of those men who are unable to withstand a woman's tears, as in former days he had been unable, despite his hatred of war, to see danger without plunging into it. He began to mumble words, which came to him at random:

"I said this . . . you understand, Madame, because we were on the subject. Otherwise it doesn't worry me and doesn't concern me. I know very little about it. And I had no intentions of saying that *Celtic's* isn't the sort of place to be frequented. Why, even Mme. Saulnois who, Guilloux assures me, is a perfectly respectable woman, was there . . ."

"And if so respectable a woman as Mme. Saulnois may safely dine at *Celtic's,* then my friends and myself certainly can, isn't that so?"

"Oh! Madame, I expressed myself badly, I wanted to say . . ."

He couldn't find the right words, blushed furiously, became silent. But he could not take his eyes from Albine's face, anxious to see her serene once more. She looked at him for a long time, without any anger whatever. She had too much experience with men and her own power over them not to feel that Roger's brutal clumsiness, of which he himself suffered now, had brought them more closely together than ten correct conversations according to social formulas. There he was, facing her, completely lost, while she had regained her poise. She said to him softly:

"When a man of your age, your strength of body and mind, and of whom Helgot Desmarais thinks what he does think, when a man like you has such violent fits of anger and so much bitter rancor, it is undoubtedly because he has suffered from life and its injustice."

"I have suffered from it," mumbled Roger Vaugrenier.

But this avowal, acting like a reflex, immediately offended his dignity. He dreaded to complain and to be pitied.

"I've suffered from it," he continued; and his tone little by little resumed its sonorous aggressiveness, "but hardly more so than other people. Just enough to realize that the world is not perfect, and that only those who take advantage of it may admire it in bulk. I am an illegitimate child. My mother, who was a governess in England, had been seduced, I believe, by her pupil's father, a respectable gentleman. My name is my mother's name. Oh! I don't mean to infer that this sort of thing is very terrible. We're no longer living in the time of the younger Dumas. The fact that I'm a bastard never hurt me. A kindly-hearted man, an English physician, who was a discreet friend of my mother's, undertook to bring me up, because my poor mother died when I was a little child. I've therefore no reason to either complain of or rejoice in my fate. Mine is a happy medium. Men have done me both harm and good, more harm than good. Naturally I bear no one any grudge, not even my father whom I do not know. Society is stifled by absurd laws. The result is a mad scramble in which the bigger and stronger element crushes down the smaller and weaker. It's very simple."

"Do you believe these laws can be changed?" asked Albine, greatly interested.

"Certainly, since they were created and enforced."

"For instance, by severely punishing the seduction of a defenseless young girl?"

"Punish? Add to the weight of laws? Never! Never! We're bursting with too many rules, too many shackles. Do you ever read Saint Paul, Madame? Saint Paul saw very well that it is the law that creates delinquency; he made no bones about saying so to the Pharisees of his time. If my father and my mother loved each other they were right a thousand times in belonging to each other, no matter what their respective situations were! It's an idiotic, fatal law, the Pharisee law of sexual morality, a law based on nothing except egotism and greed, and which made a crime of free, righteous action."

"I'm certain," said Albine, "that this is the subject of your book."

"Oh! you've guessed it? . . ."

"One speaks with such passionate precision only of subjects which are vital to one. Now will you tell me its title?"

"Yes, it's called: *'Against the morality of the sexes.'*"

These words which, a while ago had stuck in Roger's throat, seemed now easy to utter. Still, their very sound, in this drawing-room, alone with a woman, made him uncomfortable.

"Forgive me, madame, for speaking of these things to you. I've told you, I'm the absolute opposite of a society man. I'm a man of work, and if need be, perhaps, of action. But I know I'm clumsy and a bore. Forgive me."

The countess smiled. Women who have kept their beauty and sensitiveness late in life, when they become

enamored of a young man add a deep maternal feeling
to their love. The physician's last words reacted on Albine's soft sensitiveness. She longed to take this big boy
into her arms, to console him, calm him. "How captivating he is!" she thought.

"You aren't in the least bit clumsy," she answered.
"You are violent and abrupt; it isn't the same thing. As
for being a bore, you're just the opposite. Impassioned
people sometimes hurt our feelings"—she paused slightly
—"but they never bore us. What you say about laws
in general, and particularly the ones that regulate the relations between men and women, is perhaps true. But
men have created these laws. It's up to them either to
change or destroy them. We women, sentenced to submit to laws which we have neither made nor even accepted, and which consequently do not bind our conscience, we've always defended ourselves against them
by the methods that the weaker use against the stronger.
We have not rebelled openly. We have tried to cloak
our cravings with an outer respect for social conventions. Oh! it's not very creditable, I know. But we had
no choice between this compromise and moral slavery."

At this moment the door opened admitting a footman
who brought in the tea-wagon. He removed the low
stool standing between Roger and Albine and replaced it
by the tea-wagon. Conversation stopped for the time
being. "Then everything Guilloux told me is correct."
Roger thought. "A daughter of Pierre de Mestrot, a
titled artist, and of a model; an emancipated youth, a
suspicious trip abroad at the age of eighteen with a questionable friend—this Henriquette Dupont who taught her
painting. Suddenly her wanderings interrupted by her
sudden marriage to a Moldavian aristocrat, Count Anderny, dead since. Widowhood, years of gay life in

Paris and Europe. This is what she calls a compromise between the cravings of her heart and social conventions. She needn't play the virtuous lady. What nerve!''

So he mused. But he felt upset. Why did Albine's confession, so daring in its discreet revelations, tug at his heart strings so painfully?

When the liveried servant had withdrawn, Albine offered a glass of port to her guest and poured herself a cup of tea. They exchanged the usual tea-table amenities. Roger scrutinized her face, her hair, her low cut corsage with its glimpse of bare shoulders and breast, her bare arms, her hands. Despite his close scrutiny, despite a strange, jealous wish that possessed him to discover traces of age, he could find none, and it irritated him, almost like an unfathomable enigma.

"Guilloux claims that she's had her face remodeled in the United States by a great surgeon. If it's true, it's a beautiful piece of work. But it's not true. She is simply a magnificent human specimen who concentrates all her energy and uses all the means that money can purchase to preserve her beauty."

He noticed that she had not touched the cakes and put no sugar in her tea.

"Thanks to modern hygiene a woman of over forty like madame Anderny, can beat the preceding generation by ten years when it comes to appearances."

Thus he mused when suddenly his critically observant glance met Albine's. He felt that she had read his thoughts, and he was ashamed. There was in her large brown eyes no duplicity, no challenge: on the contrary, they frankly bespoke that intense desire to attract, to captivate, which makes the maturity of an infatuated woman almost irresistible to a young man. A wave of happiness swelled his heart. The shallowness of his theories, the sordidness of his own pride shocked him, and suddenly he was afraid lest the present reality become a lie, lest he had deluded himself. What attraction could he possibly have, he, a pitiful nobody, without money, fame or elegance, for this exceptional woman, rich, beautiful, acclaimed everywhere despite Guilloux's gossip, courted by kings, whom an English Duke had wanted to marry the previous year? It was true that other women had already singled him out, him, Vaugrenier, who considered himself unattractive. Thus he had had sudden love affairs which his clumsiness had invariably spoiled. . . . Now, for the first time in his life, he wanted to attract, to arouse a woman's desire.

With her shrewd knowledge of the hearts of men, Countess Anderny felt his agitation; she understood her own power. She doubted the future no longer. Her opponent would still have his rebellious moments, his angry outbursts; he would still try to fight and would only hurt himself in the struggle; but each time he would become more and more enslaved. For, in spite of his self-righteous demeanor, Albine understood him to be extremely sensitive. "He has the temperament of a believer, and the mind of an unbeliever. Nature has stuffed him with bourgeois scruples. But he has been a nihilist ever since he has been old enough to reason!" And it was his nature that she had to contend with, not his doctrines! The foreseen difficulty of the conquest roused in her the overpowering wish, a truly idealistic one, where the flesh had completely been eliminated: the need of gently curbing an indomitable will. All these thoughts were agitating both opponents while they were again engaging in conversation according to the rules of the social game, tired by the recent encounter and implicitly agreeing not to renew it. The dangerous theme of war having been put aside, the only remaining subject of con-

versation was the limited group of their mutual acquaintances.   They tackled it with the light irony which is the
usual formula of such conversations.   Albine noticed that
Vaugrenier held his ground without effort.

"The professor was entirely too pleased with himself,"
he was saying.   "He has a certain verve but seems to be
limited mentally.   His wife is far superior."

He was speaking of the Saulnois.

"You have judged correctly," answered Albine.   "My
little cousin Jeanne de Gueyze is exceptionally gifted; her
character matches her intelligence; her husband's success
is truly her own achievement.   A love match.   The
provincial girl, poor and of the nobility, marrying a professor of philosophy.   In those days Saulnois was beginning to compile learned books entitled: 'Infinite and
Infinity,' which no one read.   She guided him into other
channels.   She inspired his series: 'Psychology of a
French province,' which sold like a novel.   She introduced
him in the best social circles.   He became the philosopher
of the smart set.   He is a member of the Académie des
Sciences morales; she will manage to get him into the
Academy of the Immortals."

"Guilloux claims that the household is a bit shaky."

Albine flared up.

"Guilloux!   Don't take him seriously!   He can't forgive society for the two or three brilliant marriages which
he has missed himself!"

Then quieting down, she went on:

"Jeanne Saulnois is a faithful wife, she loves only her
Albert; it's as though she doesn't see other men.   Your
friend Guilloux is going through this experience now;
that's what embitters him so.   All his seductive charm,
his diplomatic tricks fail to disturb ever so slightly the
marital peace of this plump blonde.   So he tries different
methods now, tries to arouse my cousin's jealousy by

proclaiming everywhere that her husband is deceiving her."

"But this, at least, is true? The pretty Mme. Lorande?"

"More Guilloux nonsense!" interrupted Albine. "Saulnois has had a few light adventures; there are women in Paris who fall for celebrities wholesale. But as for Berthe Lorande; listen to me, Mr. Vaugrenier, and look straight at me. Berthe Lorande is my friend. I have known her since her first book came out, since Paris discovered a great writer in this ravishing daughter of a small dry-goods merchant of Jouy-en-Josas. I'm as well acquainted with her life as I am with my own. Well! I assure you that Mme. Lorande never resorted to the famous compromise between morality and laws, and there is no woman more virtuous than she."

"And yet, Saulnois . . ."

"Saulnois became infatuated with her, like many others. But he simply wasted his time. Don't you know that Berthe is irresistible when she chooses to be?"

"Guilloux reproaches her with choosing too often."

"Can you reproach the diamond because of its fire? Berthe Lorande is the most magnificent source of eloquence, lyricism, passion. The sparkle and heat attract both men and women; men get burned. Is it Berthe's fault? Besides, you'll judge her for yourself, because I want you to know her. I'll arrange a luncheon here, with her and my friends, Mme. de Trévoux and her son, who are both charming. Once more, don't knit your brows! Don't wind up again the mechanism of your misanthropy! Be friends with Guilloux, well and good. Be friends with him exclusively, and you will become a maniac. A man of your age and merits must not isolate himself. Have you so little faith in your own doctrines that you dare not let life test them out?"

Roger, rising slowly, answered with deep concern:

"Frankly, Madame, all doctrines aside, I feel that everything is estranging me from a society like yours. My poverty, my birth, my character."

"What romantic words! Men of your kind are the rage of the wealthiest circles of Paris, without whom these circles would perish of boredom and dearth of ideas. And they know very well that they remain your debtors. As for birth . . . I myself am a legitimized child, the daughter of a Parisian artist's model. I'm not a bit ashamed of it, and I assure you that it never closed one door to me. Finally, since you absolutely insist on being told so, you're a very delightful man, and I predict great success for you. Be brave."

These last words which under any other circumstances and coming from any one else would have made the moody physician balk, were spoken with so gracious an intonation and expressed with such simplicity that Roger felt it as he would have a caress. He stammered:

"How could one help being brave, Madame, when it is you who encourage?"

She too rose. The tea table no longer separated them. They found themselves face to face, and very close.

"Madame," resumed Roger in a low, breathless voice, "I was ridiculous and incorrect at the outset of my visit. It's my nature. When certain ideas get hold of me, I no longer remember where I am nor whom I am speaking to. But I shall leave your house disconsolate if you won't say that you forgive me."

A slender hand rested on his dark coat sleeve, and, while this perfect, living thing held him spellbound, Roger heard Albine answer:

"Of course, I forgive you. You came here all feverish from the poisons Guilloux inoculated you with. The outburst was inevitable, and I foresaw it. What he told you I don't know, and I won't ask you. A number of venomous lies, with just enough of truth in them to sway your good faith. These accusations against women are so convenient. Their very nature at once forbids all possibility of verifying them."

"Yes," said Vaugrenier, "people ought to be ashamed of uttering them and listening to them. I'll tell Guilloux what I think of it."

"Don't! Let it be our secret. It would rather please me to fool him. He lunched here to-day, and it amused me very much to see so clearly through his game while I concealed mine from him."

But Roger was no longer listening. The contact of this hand which pressed his arm to the rhythm of her words, played havoc with his nerves. Nothing brutal in his emotion: only the longing to sink at her feet, or to seek the refuge of her shoulder. In spite of all the encouragement that he had received, he could not conceive that some day he might take her into his arms, draw her face close to his. The thought of it hurt him. On the point of leaving, impelled by an inexplicable distress, he found nothing to say, he so proud and grave, nothing but a few not very masculine words, words that burst from the mouths of women on the verge of surrender:

"You'll forsake me some day!"

They were so totally unexpected, these childish, yet fervent words, that they upset her. She drew back and dabbed nervously at her eyes with her small handkerchief, rolled in a ball. Equally swayed by an emotion which they seemed to communicate to one another by an electric current, the tic-tac of the clock with the gilded cupids doled out to them beat by beat an unforgettable minute.

Albine was the first to regain self-control.

"People who know me well," she said, "—I'm not speaking of Guilloux—know that my heart is loyal. Good-by for the present."

She offered her hand which he kissed now. But this conventional kiss brought him no happiness. She was looking at him and thinking: "What grace in all his gestures! Even when he is upset he isn't at all awkward. . . ."

He had already reached the door when she said:

"Come back to see me soon. A telephone call any morning, and I'll close my door to all except you."

For a moment she saw a flash of his earlier hostility once more cross the harassed features. Then the cruel light faded. He hung his head and murmured resignedly:

"Of course, I'll come back. I know very well that I shall!"

SECOND PART

I

BETWEEN Saint-Philippe-du-Roule and the avenue de Friedland, the faubourg Saint Honoré descends in a steep, short slope. Half-way up on the right side, is an arch-like door of tremendous size. Supported on both sides by pavilions entirely devoid of any architectural style, it leads into a vast courtyard. For quite a long time this courtyard was cluttered up with incongruous old shanties, seemingly grown from the ruins of the little house whose gallant recollection Casanova evokes in his memoirs. Some years previous to the war, the Crédit Général bought up the whole lot and installed there its bond department and safe deposit vaults. Everything was demolished except the massive arch with its two pavilions, and on the cleared ground sprang up a real American building, a skyscraper within the limits of the building laws, equipped with the last word in industrial comfort: lights, heat, constant hot and cold water, telephones, special telegraph wires, moving stairways, dumbwaiters; finally elevators which soon became known in the world of finance as the swiftest in Paris; one felt as though traveling in a high-powered shell, when riding in them, people said.

When a visitor, having obtained an interview with the mysterious queen who presided over this brick, iron and glass palace, stepped out of the elevator on the top landing and was being ushered into Camille Englemann's office by a purple-and-silver liveried footman, he admired the sudden change in furnishings. Past a certain door, Turkestan rugs were spread over the parquet floors, wainscoting done by old masters covered the walls, pieces of

67

furniture and paintings which were few but well-chosen and grouped with unerring taste, gave the impression of a museum.   The first two of these rooms were well-known to art collectors.   At the threshold of the third the purple-and-silver clad footman consulted a plate of old enamel framed against the door post.   This plate flashed at an electric touch from within one of the following monosyl-lables, *"in," "out," "wait."*   If it was: *"in,"* the foot-man, without knocking, showed the visitor into Mme. Englemann's office; if it was *"wait,"* he waited until *"wait"* was replaced by *"in."*   If it was *"out,"* the foot-man picked up a near-by telephone for instructions.

One morning in early February, less than two months after Albine and Roger's meeting, Camille Englemann was seated from nine o'clock on at her desk in this well-guarded office.   The medium-sized room was laid out so as to overlook through large bay-windows the gardens of a handsome adjoining house.   From her table, an exact replica of the one that graced the study of the Minister of the Interior in the Place Beauvau, Camille saw only tree tops outlined against an immense horizon.   No portfolios, files or pigeon-holes; nothing reminiscent of ordinary office furniture.   This elegant room, a Louis XV salon, where only the size of the writing table and the book-case which covered an entire panel facing the windows evoked the thought of work, could just as well have been the studio of a writer or a scientist.   It was here, however, that Camille Englemann studied and transacted the bank's business, dictated and signed her mail.   But all traces of finished transactions, inspected files or letters written, disappeared immediately.   It was the rule.   A charming, chiseled and gilded bronze urn resting on a near-by stand swallowed up these documents which, on the floor below, a secretary collected, classified, and distributed.

In her empty, silent office (only one of her senior

employees had the special duty to telephone her, and only at certain given hours, unless absolutely necessary) Camille Englemann, in a dark-gray, tailored suit which partly concealed her thinness, sat upright in her arm chair, her elbows leaning on the table. She was deep in thought. A file containing two typewritten reports and a hand-written letter pulled out of its envelope, were spread before her. Camille was thinking. Her ravaged face, with the head-band which concealed her scar, that glorious souvenir of Souilly, her face which she no longer watched when alone and the muscles of which she no longer strained, was what prolonged illness resulting from war wounds had made it. In addition to the burn on her face, she had been shot in the stomach. Acute peritonitis had set in and had yielded to treatment only after ten days of high fever; and, finally, restored to health, Camille had found that she had become a sort of ghastly shadow of her former self. Rightfully proud of her figure, previously, she was but a bony skeleton now. She had never been pretty: her features were neither regular nor graceful. But her smooth, olive complexion, her luxuriant hair, her radiant mouth and the intense fire of her dark eyes had formerly always won her masculine attention. And if, too imperiously tyrannical, she had not found love, at least she was certain of having aroused passionately sincere desires many a time. The stupid violence of an aeroplane bomb, after imperiling her life, had seemed to dry all this up, leaving, so to speak, nothing but the frame. Camille's vision was entirely too clear and her soul too noble to fail to realize the extent of the damage done. She fought as well as she knew how, in order to repair and dissemble it. She made special efforts to forget it, as she waved aside all worries about hopeless things, worries that absorb energy needed for the present. Yet, facts kept on reminding her of it.

First, it was the indifference of the men whom she met, an indifference which was so cruel a blow to her vanity that she, a tireless walker, practically gave up strolling through Paris. Too, it was the amazement which she read in the eyes of those who had known her before the war, and who, seeing her for the first time since, hesitated to recognize her. There were whisperings of "how she's changed," overheard in the small-talk of some drawing-room or other. . . .

This time the shock of reality had hurt her even more. And she re-read the hand-written letter with breathless attention, as though trying to digest the words and reconcile herself to facts.

Suddenly she threw it down, took a few steps toward the book-case, retraced them, looked through one of the windows at the bare tree-tops close by and the clear sky, the pale sunshine of the waning winter day. But her real gaze was turned to the depths of her own heart. She beheld its tumult and confusion. Then like a fighter who feels near the breaking point, she gathered all her strength by sheer will-power which she had exercised since her girlhood days.

"Well, what of it? I'm no longer what I used to be, there's no deluding myself about it. I'll remain wounded and scarred till the end of my days. If there are rogues who jest about it, there are also noble hearts who admire it. For instance this charming Laurent Sixte tells me whenever we meet and without the least flattery, things which exalt me. His admiration for my war record isn't simulated. What fire there is in his words!"

Her trend of thought swerved. She was no longer able to control it; something strong and bitter like a sob made her gasp. "I've sacrificed the woman I was, I've sacrificed the peace and joy of my life to an obscure

impulse which I called my duty. Did I trick myself?
The reputation of having behaved courageously at times
brings love to a man, never to a woman. . . ."

And yet, Laurent Sixte? She remembered, with what
tender concern his eyes rested on hers whenever they
chanced to meet.

"Perhaps," she said to herself, "with a certain fine
type of man, admiration creates desire, as it does with
us women."

Having fully regained her self-control, she went back
to her table and sat down. A small ivory board with
several gilded switches was fastened to the edge of the
table. Camille turned one of them. A voice seeming to
come from nowhere, spoke:

"Madame?"

From where she sat Camille answered as though speaking to some one actually in the room:

"Marguerite, at half-past ten, in a half-hour, I expect
Mme. Lorande. She is to be brought up and shown in
at once. Instruct them to do so."

"Yes, Madame."

"Now, send for Mr. Dutrier. Let him be here in five
minutes."

"Yes, Madame."

The switch, manipulated in the opposite direction, cut
the mysterious communication between the two parties.
Camille immediately pressed another one, the one which
put into play the word "*in*," on the indicator in the anteroom. This done, she folded back the open file and took
a seat between the bookcase and the windows on a soft-
cushioned sofa upholstered in purple silk and embroidered
in gold Chinese fashion. She rolled a cigarette, lit it,
waited calmly. A moment after the door opened and
Dutrier came in, correct, slightly ceremonious.

"Madame, I pay you my respects. . . ."

"Close the door and signal *'out,'*" she answered.

Dutrier, with the air of a man familiar with such orders, bolted the door, approached the table, and moved a switch. Camille watched him: a handsome man about forty-five years old, solid and graceful, somewhat of a sportsman, very well groomed, with thick and wavy hair and well-manicured nails. As he bent over the table Camille's eyes fell upon the pear-shaped pearl in his necktie, a pearl costing one thousand louis. She smiled to herself.

Dutrier, coming towards her, was smiling also. His attitude was a clever mixture of flattery and respect. With the tip of her cigarette, Camille indicated an arm-chair opposite her. He caught her hand in mid-air and kissed it with deliberate slowness. She let him do it.

"You're kind," he said in a restrained voice, "to send for me this morning. It reminds me of our first meetings. . . ."

Camille Englemann shuddered imperceptibly at the familiar note in his voice, but said nothing. Then he began to show astonishment, and a shadow of anxiety crossed his complacent face. His was one of those natures that are strong and aggressive only as long as they are successful. Somewhat upset, he said at once what he should not have said:

"But you seem so strange . . . as though you hold something against me?"

As she threw down her cigarette without replying he drew his chair closer and took the long, thin hands between his own fleshy fingers.

"Something against you?" Camille spoke so naturally that he became reassured. "Why?"

She looked at his face, glowing with health which he was lifting towards her, alive with the most ardent expression of tender desire. "And they say," she thought, "that women are the best pretenders! . . ." Still, she allowed him to caress her hands, her wrists, her arms up to her elbows.

"I've an idea," said Dutrier, "that you bear me a grudge because of the offers made to me by the Banque Provinciale?" Camille shrugged her shoulders.

He continued:

"Of course I could have refused without telling you, since I've decided to refuse! But, dearest, every one has his pride! They offer me one half more to do the same thing I'm doing here. Well, it flatters me, and I'm pleased to be able to show my charming chief that her employee is not a fool. . . ."

"How common he is!" thought Camille. "And how could I have done it? . . ." A sort of humiliation frequent with men who realize that the tyranny of the flesh has made them the slaves of a vulgar mistress. She controlled herself, forcing herself to speak.

"So, you haven't answered?"

He accentuated the amorous pressure of his fingers on the muscles of her forearm. Camille thought: "Good! —his caresses revolt me. I was afraid I would be affected, I'm only disgusted."

She was so little affected that she followed and read on the man's face the eager hope that he had reached his goal, and that she would say, as she had already said twice within the same year: "Very well, I shall raise your salary by half!"

"I didn't answer," said Dutrier. The woman's two slender hands slid through his fingers like snakes.

"Well! Tell them you accept."

His flushed face suddenly turned pale, and under the stress of emotion he reverted to the common language of his youth, saying:

"Beg pardon?"

"I tell you to accept," said Camille, moving away from him.

He was struck by the sudden intuition of the guilty who feel that their secret is in danger of being discovered.

"Ah!" he said—"I've been slandered!"

"No. If I had wanted to credit more or less veiled hints and anonymous accusations I would have done so quite a while back. But never mind! I preferred to trust you. To-day, however . . . there! Go. . . . On my table! That file, open it. . . . Well, go on!" She repeated brusquely, rising and stamping her foot.

Partly through obedience and partly through anxious curiosity, he carried out her orders. Camille Englemann watched him. She saw him stagger as though he were seasick, snatch the handwritten letter without even glancing at the typed report. He read it at a glance, hesitated, then recovered his nerve, the blood once more coloring his cheeks.

"Well?"

"I did write this letter, it's true," he replied, "but I was forced to . . . a moral obligation . . . stronger than the pressure of a pistol against one's head. And so, I wrote it for . . . your sake. Yes, for your sake, Camille—"

She interrupted him with an outburst of laughter:

"Really? It's for my sake that you vow eternal faithfulness to Mlle. Juliette Combier, a model at Lenter's, that you describe to her the horrible servitude imposed upon you, in the interest of her and your future, by my set—madness. . . . These pretty words are in your letter."

A dry sob broke her voice.

"Swine!" she mumbled. "And I loved you once!"

He stood the blow without retorting. He still clung to his last chance.

"I have written this letter and others like it, I own up. I have written them to spare you a great deal of annoyance, possibly to ward off an attempt on your life. This woman has been my mistress for five years. I am the father of her child. She was told of our attachment. She lost her head. She threatens. She wants to kill everybody. Naturally, I'm trying to pacify her as well as I can. Anything rather than a scandal. . . ."

"Read the two reports in the file," Camille interrupted him "concerning Mlle. Juliette Combier, and spare yourself these pitiful lies. You have known her three months. She was a decent girl. She became your mistress six weeks ago. She knows what you are to me. She hopes to benefit by it, as well as you. There is a perfect understanding between you two."

This time Dutrier became nonplussed. He could only stammer awkwardly.

"Well! . . . It's true . . . I was unworthy. I was insane. . . . Can one control one's passions? There are moments when I'm no longer master of myself, I'm like a drunkard. . . . I act, I speak, I write at random." He drew nearer to her. "You know very well that at such moments I'm a brute. . . ."

His eyes were close to hers; he tried to seize her. Her fist striking him between the eyes sent him reeling backward. It was a blow betraying the strength of a woman long trained in the art of self-defense.

"Beast!" she gasped.

In the horrible silence which followed both regained their self-control. Dutrier remained standing at a distance. Camille resumed her seat on the couch. From a small case within reach of her hand she took out a mirror, some powder, and slowly repaired the slight disorder of her face and hair. Then she said:

"Monsieur Dutrier, you will leave the bank this very day."

"But my contract . . ."

"Your contract which I re-read just a while ago gives me the right to dispense with your services when I please, on condition that I pay you six months' salary. That makes twenty-five thousand francs. The treasury has been instructed to pay you fifty thousand."

She remained silent for a moment and then added:

"You've fully earned it!"

Her eyes dominated his; and she read in them as on a screen, the film of his thoughts following one another: "Fifty thousand. . . . She's some sport! . . . But the loss is mine, anyway . . . and, after all, I have the goods on her, I can make trouble for her. Bah! She's too powerful, I'll not succeed. . . ."

It ended with a noble attitude of offended dignity. The blood once more colored his rounded cheeks; his torso straightened, his voice became emotional:

"Madame, I can do nothing but submit. For three years I gave this firm all the endeavor of my brain and my work. I realize that I am being dismissed for reasons which should not bear the slightest influence upon . . ."

Camille passing by him abruptly cut his sentence short. She unbolted the door herself, opened it:

"Get the hell out of here!" she said crudely.

He hesitated a moment, then obeyed.

She shut the door and glanced at her watch. The platinum-encircled wrist shook ever so little. Twelve minutes past ten, she read on the narrow, oval dial. Before the arrival of Mme. Lorande she still had over a quarter of an hour of respite. She must make judicious use of it in order to quiet down completely. Resuming her seat at the table she busied herself methodically. Slipping the Dutrier file into an envelope, she sealed it herself with several seals; a minute task which relaxed her nerves. But one cannot seal one's thoughts with wax. Her rebellious mind dwelt obstinately upon Dutrier, not to regret him, but to wonder and chide herself. Can passion enslave, blind one to such an extent? "Yes, it's a shame," she thought. "But such things happen to all men. . . ." The excuse seemed sufficient because she was accustomed to assume a man's rights, duties, and social functions.

"And I feel now," she went on musing, while she smelled the fragrant odor of the melting wax, "I feel this disgust with my own self which some men spoke of to me in confidence. *Animalis homo!* Besides, let me be frank. Did I have any regard for Dutrier, formerly? Didn't I know what he was? Ah! if he has from now on lost all power over me, if there is nothing of him which I regret, it is not because of his unworthiness; it is because I know that his passion was not genuine!"

Seeing that the seals had cooled, she rose and locked the envelope in a secret vault hidden by a tapestry. Then she meditated, standing, her hands hanging idly. For the first time, she wished to free herself from a bondage whose thrills must be paid for so dearly. To treat "it" as men did had been her doctrine till this day. Desire pricks you; if you allow it to grow into discomfort it upsets your balance, blurs your vision, hinders you in your work. It must be satisfied just as hunger is appeased by a meal; it is the vulgar masculine doctrine. Because a woman fills a man's place in society, assumes the task and responsibilities of a man, is she rightfully entitled to appropriate man's doctrine and put it into practice? Yesterday Camille Englemann would have

answered: "Yes" without hesitation. To-day, she
wondered. "It's my disgust for this discharged valet,"
she thought. And yet, no! The moral hesitation, the
restless mind, were partly Dutrier's doing, but partly
only. "I felt it much before I ever laid eyes on that
letter. Ah! let's not be afraid to look at it squarely.
I felt it since I met Laurent Sixte. His respectful admiration makes me uncomfortable. I imagine that he is
deceiving himself concerning me. It embarrasses and
humiliates me. . . . I want to say to him: I am this
and that . . . and I dare not! Ah, what a mess in this
pitiful heart of mine!"

The discreet ringing of a muffled bell informed her that
some one was crossing the anteroom. "It's Berthe,"
thought Camille. And glad of this visit, she did something which she did very rarely: she ran to the door and
opened it.

They were now sitting side by side on the purple couch
embroidered in Chinese gold. Camille, with tender admiration in her eyes for the other's amazing charm, a
mingling of mental brilliancy and physical beauty, stared
at her friend who was saying:

"Yes, there you are. . . . I've suddenly awakened, a
coquette, longing to adorn my home and myself. . . .
Oh! I want the most lustrous pearls about my throat,
and the choicest sapphires and emeralds on my fingers.
I visit the dressmakers. Triumphantly they display
barbarous finery for me to choose from. I remember
immediately their creations worn by the handsome
Mme. Jeumout or the Countess de Nivernois, and I run
away in despair. Likewise, at home, my entire little
fourth floor, which I had arranged to my taste . . ."

"And delightfully so," said Camille.

"Now it seems so poor, incongruous, devoid of all

harmony and style. Jean has so much finesse. You
can't imagine . . . and his taste is so absolutely unerring.
I have not as yet had the courage to invite him to my
house, and he constantly begs me to."

"So it's real passion?"

"Skeptic! You smile while you utter this word, so full
of heavenly meaning! Do you know its significance?
As for me, it frightens me and sharpens my desire; but
its real meaning I am ignorant of. To love, to be loved?
. . . To me these are mysterious words, which I do not
understand."

"Ungrateful child! So many men have entreated
you!"

"What of it? What were they risking? It amused
me to have them like me; is the time I gave them wasted?
I want to be liked by you, too; do you reproach me with
the fact? Is it giving nothing to spend on a man this
desire to charm? And I gave them this advantage, for
instance to this Saulnois, who is beginning to protest, and
is becoming unbearable. I gave them the time and the
liberty to charm me themselves. Had one of them
succeeded, believe me, I wouldn't have bargained with
myself. All of me! My whole life!"

She burst into childish laughter.

"Alas! They give up the race, and afterwards they
hate me and slander me. They ought to thank me on
their bended knees for having for a time roused them
from their triteness, for having lifted them above their
own petty natures. . . ."

"And this Jean de Trévoux who to-day occupies all
your thoughts," interrupted Camille, "he will meet with
the same fate as the others. You are beginning to like
him. Soon you will like him still more. A day will
come when you'll like him less than the previous day . . .
and you will not be charmed. And he will curse you."

"With him, it's different."

"You imagine so."

"It *is* different!"

Her pretty face grew pensive, all aglow with thought trying to formulate itself into words.

"I try to charm him, just like the others. But the others. . . . All of them . . . I was certain I could charm them. As for him, I am afraid I won't succeed."

"Nonsense, he's mad about you, it's plain."

She shook her russet head gently:

"He's mad about an image of myself, dwelling in his mind. But this image is not I."

"I don't understand you."

Berthe threw her arms about her friend and kissed her, nestling close for a moment.

"Don't ask me to explain, not yet. Some day you'll understand; I'll tell you everything. To-day, I haven't the courage. Let me live the present, which is delightful. Yes. Jean adores me. If I should say to him to-morrow: 'marry me!' this twenty-year old child, this righteous, pious son who has a father confessor wouldn't hesitate. He knows I am an unbeliever; and he knows my age, which is in the Who's Who. Oh! why did I admit it, this birth date of mine, at an age when, to see it in print, was to me like looking at my face—a young girl— in a mirror! I should like to burn all encyclopedias. My features, my hair, my body. . . . I know that time has by some miracle spared them. But the flight of time is merciless, and men ruthlessly persist in enumerating its stages publicly! Here, all my books, and what you call my fame, I'd give it all to be as old as I look. But I didn't come to disturb you in your work just to spin this yarn to you."

"You do not disturb me. Your visit did me a lot of good. I was downcast."

"Oh! You have worries?"

"No. . . . Some annoyances that flit to and fro, and that only work or friends can dispel. Don't leave me too soon! Let's lunch together, do you want to? I also have some things to tell you. But first what is the nature of your visit?"

"It's a visit to my banker. What available funds have I here?"

"We'll get the information if you insist. But to simplify matters, how much do you need?"

Berthe's face took on the expression of a worried child:

"Listen. My new book is being brought out by Naudin. Also I've accepted a series of monthly articles paid very highly in the *Wide World*, a big American review. That'll come to about fifty thousand francs in no time."

"I'm not in the least afraid of an overdraft," said Camille, laughing. "Come, tell me the amount you need, and it's yours."

"No! You know I've inherited from my parents who were small, honest merchants, the fear of debt. But surely, I'm good for about a hundred thousand francs between now and the end of the year. If you don't mind lending me this amount, you'll get it back soon."

Lowering her head, and utterly charming in her confusion, she confessed:

"I'm going to buy a beautiful automobile and take a trip to the Rhineland. Yes . . . of course, to see Jean and be with him. But I want to do him honor. . . . I want to surround myself with luxury, to dazzle him. Ah! You think I'm crazy . . . say it, go on, it's true!"

Both were frankly laughing, patting each other's hands with that tender gracefulness which imbues friendship between women with the sparkle and frailty of love.

"Whatever you wish, dearest," said Camille. "Buy all the pearls and automobiles you want: My credit here covers yours. It's such fun watching you who are so careful, become reckless! But rest assured that I envy you."

"I'm to be envied, it's true," said Berthe. "The day before yesterday after a two hours' lark with Jean in the woods of Saint-Cloud—deserted and sooty and rust-colored beneath a timid, wintery sun—I felt so light, so ethereal, so chaste. It was an outing of children in love. Not a single caress beyond kisses . . . kisses wherein I feel much more timid than he does."

Camille was listening intently; Berthe nestled close to her and whispered:

"Imagine, I didn't have the courage, after leaving him, to go back to my bachelor diggings. To speak, speak of him to some one who would understand me, who wouldn't ridicule me. . . . I had to. It happened to be the hour when you are inaccessible, when you conclude important transactions at the end of the day. So I fled to Albine Anderny. And the wonder is that I not only found a sympathetic listener in Albine, but the understanding of another woman-angel. . . . Yes" her childish laughter rang out—"a woman-angel, with sprouting wings, like myself. . . ."

"Like yourself! You exaggerate. In spite of what is being said about you you are purity itself and you always had angel's wings. While Albine's wings burnt their feathers a long time ago at all sort of flames."

"I tell you they're sprouting again! And, listen! Let's not joke.—The crisis through which Albine is now passing is sublime, like all outbursts of her soul. Albine is one of the rarest and most perfect examples of woman-hood I have ever known. Take her beauty: even to-day, not a single young woman can compare with her. She has a lofty mind, her culture is far superior to mine, I whose profession it is to be cultured. She knows, she understands everything. In the arts, which she approached as an amateur, music, painting, poetry, she has shown that she could become a master if her social position did not forbid her to compete with artists. In love . . ."

Berthe Lorande hesitated a moment as she always did when striving to mold her thoughts into strictly logical words.

"In love," interrupted Camille, "she has had a number of experiences."

"Several. But never anything vulgar," replied Berthe without noticing that Camille had paled as though she had been stabbed in the heart.

"Alas!" Camille murmured: "There's a certain amount of vulgarity in the love of every man."

"A heart like Albine's succeeds in sublimating this residue, it is so fiery! Listen. You'll understand. Guilloux, the diplomat—you know? Maurice de Guilloux amuses himself by spreading at large that word invented by Mercueil; the 'Don Juanes.' Incidentally he applies it right and left, to you, to me, to the Grand-Duchess Hilda, to Albine. It doesn't matter to us, does it? The word, if it has any significance at all, really fits only Albine. She alone is a Don Juane. Had Don Juan been a woman he would have been Albine. I feel that, like Don Juan, she is the victim of a relentless fate. She pursues an elusive ideal through deceptive temptations: but there is nothing base, nothing material in her fervent wish. No similarity whatever between this restless soul and a weary yet unsatisfied Messalina. Albine, obviously created by nature to inspire love, is striving to reach her natural goal like all normal beings. It isn't her fault that the love of men has failed to overwhelm her.

The fault lies in the moral disproportion between these men and herself. . . ."

All Berthe's fiery words touched a sore spot in Camille's heart, and although she was quite fond of Mme. Anderny and paid no heed to slanderous talk, irritation prompted her to say:

"If she has not achieved love, she has at least in the course of her experiences acquired money."

"Money!" protested Berthe. "There is no woman on earth less mercenary than Albine. You know very well that she was a rich young girl. Her mother's second husband left her at least a cold solid million. Later, at the time of their marriage Anderny settled upon her a million florins which she luckily—and on your wise advice —exchanged into pounds and dollars in the nick of time. Albine's averred wealth, in spite of what Guilloux says, justifies her mode of life perfectly. Albine mercenary? Oh! No! The day on which she will be able to grasp her elusive happiness, should she have to sacrifice all her wealth and earn her own living, she will throw her fortune away and go to work." After a silence she added: "And this is perhaps what is going to happen."

"For that little physician?"

"In that little physician, who by the way has a sterling character, she thinks she has met what she has looked for all her life: an unselfish, shadowy, passionate nature. The other men knelt at her feet, begging her to be their prey for one moment. With this one, it is everything or nothing. For the time being, there is nothing, absolutely nothing between them, not even highschool girl and boy kisses, as between Jean and myself. I have it from her own lips, she confides in me absolutely. Thorough decency. But they see each other every day because they can't live without each other. Haven't you noticed that she is no longer seen in public, at restaurants, theaters, races? She even goes very little in society, manages to have Vaugrenier invited wherever she goes. He is making life unbearable for her, with his jealousy, queries as to her past, fits of anger, repentance, apologies, entreaties. She suffers . . . she has never been so happy. Anyway, she admits that this situation can't last."

"A break?" asked Camille.

"Or marriage," replied Berthe. "She did not say so to me positively, but I'm convinced that she is thinking of it. Only, Roger would have to be brought around to it. It isn't easy!"

"I can conceive that. Twenty years younger than his fiancée."

"Oh! this wouldn't stop him! He professes to hold in contempt all prejudices and conventions that are purely worldly. Only, there is Albine's past and her wealth to be reckoned with."

"But since he has no prejudices!"

"In the main I think he has them all; that's Albine's opinion. But it is no prejudice for a decent man earning his own living not to want to be labeled with a certain word."

Camille's heart contracted at the recollection of the word with which she herself had branded Dutrier.

"For the present," went on Mme. Lorande, "it's the climax of the crisis. Both having felt the necessity of a short separation in order to think, Vaugrenier is in England for a fortnight. He went to visit the English physician who was his tutor, a certain doctor Hobson, who lives in Penzance. You know, Vaugrenier is the natural child of a French governess who died in London a long time ago. All this, by the way, is rather hazy. Albine suspects that Roger's real father is precisely this

doctor Hobson? But Roger sincerely believes that he is
the son of an English society man; his mother told him
so, years ago. Frankly, in spite of the fact that he
shaves, as does everybody else, this brown, bushy-haired
chap does not look British in either body or face."

"In demeanor somewhat."

"Don't forget that he was brought up in London. Besides, no matter whose son he is he is a thoroughbred.
And, deep down, I understand Albine."

"So do I," said Camille. "But you must excuse me. I
have a directors' meeting here in five minutes. Shall I
make you comfortable in my little drawing room till
luncheon?"

"No," said Berthe rising. "I'll drive to the Bois and
take my constitutional. I'll come back at one o'clock."

"The money for the follies that you are planning will
be ready, spendthrift."

"Thanks."

When the novelist had gone, Camille quickly sat down
at her table, and after a moment's thought wrote the
following note on a Crédit Général letter-head, and in a
strictly business-like form:

"*Monsieur Laurent Sixte, Director of the Bond Department, Banque des Vosges, Paris.*

*The head of the Bond Department of the Crédit Général
is leaving our firm to occupy a more important post at
the Banque Nationale. I have thought of you as his possible successor. You would of course receive the same
salary that he did, namely three thousand francs per
month, plus an interest in the yearly profits, the percent-
age of which is decided upon annually by the Administra-
tive Council, and which varies of course. Mr. Dutrier, in
this manner, received about twenty thousand francs in
1919.*

*I will be very much obliged to you for a quick answer,
in as much as the position is open from to-day on.*

Sincerely yours,

(Signed:)   Camille Englemann."

II

*Half Moon Cottage, Penzance
February 16th, 1920.*

*One thing above all else: my thoughts are full of you.
The five days gone by and the great distance between us
have changed nothing: my thoughts are full of you.   I
realize this, I confess, with irritation.   But have I not
promised to tell you everything?   The object of our self-
imposed separation was to fathom our hearts.   If we do
not say to each other: "This is what I found in it,"
what was the use of parting?*

*I hoped that my return here where I lived as a child
and a youth, and where I have not been in twelve years,
would bring about what we call a revulsion in
therapeutics.   How frequently, in former times, I succeeded in curing myself of a caprice by this means!   How
many times I saved my threatened freedom with only the
help of absence!   A new horizon, a strange city, a chance
meeting with an old friend would suffice to dispel the
shadow of absent images.   And I would then scoff at
myself, thinking: "Was it really so little?"*

*To-day on the contrary things, people who are before
me, all present realities are the ones to fade away: the
image I left in Paris eclipses everything.   I crossed the
channel and London like a somnambulist.   Even this
little English house of dear memory; even the sight
of dear Sam Hobson, with his greying hair and ruddy
face, the only being who has loved me all my life, why,*

all this failed to awaken me from my dream. I say to myself with anguish: "Is it so strong this time! . . ."

Still, our separation will not have been useless. It has brought me neither oblivion nor peace, but it has enabled me to think and see clearly. In Paris the possibility of meeting you at any moment of the day made my life hang on these meetings. In between times I waited. How can you think, get your bearings, when an incessant fever consumes you? Here I arise in the morning knowing that the whole day will pass without my seeing you. The result of it is a feeling of infinite distress; but within this void I can think, ponder, test myself. Some facts which escaped me in Paris loom up forcefully. One of them is that our meeting was for both of us a dreadful caprice of destiny. Another is that the present time, while we are not yet lovers, is the time when parting, no matter how hard, will torture us least. The last is that, even if we do postpone parting until the irreparable has happened, we shall have to part just the same, and do so in mutual despair and hatred.

Unless . . .

I can not as yet utter the condition which would make a real, solid, lasting union possible between us.

This condition depends on you. I do not believe for one moment that you will live up to it; I am even quite certain that it will never materialize. This is the result of my bitter ponderings. Now I am going to explain, as clearly as though I were establishing a diagnosis. You know my genuine horror of literary phrases applied to life; besides neither time nor subject lend themselves to it. If I hurt you, forgive me. Knowing your heart as I do now, I would only cause it greater pain by remaining silent.

From our very first meeting, and increasingly so as we came to know each other better, something in me has been your enemy. I detested that portion of your past which I have not known, and I detested your luxury, your wealth, your ordinary routine, your mode of life. I have absolutely no right to tell you this, I agree, but it had to be told.

I have tried out all sensible objections. I do not believe in what is called morality of the sexes. Not only do I not believe in it, but I deem it absurd and petty. Woman is not less mistress of her body than man. It is men who invented the contrary doctrine in order to own women as one owns a field. Nothing so far has shaken this conviction in me. But I met you, and at once I felt conscious of this hated prejudice within myself for you rather than against you.

Your right to love, even in the past, shocked me as though it were a monstrosity. It tortures me to think that you have refuted the very conventions which my reason impeaches. I find it quite natural that Camille Englemann or the Grand Duchess Hilda should have passed from embrace to embrace, as men are wont to do; but one glance given by you to another, in the remotest past, fills me with agony. Contradictions, madness, call it whatever you will! It is so. Theoretically one may free oneself from hereditary errors; they hold you powerless when you yourself are at stake.

You have loved, Albine. You have brought happiness to others. What is to me more atrocious still: you were given happiness in return. Ah! I wish I could come face to face with these men and kill them, kill them as a brutish peasant kills his opponent, like a savage wolf rips another wolf open. This is what I have come to. This hateful reaction—there is no other word—which the

*Albine of bygone days, the Albine I did not know brings
about in me, is so strong that it fills me with enough
strength against the Albine whom I know and who
possesses me. Do you want proof of this? Several
times already, I found myself alone, face to face with
you, in your home. I love you, and I know that you love
me. Not only was I not even touched by desire, but it
was at these very moments, when we were alone, that I
was most moody, more than ever your enemy. I thought:
"One day in the past another man occupied the place where
I am now sitting opposite her; and this adorable face said
to him as it does to me: Dare! . . . And he dared!
They dared. . . ." Then all desire would vanish, and
thoughts of murder would haunt me.*

*Albine, I will not, I can not any longer visit that house
in which Paris has known you, worshipped you, judged
and slandered you so many years. I have suffered too
much in it. When I meet these people of your own
world I imagine that they look at me in a knowing
manner and couple our names in vile comments. I have
heard whispered behind my back: "He is the latest
one. . . ." When chance spares me such humiliation then
I am made to witness a conversation wherein you partic-
ipate, where names totally unknown to me are mentioned,
where they praise the charm of a certain crown prince,
of an Italian nobleman neither of whom I have ever
seen, yet whom you know or have known more intimately
than myself. Do I find you alone? The walls, the
pictures, the furniture and the bric-à-brac, the servants,
all this luxury about you testifies, like stage scenery
shoved aside during the intermission, to an existence of
which these strangers who were your admirers, your
slaves, were a part. They at least were your equals in
origin, wealth, mode of life instead of being like myself an intruder whom it astonishes and amuses every one*

to find in your home. *Albine, I know the valor of your
mind, the strength of your soul; you understand me.
You understood me even before I spoke to you as I do
to-day. I am not insane enough to reproach you for not
having kept yourself for me, when you did not know me.
But the fact that this past continues on to the present,
that these same people, their friends and companions
gravitate around you, that your surroundings are the
same to-day as they were yesterday, that your name is
whispered around me in a certain fashion, in one word
that Albine will always be "the celebrated Countess
Anderny," this is what is banishing me from your life.
I bore it when I did not as yet love you, and while I
unresistingly drifted without knowing where. To-day
it is time to come to a decision.*

*I will not return to Paris and live once more through
the preceding weeks. And in order for me not to live
through them again, everything about you would have to
undergo a sudden change.*

*But this I know is impossible. The ridiculous
romanticism of visualizing the Countess Anderny fleeing
her sumptuous and festive life, relinquishing everything
she held from the past, even maritally, in order to unite
her life to the precarious life of a little physician of
twenty-three, neither good-looking, nor well-known, nor
of a pleasant disposition, and poor into the bargain—
why—I am not a fool! Such a turn-about is impossible.
I do not even know whether it can actually be done, for
I can see all the material difficulties that will arise.*

*Well! It proves that our lives can not be united, be-
cause this is the only thing which would make a union
between us possible.*

*Solitude was necessary so that I could see this clearly
and dare say it. In Paris, several times I vowed either to
tell you or write you so; I tried to broach the subject as*

*best I could; and then at the last moment I faltered . . .
and I could only show you my unfair resentment or my
silent despair. Now I have told what had to be told.*

*And now that I have said it with sincere firmness, let
me add that with you out of my life I shall continue to
live only by the memory of you. Do not think that a
grudge against you will take root within me, you who
will have upset this pitiful life. To have been, and I so
insignificant, an episode in your life is worth the suffering. Albine, I did not know that an Albine could exist.
This witching beauty, this lofty character, this impression
you give of being really made of a substance more than
human, different from ours—I had been told about it:
I thought it was fiction or legend. And I convinced myself; it is true. At first it irritated me; then I submitted
to it, and I found that subjection was sweet. With delightful surprise I had to admit that this superhuman person had a tender heart; dare I tell you all my thought?—
a motherly heart, full of understanding and indulgence
for the pitiful wreck I am. How well you knew how to
disarm, appease, console me! How quickly you grasped
my contradictory nature! How easily you discerned the
innate from the factitious in me! I am saying all this to
you at random as it comes to my mind. Do you remember two nights before my departure when you kept me
so late with you in the library? I had made you cry;
then I had begged and was granted forgiveness; and suddenly I was at your feet, crouching on the purple stool,
my head in your lap. Your hands rested on my coarse
hair which seemed to soften under your touch. It is absurd and ridiculous to write this to the woman you love;
but what I chiefly felt then was an unbelievable peace.
My journey was ended, I had arrived, nothing would ever
trouble me again. I was happy. God is my witness that
often enough, in speech and thoughts I ridiculed platonic*

love; I perceived in it merely another, cleverer trap of nature! But of what avail are theories? During the extraordinary minutes spent at your feet I felt a bliss which no physical possession on earth can equal; entirely remote from all ideas of physical voluptuousness. I had no desire whatever to play the saint; but the beast within me was dead or drugged. We had become so spiritualized that our minds communicated without words; I understood that your happiness equaled mine and that it was of the same spiritual quality. I felt that, like myself, it was the first time that you experienced something of the sort and that your gratitude equaled mine. Did it not seem to us that this happiness stretched its roots into depths of time which we could not fathom, into a sort of previous life where our beings already had united, merged into one? It was bliss, mingled with the amazement that without action, almost without thought, each moment increased the preceding moment's delight. The same evening, when I had taken leave of you, when I was once more alone in my rooms, I realized what our lives could be if united free from everything separating and hindering them. And I was in extreme turmoil, I did not have the courage to give up. Yet I was lucid enough to weigh the obstacles. What was to be done? It was then that I decided to isolate myself, and you permitted me to do so.

I am writing these incoherent pages in the same little room where less than ten years ago I used to spend my school vacations. Through the window I see a landscape of green groves and villas, a narrow stretch of sea between two rocks, all this shining through a sunlit mist. My studious, restless, adolescent life seems to be recorded between these four yellow-painted walls, adorned with the ingenious and modest trimmings of the British home, not the one you have known, Albine, in "palaces" and "estates," but the home of that England which works and thinks, and which is the real England. Here are my text books, my note books; here are my tennis rackets and an oar, also a cup won at a regatta. My mother's portrait is faintly outlined under the glass which protects it: her thin profile and the dark mass of her too heavy hair. More recent and clearer, here is the picture of my dear godfather Hobson, solid and martial in his uniform: my godfather Hobson who assures me that he has found me a fiancée, and who is disconsolate because I refuse to meet her! Oh! I know that all this is unworthy of the slightest attention. I have been a little bourgeois college boy just like the others, who used to spend his vacation in the home —like many others—of a kindly country doctor. However, I ask you to give a moment's thought to this lonely child, dreamy, restless, vaguely embittered against his fate. This child, and the wounded man you nursed at the hospital in Jellicoe, it is my whole life. How little it seems! Ah! dear, dear Albine! Why can I not see thus, in a monotonous, commonplace epitome, all of your life? There must have been a time when your life was as simple and could be fathomed in one glance. The initial curiosity, the first emotion had not yet touched you; you were an ignorant young girl. A man, other than myself, approached you then. . . .

But why picture, why express these things to you? It is far better to cut my letter short so that at least it will not grow loathsome to you. I have been feeling terribly sad the last few moments; suddenly the intuition came to me that this letter will sever all bonds between us, that I will never again see you, Albine. Have mercy on me!

Roger.

III

"He is extraordinary, don't you think, princess? He succeeds in everything which he undertakes. Even the four seasons can not resist him. Who then would dare give such a garden-party on the fifteenth of April? *Ach Gott!* He has the audacity to do it, and look at the beautiful June day that it turned out to be, just for the party! *Ist es nicht schön, hier?* In the heart of Passy, this house which looks like a little provincial castle, the small garden with its lawn and big trees, so tall that it seems to be hanging! Yes—a tiny hanging garden, one might say. These clusters of lilacs . . . all these flowers. They were planted only yesterday, for fear of the lingering frost; all this comes from hot-houses. *Er hat furchtbar viel Gelt bezahlt!* He never reckons, he is truly a lord. Everywhere, in Europe and elsewhere, he is held in such high regard. Look about his drawing-room where he has such exquisite, costly furniture; on all the stands, nothing but photographs of royal personages, so flatteringly autographed. '*Zu meinem lieben Ramon Genaz,*' says this poor Ferdinand of Bulgaria who was— what do you call it?—ousted out, and is now in Munich . . . I'm delighted you came, dear princess; you will meet all your friends here, our set, and also some Parisian types, painters, writers . . . *Sehen Sie! Hier ist Lady de Stone—la grande dame en rose: elle a l'air d'une cuisinière, nicht wahr?* She courts Ramon who doesn't give a rap, you can imagine. *Et derrière elle le secrétaire der Spanischen Gesandschaft.* A handsome chap, don't you think? Somewhat on the style of Ramon, but less refined. Go and have him presented to you. He likes comfortable blondes like yourself. Ah! count Primoli . . . *Come va, gentilissimo?*"

Leaving the Greek princess whose name she had not succeeded in recollecting, the Grand-Duchess Hilda gave her hand to the count. They exchanged a few remarks, and he took leave of her with the following words the irony of which she did not in the least understand:

"I leave your Highness to go on receiving your guests."

It was indeed she who was receiving, with the naïve impertinence of a "royal personage," as she was wont to call herself, accustomed to having her caprices become laws. With Ramon Genaz she had planned all the details of this party where crowded, if not the best people of Paris society, at least that brilliant group of best people which enjoys Paris mostly in its contrasts and who enjoy a party the more it seems the result of a wager. Genaz's crush, presided over by a Royal Highness, put the finishing touch to this kind of wager. There were café-concert stars and duchesses, spectacled scientists and lounge lizards, a few young men too well dressed with dyed hair and rouged lips—and a few ambassadors. There was Berthe Lorande. There were two negroes. There was a Protestant clergyman who was the author of a metaphysical treatise. There was an illustrious French war lord; another one, English, was being expected. There was Jeanne Saulnois monopolized by Guilloux in Ramon's den; there was Saulnois planted all by himself in a corner of the garden and watching Berthe Lorande who, instinctively and without any object whatever, was trying her best to win the great French war lord, yet never losing sight of the entrance steps with the hope of seeing Jean de Trévoux appear. There was, of course, the Prince of Mozambique, with a few samples of his posterity. There was a Monsignor, very handsome, very elegant, with a crimson cassock and a Jewish name. There was Camille Engelmann, so artistically gowned, so skillfully semi-masqued by her fur hat that she seemed pretty. Seated under one of the big trees, she was bending over Laurent Sixte whose pleasant, youthful face beneath the grayish hair, open smile, and graceful elegance already caused women to ask: "Who is it?" and to receive whispered replies. There were two newspaper editors, middle-aged and rich, and the director of an art theater, young and poor. Three exquisite-looking women, belonging to this privileged generation of real *mondaines* which blossomed forth right after the war, divinely dressed, crowded about a very celebrated little scientist who was explaining to them the theory of relativity. There was Mistinguett. There was Cécile Sorel. All this rattled, cackled, nibbled at small cakes served under an Arab tent, sipped port wine and champagne, smoked amber-flavored cigarettes, flirted, gossiped, plotted, ingratiated itself in business, politics, love, or simply, like Count Primoli, watched philosophically a Parisian ant-nest swarming beneath a spring sunshine in a setting that smacked partly of the stage and partly of the gambling house, and where everything upset nature's fundamental laws from premature flowers to paradoxical sunshine.

At this party the real host's inobtrusiveness equaled the ostentation with which the grand-duchess exhibited herself. Occasionally the smart set wonders at certain dazzling successes which no rare merit seems to justify. Look at it more closely, and you will see that almost invariably the lucky beneficiary possesses to the nth degree one quality at least, but which proves sufficient; a quality so difficult to define that in order to formulate it the logic of language has to resort to an image, by the way incomplete: Tact. Ramon Genaz had tact. This party which, to-morrow, through the gossip of the guests and newspaper reports would confirm his social success, this party carefully planned by him months ahead, this party

at which the presence of some people was the result of
efforts and negotiations worthy of a Talleyrand, seemed
to have lost all interest for him.   Except to talk to three
or four exceptional people he never left the discreet corner
in the small drawing-room where he was the center of a
group of elderly and conservatively dressed ladies, but
who represented the "cream" of the French race and very
rarely left their exclusive quarters to attend a private reception.   This group included Mme. de Juvigny, an elder
sister of Mme. de Trévoux, the "beautiful" Countess de
Mers who was almost seventy, the Marquise de Bugey,
still dazzlingly attractive, a halo of snowy hair framing
her face.   These dowagers were the ones that Ramon
Genaz really courted, incidentally applying without ever
having heard of it—for, in spite of the fact that this conversation bristled with the names of ultra-modern artists
he was as ignorant as a stable boy—the advice which
Mme. de Mortsauf gave to Vandenesse: "The woman
of fifty will do everything for you, the woman of twenty
nothing."   Thus guarded against the familiarity of his
guests, he welcomed from a distance, with a smile, a
wave of the hand, making as if to rise only to sit down
again at once, the new arrivals who dared not intrude
upon this respectable circle, and signaled to him of their
own accord: "See you later."   Otherwise, how could he
have avoided asides with young women, which would result in dreadful scenes with the grand-duchess?   In this
manner at the end of the reception he would be able to say
to her: "This party was yours, and I saw only you
there. . . ."   And so among these smart feminine parrots
that were fascinated by his truly incomparable art as
tangoist, he maintained a delicate balance which the
slightest show of favoritism would have transformed into
a cabal of venomous jealousy.   For the moment motionless and almost hidden from sight, he still remained to all

of them the center and life of the party, certain of rally-
ing them when, at the planned moment—a narrow board-
floor thrown on the lawn like a theatrical prop—he would
appear, his finger tips touching the ones of his professional
rival, La Vitzina, a Hungarian who, for the first and only
time—it was the surprise of the party—would publicly
dance a tango with him. However, the smart women
watched him, each one determined to pluck him as soon
as he escaped the old guard. They watched him, through
their gossiping and flirting, not because of sentimental
desire, less yet through sensual tyranny, but rather
through fascination, fad, snobbish rivalry. How long
would people go on saying that this glorious foreigner
with the profile of a young Roman emperor, with hair of
such a shining black that he touched his temples with gray
powder to subdue its brilliancy, the eyes of an odalisque,
a body as supple as a young girl's and robust as an
athlete's, how much longer would people go on saying
that this demi-god of the dance belonged exclusively to
that lanky, dried-up grand-duchess? They were all
ready to sacrifice themselves, these smart mondaines, to
put a stop to such scandal, and this lofty rivalry gave to
their delicate nerves the illusion of love. Ah! as the
poilus were wont to say, the Grand-Duchess Hilda von
Finsburg certainly "got hers" in the conversation of the
mondaines!

In the meanwhile, seated near Maurice de Guilloux
in a cosy corner of the English library, which Ramon
called his "den," Jeanne Saulnois, dressed with girlish
simplicity in a loose frock of purple chiffon, without a
single jewel at neck or wrists, and so fresh, so calm of
face and serene of manner that she actually looked like
a young girl, was giving imperturbable answers to the
diplomat who was becoming unnerved. The cause of his
agitation was this very tranquillity which Jeanne op-

posed to the various forms of his amorous offensive. Its present form was to excite Jeanne's jealousy of Berthe Lorande. But Jeanne had such an easy, clever way of changing the subject that he finally lost patience, became irritated and exclaimed:

"But, after all, what sort of a spell has your husband cast upon you? He is intelligent, I grant you, but much less so than yourself. Physically he isn't bad, but . . ."

"My poor Guilloux, stop pleading," interrupted Jeanne smilingly. "You want to prove to me that there are better-looking and more brilliant men than my husband, yourself for instance?"

"No, not I, but . . ."

"You or others, it makes no difference to me. Do you think love is a currency with which one bargains for a given lot of human qualities? It would be charming if a woman were to trade one love affair for another every time she sees a more desirable object. Oh! no, friend Guilloux. I fell in love with Albert at sight, or at least, from our very first meeting, I felt that he attracted me as no one had ever done before. And yet he is not very fascinating according to your standards, this young professor at the Auch college, with his curly beard and his cheap spectacles. Hello! is there music?"

A small, reminiscent of old-time serenaders, orchestra, guitar, zither and 'cello, began to strum languorous Neapolitan melodies beneath the trees, and suddenly the drawing-rooms emptied their crowds into the garden.

"Let's go!" said Jeanne rising.

"No, not yet!" begged Guilloux. "It's very interesting what you were saying. You don't care about this silly music any more than I do, do you? So your Albert looked—ah—rather middle-class when you first met him?"

Jeanne's laughter, the laughter of a clear conscience, of a young novice, rang out gaily.

"No, my Albert didn't look at all middle-class. He had his fine physique, his blond hair, his sensitive features . . . his nice, warm voice. Still—he was a bit gawky . . . his clothes, his general appearance smacked rather of the provinces."

"Then what made you desire him?"

"Look here, Guilloux, you don't understand the first thing about it. Desire him? I did not desire him! Do you for a moment imagine that a young French girl of good family, and well-bred, desires a young man as an old roué thrills to a little shop girl? I happened to be present at some commencement exercises where Albert made a speech. His way of talking, of thinking, impressed me. I desired—to use your own word—to know him, speak to him, to have him devote himself to me and devote myself to him . . . if only to have him trim his beard and change his eyeglasses and his tailor. Yes, such were my first desires regarding him, and really, they are quite typical of the average young girl."

"Yes . . . undoubtedly," mumbled Guilloux, too shrewd not to understand the delicate nuances.

In the garden a brittle, clear tenor voice, accompanied by a melting 'cello and the *pizziccatio* of a guitar, modulated a Neapolitan song:

> *"Come porti capelli, bella bionda?*
> *Io le porto a l'uso marinaio. . . ."*

Jeanne and Guilloux were alone in the den; their voices were loud, unwary.

"And how did you manage to have all your various desires fulfilled?" continued the diplomat.

"Ah! that was not easy. I led my poor old parents round by the nose. I was an only child. But even so, how persuade them to receive a college professor in their home? So with the help of a few young girls and young society women I organized a weekly course of modern literature, which met at the residence of my aunt Madame de Bruin. She owned, near the cathedral, a spacious home with a beautiful ballroom. And that's all. The moment we were able to talk to each other, everything went along swimmingly. He is clever. As soon as he learned papa's and mama's little weaknesses he began his campaign and reached his goal inside of six months."

"I can easily see what Albert gained by it. Without you he would still be busy scribbling books as unintelligible as his doctor's thesis; he would lecture at the College de France to a class of four young Wallachians and five old Englishwomen; he would still buy his suits and his eyeglasses in a department store; he would not be a member of the Institut; he would not be received in the best society, and at this very moment he would not be flirting with Berthe Lorande. For he is flirting with Berthe Lorande just now; he even seems to be upbraiding her, which is the climax of a flirtation. I can see them from here. Bend over a little, and you'll see them too."

"I will not bend over, I do not want to see them," protested Jeanne: "my husband is absolutely at liberty to say gracious or even disagreeable things to Mme. Lorande. . . ."

"All right, you're stubborn. But what was I telling you? Ah! I was saying that I see perfectly what Saulnois gained by marrying you. But you, who are an exceptional woman, who possess beauty, intelligence, race, a certain social savoir-faire in the highest sense of the word . . . think what you undoubtedly would have become had you waited for a man really worthy of you!"

"If I had not married Albert? Oh! I know quite well what I would have become. I would have become an

old maid, as yellow and sour as a dried lemon; I would
be making prune jelly and tomato preserves at Fersac in
the old shack of my ancestors, which our peasants have
the kindness to call *lou castet.* Or I might have married
one of my neighbors, as poor as my parents, a gentleman
with a handle in front of his name, who within ten
years' time would have squandered my meager dowry
at the royalist club of Auch and who would sleep with
my farm-girls . . . I prefer being Mme. Saulnois."

The tenor's clear, brittle voice was thrilling out a gay
tune from beneath the trees;

> *"Tiritomba!*
> *Tiritomba!*
> *Tiritomba, l'aria va!"*

"Granted!" said Guilloux. . . . "But would you be any
the less Mme. Saulnois if . . ."

"If I listened to you, my charming serpent? Yes, I
would be much less Mme. Saulnois. The greatest element
of our happiness is not the Institut; nor our social
position, nor the money which finally came to us. It is
the fact that we are truly a couple where each is to the
other what the latter desires most. Try to understand
this, friend Guilloux, you who frequent too many Don
Juanes and believe too freely in the Don-Juanisme of all
women. Belong to any man other than my husband?
Why? My complete happiness consists in belonging to
him only. This happiness would vanish, I feel it, were I
to experiment with any one else. Well then? I ask you
would I destroy the full joy of my life in order to taste
something which does not tempt me? I deserve no credit
for resisting, believe me. It angers you? Why? I
like you very much all the same, I assure you."

Guilloux rose and remained in thought for a few moments; fear of ridicule stifled the harsh words that rose to his lips.

"Very well," he said. "Keep the happiness that appeals to you. You are right. Only this happiness does not depend solely upon you. I do not desire a revenge which would hurt you; but I'm afraid I will have it just the same."

His customary bantering tone had given way to a sort of evidently sincere asperity. He experienced the perverse pleasure of seeing Jeanne grow pale. She rose in turn:

"What do you mean?"

"Nothing. If you value your household as much as you say, keep your eyes wide open."

They were unable to continue; the music having stopped, the guests were flowing back into the house with exclamations of "Charming, isn't it?" or "Lovely voice this Ripardi has!" and: "What a bore! How stupid to permit such clap-trap in the land of Debussy!" or, "Is that the sort of rot that the grand-duchess and her tangoist need to get a thrill?" All these remarks were thrown about aloud and carelessly. Jeanne and Guilloux were separated by the crowd, Guilloux being stopped in passing by Lady de Stone one of whose admirers he had been in London. Jeanne, put on her guard somewhat by the diplomat's last words, finally took in all the details of the following short scene which took place in the garden near the buffet. Berthe Lorande had suddenly left Albert and glided like an adder through the crowds to greet two newcomers who were coming slowly down the entrance steps.

Both were searching the crowd with their eyes; they were Jean de Trévoux and Roger Vaugrenier.

Berthe joined them and almost immediately isolated herself with Jean de Trévoux, while Roger remained standing motionless, his eyes still seeking.

Was it the effect of Guilloux's insinuations? Jeanne was struck by the anguish depicted on her husband's features. Albert had not missed a single one of Berthe's movements. The novelist had drawn Trévoux under the trees, had made him sit down, sat down herself, close to him. Like most infatuated women she could not resist parading her love: she caressed him with eyes and voice: and even her tiny, childish hands, were constantly reaching to touch his. Albert saw it all. His emotions too, were overwhelming. He could not conceal them. . . .

"What?" thought Jeanne Saulnois. "Can Guilloux be right? Does she take pleasure in torturing my husband? Well, she'll have to reckon with me. . . ."

Briskly she crossed the width of the garden just as some servants in baroque livery were putting up a narrow platform of polished boards on supports prepared in advance and concealed by masses of flowers. The onlookers were amused by these preparations. They crowded around, watched; no one noticed the meeting of man and wife, she unruffled and smiling as though she had seen nothing of his strange behavior, while he suddenly became serene once more, and, as though relieved by her familiar and protecting presence, clung with both his hands to Jeanne's bare arms, drawing close to her, like a restless child. For Albert Saulnois was one of those husbands who are rather more constant than faithful, who will not because of an illicit caprice encroach upon the share of love reserved for their wives, who suffer from the inability of confiding to the latter worries of this nature as they do all other worries, and who if they dared would appeal to them for protection in their amorous disappointments; just like those devout rogues who burn a candle at the altar in order to win the patron saint's indulgent support for their peccadilloes.

The installing of the stage which had diverted the attention of the crowd from this marital intermezzo, also cloaked the arrival of Roger and the anxious, disappointed air with which he inspected the garden, then searched the drawing-rooms. Only a few intimates among the guests of the rue Raynouard knew him, as did also a few of Jean de Trévoux' personal friends; for the two young men, in spite of the four years which separated their ages—*longum aevi spatium,* between twenty and twenty-four—had, according to the current slang, "hooked up to each other," ever since their first meeting at Albine's. Totally unlike in appearance, their doctrines and habits in complete contrast, a latent affinity had drawn them close together. Trévoux, sentimental, conservative, religious, unconsciously admired in Vaugrenier his own nature freed from all shackles. Discussing with him all matters, he would hear within himself unsuspected echoes repeat the statements of the unbeliever, the rebel. Roger loved in Trévoux the Roger that he would have been—he realized it now that Albine's perspicacity had explained him to himself—if, like Jean de Trévoux he had been born of old French stock, settled for the past three hundred years in a certain corner of the Rouergue country, thus carrying on, during these three centuries, the same spiritual struggle under the same flag. He scoffed deliberately at the idealistic fervor, the hereditary scruples, the faith in love professed by his junior, and refused to admit to himself the comfort which he derived, in the fact of his very confusion, from Jean's trusting, fervent words. Jean spoke ceaselessly of Berthe, with the petulant ardor of a fiancé.

Roger never mentioned Albine. But instinctively he would ascribe to Albine whatever Jean said of Berthe, his entire heated, generous defense of her against the world. Assuredly, Jean had guessed the love drama which was taking place between Albine and Roger; but Roger was grateful to Jean for being silent on the subject, for confining himself to expressions of admiration, obviously sincere, towards Albine. At the time of his departure for Cornwall, Jean stood on the platform smiling at him as the train pulled out, and on the morning of his return after ten days' absence Roger called on him at once.

This time his heart was too heavy. He had revealed his whole secret to his anxious friend; the real cause of his departure, his letter to Albine, the ultimatum it contained, and chiefly the frightened anguish in which the countess' silence, for nearly a week since he had sent the letter, had plunged him. He had interpreted her silence beforehand. It meant: "Step out of my life." And this decree which he accepted, which he was responsible for, he no longer had the will-power to submit to.

"This is how matters stand," he had concluded. "Oh! I'm not proud of myself, old man! I am rather like Baron Hulot. Even so, Hulot had the excuse of being old and of having possessed his mistress "

"Go to see her!" Trévoux had answered. "You know quite well that she is waiting for you."

"And say to her: Forgive me! I exacted something of vital importance, you refused it . . . forgive me! Forgive me! I ask nothing now! No, after all, I have not fallen so low!"

"Do you want me to tell Berthe? She will bring you two together."

"It would amount to the same thing."

"Wait! This afternoon Ramon Genaz is giving a

party at his home in Passy. I have been asked to bring some friends. Come! The countess will certainly be there, since the grand-duchess is her intimate friend. You will meet quite naturally, and five minutes later there will be perfect harmony between you two. Why—what separates you is nothing but a lovers' misunderstanding."

At first Roger had made weak objections for the sake of appearances. But when a few hours later Trévoux had come for him the latter had found him all ready to start and vibrating with impatience.

So here he is now at this party which two weeks ago he would have decried sarcastically, in the heart of this mixed society, a result of the war, and which he loathes. There he is, witnessing the preliminaries to an exhibition by contemptible puppets, and he does not even try to be amazed at it, he scorns no longer this social quagmire with its artificial gayety, its craze for costly pleasures, its wanton insipidities. The cadaverous, grave-like scent which emanates from it no longer offends his nostrils. What matter frigid observations, harsh theories, rebellious preachings? Why play the part of the philosopher in Couture's painting? Why drape himself in his dignity? The most important thing in the world just now to this philosopher, this student, this rebel, is to find a certain woman whose presence suddenly has become necessary to him, as necessary as air to the lungs. In order to see her again, even should she repel him, he had suddenly left England on the previous day and come back to Paris by aeroplane, as though this meeting could not be postponed another fifteen minutes! Yet this woman was not his mistress; she had not yielded herself to him even in the slightest degree. Therefore it was not the tyranny of the flesh that fettered him. It was something more mysterious and more compelling; the promise and vision of a life which he could only live by her side, with her, mated to her. Oh! If she would only come! If he could only see her! Even if she repelled him, scorned to look at him, even so he felt that the fever in his blood would subside at the mere sight of her.

But he scrutinizes in vain the ebbing sea of faces. His eyes do not find the one face that eclipses all others. By contrast it seems that all the other faces outline themselves with an extraordinary clearness and precision, as though illuminated by an inward light, and reveal all in one breath the physical blemishes more or less concealed, the intimate workings of the brain, secret thoughts, souls. While the grand-duchess unsparingly resorts to naïve humbug in order to rally the spectators around the lawn, and cries: "He is going to dance! A tango with La Vitzina, a tango for us alone that no one has ever seen or will ever see again!", Roger reads behind her dry, horse-like face shrouded in heavy, Teutonic sensuality, the brain of a backward child created to become the prey of intrigue. Ramon Genaz's smooth forehead, at times furrowed by three anxious wrinkles, his large eyes which, suddenly restless, roll in their sockets from right to left, his demeanor betraying a nervous man who restrains himself and tries to appear impassive—all this reveals a human being morally disguised, full of audacity and anguish, still deliberating as to what means he should employ, but capable of using the worst. A divine light suffuses Berthe Lorande's features, offering herself to Trévoux like a Host. What witching spell blinds Jean to the thing which Roger sees so clearly: the nonhappiness, the horrible anxiety of her who thus offers herself? Likewise Roger imagines that he can read as in a clearly printed book the integrity of heart written on Laurent Sixte's face, the bloom of sentimental youthfulness in Camille Englemann, Guilloux's game between Saulnois and his

wife appears to him like an easy chess problem on an un-
obstructed board, where three figures only are left to
battle.   The grand-duchess' dragooning command jerks
the crowd into motion.   Everybody gathers about the
lawn.   The circle, the people in front seated, those in
back standing, closes about the green grass which edges
the dancing-floor made of boards, barely the size of a
floor of an ordinary room.   A gangplank stretched across
the grass joins the dancing floor to the gravel of the alley.

It was on this diminutive square that La Vitzina and
Genaz were going to perform; and the grand-duchess
proclaimed loudly that in the very narrowness of the
dancing space lay the thrill of the thing, the finest of the
superfine, the masterpiece.   Do not the Argentines state
one should be able to dance the tango on a dinner plate?
And there in a nutshell, was the childish naïveté of gay
Paris; everybody, men and women, were positively electrified at the thought that they were going to witness this
unique, admirable, fascinating performance—a tango
danced on a floor measuring a few square yards.   There
was something worthwhile having lived for as far as
1920, through the agony of the invasion, the perils of
war, the intoxication of victory and the bitter come-
back of peace.

While the orchestra, 'cello, guitar and zither, preludes
softly, the two virtuosos appear clasping each other's
finger tips.   They easily solve the problem of crossing the
gangplank, before any one has the time to notice whether
they follow one another or whether they come forward
together.   La Vitzina is flat, sexless; the face of a young
boy, slightly worn, daringly made up in ochre powder:
she seems almost nude, in the straight tunic of gray chiffon which leaves her arms bare to the elbows, bare almost
to the knees, her legs clad in sheer black silk through

which glistens her skin. A toque with drooping feathers covers her rust-colored hair. Genaz is dressed in a cutaway, dark gray trousers, a shirt with frill; he is bareheaded. Immediately before reaching the dancing floor, their gloveless hands, the man's left and the woman's right, clasp tightly and are brought back to shoulder level; the woman's left hand rests lightly on the man's shoulder; the man's right hand, upturned, brushes with its back the lower part of the corsage modestly cut in a point towards the waist. Incidentally, nothing more decent than these preliminaries; wanton curiosities, if there are any in the audience, are disappointed; plainly, the two bodies hardly touch each other. They stand motionless for a moment, not against each other, but close to one another, their faces turned in the same direction are superposed like double-profile medals, the Vitzina's tiny stray curls brush Ramon's smooth black hair, yet their cheeks do not touch. The voluptuous cadences of the music become more intense. Are they dancing? One can not tell. Perfectly motionless a moment ago, the double statue gradually seems to grow animated by an imperceptible rhythm. Therein lies the acme of the art of these two virtuosos, and it is an art, indeed; they have divested the celebrated dance of all gesture, all swaying; they have transformed it into a synthesis. Thanks to them, every one will understand the world-wide fascination of the tango. Their dancing is a poem depicting human love, delicate and voluptuous, ardent yet varying. Their feet move now in such perfect harmony that one imagines the tips of the man's pumps and the woman's buckled slippers to be actuated by a fluid; a magnetic needle opposite an iron one. How could conquest, possession be indicated more chastely than by this passive obedience of the feminine foot to the masculine foot, one following the other step by step without ever touching it?

. . . But their bodies are no longer motionless. Still keeping their imperceptible distance, very close yet not clasped, one guesses that they have become electrified by the same rhythmic vibrations; the spectators, as though witnessing a love scene superbly enacted, share their emotion. They see the lovers hesitating on the brink of passion; they share their anguish, wait for the embrace to come. . . . And at the paroxysm of this expectation suddenly the music softens, quiets down; the couple loosens their grip on each other; it is now but a gallant lover guiding his companion's steps. By their incredible virtuosity Genaz and Vitzina create on this narrow space the illusion of a long, sinuous walk. Over a few square feet of board they simulate the flight of two lovers along a woodlane or crossing the dry stones of a ford. Then, with a sudden gesture emphasized by the 'cello, the two lovers stop walking; they stand still for a moment, look into each other's eyes, and, with an irresistible outburst which lasts but two seconds—and yet molds into a definite curve, the gesture still retaining a peculiar, shy resistance—they cling to each other, face to face, body to body; the fatality of love has conquered. From now on their eyes remain fastened on one another as well do their bodies; their motionless stare seems to search their souls, to watch out for signs of passion or treachery in each other; their bodies no longer observe the discreet distance, the calculated grace of the earlier measures; they caress and coax or abandon themselves, suddenly giving way, the woman at times resting, as if her strength were gone, against the breast of the victorious lover. . . .

"The novelty of their dance," Mercueil murmured in Camille Englemann's ear, "is the contrast between the voluptuousness of their postures and—how shall I say?—the mastery of self, the impersonality, the detachment

. . . you understand what I mean . . . of the dancers. Watch these two aces at it. Their tango never becomes indecent, swaying, à la Fatima; everything is visibly planned and regulated down to their least movements. Can one think of doing something foolish when a moment of carelessness can spoil everything? And their faces! Please look at them: frozen immobility! Marble! The staring eyes alone are alive. . . . Not a trace of emotion, not a sigh! At times one could not even slip a bit of cigarette paper between their mouths, and yet one feels they no more want to kiss than do the Apollo Citharedes and the Venus Callipyges in the Museum. This is the real tango. An admirable dance! Too bad there should be so many fools of both sexes to spoil it, even among the best people. . . . Ah! it's over! Let's applaud! Look, the grand-duchess does not seem pleased. Oh! well, of course! She would have liked to be in Vitzina's shoes!"

Amidst the cheers, the handshakes with Genaz, the women kissing Vitzina's ochre-powdered cheeks, the couple separated and returned to the house. Not a bead of perspiration on their faces, not a crease in Genaz's cutaway or Vitzina's tunic-dress, not one hair disturbed either in her short curls or on his sleek head. With something like respect the people stood aside a bit, while Genaz went to the grand-duchess who was awaiting her hero near the "den," her naïve face worried. But the clever Mercueil was professionally too curious and had preceded Genaz. Hidden behind the casing of the door that opened from the large drawing-room into the "den," he heard the following conversation:

"My queen! You seem displeased with your subject? What is it?"

"*Ach!* that Vitzina! She is a slut! The immodest

way in which she pressed her body against yours!
Damned bitch! And you, you looked at her as though
you wanted to eat her!"

The dancer remained unruffled.

"My queen! When your eyes have condescended
to look upon a man can there be other women's eyes
for him? Vitzina is horrible; I was clasping a skeleton."

"Really and truly?" murmured her Highness, soothed
as quickly as a child. "Vitzina a skeleton! Yes, indeed,
that's just it. A skeleton! How amusing and witty
you are, Ramon!"

Ramon bent down and whispered in her ear, but
Mercueil caught the words all the same:

"And what a foul breath! I'll dash upstairs and rinse
my mouth!"

Leaning against the banister, Roger Vaugrenier had
stood at the top of the landing and had watched the
evolutions of the dancers with that minute, restless attention with which a sick man observes the delirious mirages
of his dreams.

When it was all over, driven from his vantage point
by the swarming crowd, he wandered about the drawing rooms and the smoking room for a while, almost ran
to the garden in pursuit of a glimpsed silhouette, stopped
short in front of the astonished face of a strange woman,
and remained motionless on the spot, broken-hearted, in
despair. What was he to do? Trévoux was the only one
in this crowd to whom he could confide his predicament:
but Trévoux had not left Berthe Lorande's side; they
seemed to have forgotten the time, the place, and the
people; how could he disturb them?

"Well," he thought, "I shall go to rue Raynouard. . . ."

All pride was forgotten; he could not conceive life another hour without seeing Albine. What would ensue, what the result of the interview would be he totally ignored: but he had to see her, and find out. Already the crowd was thinning, her Highness having formally given permission to leave without waiting for her to do so first. Was she not at home? Around the small villa was heard the purring of departing automobiles.

"Did the success of these mountebanks petrify you?" sneered a voice behind him.

A hand was brushing his shoulder. He turned round: "Ah, Guilloux!"

Their relations had become less intimate, from the moment of Roger and Albine's friendship. Some of Guilloux's words stuck in Vaugrenier's memory like thistle pricks. And if Albine had not hinted that it was best for him not to quarrel with this dangerous friend, a complete break between the two war comrades would have already taken place. But so distressed was the unhappy lover that now he welcomed this meeting. They talked. In a few quick, ironic phrases, Guilloux dissected the affairs of his host, Vitzina, the grand-duchess, Berthe Lorande, Camille Englemann, Albert Saulnois. It was done so sharply that Roger felt somewhat ashamed to be there, and awkwardly sought to excuse his presence.

"Trévoux came for me," he said, "and brought me here almost by force."

"My dear fellow," answered Guilloux, "I am not in the least surprised to find you here, since our good, mutual friend is here too."

"What good friend? Is Albine here?" the question escaped from Vaugrenier's lips.

"The Countess Anderny is here," corrected Guilloux, barely refraining from laughter.

But Roger was neither in the mood nor the condition to take exception to a jest. He only said:

"Where did you see her?"

"In the small English drawing room which this clown of a Genaz calls his 'den.' She was talking to the Finsburg woman. As a matter of fact I think she had just arr . . ."

He stopped short. Vaugrenier was no longer by his side, he had rushed off towards the house.

"Bravo, Albine!" mumbled Guilloux to himself. "Fast work!"

Roger had run into the house and, jostling people on his way, had reached the "den." The group of dowagers, as Guilloux called them, including Mmes. de Juvigny, de Mers, de Bugey, blocked the way between the "den" and the drawing-room with middle-aged, self-importance. Planted firmly on their feet, their stomachs protruding, their bloodless, blotched fingers toying with their long pearl necklaces, they were waiting for the grand-duchess to end her tête-à-tête before taking leave of her.

Seated on the sofa in the cozy corner, she was no longer speaking to Genaz. A very elegant woman was facing her on a low chair. Of the latter only the haughty silhouette was visible and, emerging from the silver fox collar, the dazzling nape of the neck, the frizzed tendrils of brown hair, the horse-hair hat likewise trimmed with fur.

Roger's heart contracted: it was Albine.

Like the dowagers, and standing near them, he listened. Besides, Hilda was speaking at the top of her voice.

"Dear! Oh! dear! I was so anxious to see you! A nasty tire puncture? How dreadful! The very same thing happened to me last week as I was being expected at the Swedish legation. The entire party held in suspense because of me, can you picture it? Oh! this is

why I was so anxious to see you! You know intimately,
I believe, this gentleman who is your minister of foreign
affairs. Monsieur . . . What do you call him? Cor-
nillier, Carnoullier, which is it?"

"Mr. Cordelier."

"That's it, Cordelier. I do not want to ask anything of
him, because he was uncivil to Ramon. He annoyed
him with permits, passports, as though he were an im-
migrant. Now really isn't that outrageous? A man
like Genaz, on a friendly footing with kings? There
really ought to be limits!"

"Mr. Cordelier obliged some friends of mine several
times," said Albine.

"Oh! that's splendid. I will ask you something
concerning his department one of these days. I
will not tell it to you here because of all these ears
listening to us"—the dowagers never budged—"I will
come to your house. . . . Yes, yes, I want to! . . . A
telephone call and I will come, personally, with my faithful Lelièvre."

She rose suddenly. At the far end of the drawing
room she had spied Vitzina taking leave of her host.

"What! She is here yet, that pervert? *Schrecklich!*
. . . And he told me that she was going at once!"

She came out of the den so quickly that she bumped
into the dowagers. The latter hastened to drop a curtsey
to which Hilda did not respond, and then started toward
the door with a heavy step. Albine turned round without undue haste, and found herself face to face with
Roger.

She showed no surprise whatever. He came forward
unsteadily, hesitatingly. She offered him her hand. He
took it, and immediately, although her beautiful face
remained motionless and her stare inscrutable, he felt his
anguish melting into tenderness.

"You left me!" he stammered. "You forsook me. . . ."

He could have wept, thrown himself at her feet, oblivious of the people who still lingered in the garden and the house. But she recalled him to reality with one look. And, very simply:

"Come and sit down near me," she said.

In the adjoining room the grand-duchess, superbly unceremonious and much to the amusement of the last departing guests, was in the act of expelling Vitzina, while saying to her "that she had really earned her fee to-day, with her dancing; that truly, she must not give any more of her time than had been agreed upon, and that doubtless a score of pupils were waiting for her at her apartment to take their lessons!" Roger and Albine found themselves completely alone in the narrow library.

Their eyes, once more, took possession of each other's face. They could not conceal their mutual happiness at being together again. Their peaceful harmony like a mysterious fluid passed through their clasped hands. Roger was coming back to life, experiencing the same relief as he had one day at the Somme front when, buried alive under a caved-in mine, the weight on his breast had seemed to evaporate when the hands of his rescuers had cleared away earth and wreckage.

He repeated:

"You forsook me! You should have written me. I suffered too much."

In spite of the violent change that this new love had wrought within her, the satisfaction of conquering the man was strong enough in Albine to permit her to enjoy her victory. He had wanted to resist. He had opposed to her dominance an astonishingly powerful will. He had had the supreme courage to run away. Yet here he was, like all his predecessors, resigned, panting, at her mercy.

But the tenderness which she felt towards this captive was stronger than her pride.

"What a child you are!" she murmured.

He hung his head; a sob of emotion and joy rose from his throat. Let her say whatever she pleased now. He was happy.

She continued:

"Your letter was the letter of a child. So you were really expecting an answer? What answer? Is it worthy of you and me to sign contracts, to stipulate and accept conditions? Is that the way you conceive the union of two hearts?"

He motioned with his head that he did not, that he renounced, accepted everything.

"Had I answered your letter in the same spirit, do you think that upon your return we could have shaken hands, feeling that our love remained intact as we do now?"

"No," he mumbled. "Do not speak to me of this absurd letter. I was far away from you, I was desperate, I was insane."

She insisted in her beautiful contralto voice:

"Can you picture me giving you accounts, discussing my business with you as though you were a notary? Because that is what you proposed to have me do. In other words what you proposed was absolutely senseless. I will not consent to humiliate myself before any one, least of all before the man I love."

"You must forgive me," said Roger. "I rely on you completely."

"Yes, you may rely on me to uphold our mutual dignity. Oh! brooding heart! The worries and scruples that torment you, do you think I do not know them? Why—I feel them as well as you do! If you think me unworthy of you I shall not permit you to love me. Leave me.

Go away. I shall not consent to see Roger Vaugrenier
degrading himself."

While speaking with this unfailing, ever-present attention, if one may say so, which a woman of real breed-
ing never loses, she scrutinized the big drawing-room,
beyond the open bay-window. She saw no one except
two footmen standing with their backs to her, and
whispering to each other while waiting for orders. A
faint clamor of voices came from the small salon which
had been turned into a smoking-room: evidently a few
tardy guests had gathered there. And suddenly a voice
rose, a voice that whispered rather than sang: the way of
Genaz, when, guitar in hand, he would consent to sing
some Spanish or Argentine song. It was indeed he.
For a few intimates, grouped around the Duchess Hilda,
he had consented to sing. From a distance, one could
not make the words out through the humming. Albine
however recognized a malagueña heard years ago in
Andalusia:

> *La camicia de la Lola*
> *Un chulo se le llevo!*
> *Un chulo se llevo. . . ."*

Roger, intensely absorbed in the turmoil of his own
thoughts and emotions, heard nothing. With a movement so tender that it was chaste, Albine seized his
humbly bent head between her hands, and lifted it.

"Albine!" he sighed.

"I do not want to humiliate myself," she continued.
"But to see *you* humiliated, you whom I love, and because of me. . . . I'd rather lose you. Do not fear anything! You know my age, my past . . . do not protest!
I am certain you were better informed than you really
wished to be. There is undoubtedly some truth in what

you were told. I have lived freely. But if you were
told that there has been something vile or base in my
life, a fall, a compromise, something unspeakable, that is
a lie. Just look: rather than fall in my own estimation,
I was ready to give you up, you whom I love better than
anybody. Well, such as you see me in this test I have
always been. Disregard all this slanderous talk which
is gnawing at your heart; I refuse to give accounts to
any one. But since I love you and do not want you to
suffer, listen."

A louder guitar chord made Roger look up inquiringly.

"It is nothing," said Albine. "These puppets are amusing themselves: so much the better. In the meanwhile
they let us alone. Listen. Half of Countess Anderny's
wealth she inherited from her father, Pierre de Mestrot,
and her mother, Germaine de Mestrot, who afterwards
married Philippe Ambezac and whose heiress she became.
As for the other half of Countess Anderny's wealth, it
was given to her by her husband, Count Anderny, on their
wedding day. He confirmed this gift in his will regardless of the estrangement which had occurred two years
before his death. That is all. . . . And now, let this
question never arise between us again."

"Ah, never again!" whispered Roger.

The shrill twanging of the guitar had started once
more accompanied by Genaz' melodious humming. The
footmen, eager to listen, crept towards the room and
concealed themselves between the window draperies. The
lights had been turned on in the smoker and the drawing-room, but no one thought of doing so in the den.
Albine and Roger were now shrouded in a semi-darkness
penetrated only by reflections from the lights in the
adjoining rooms.

"Child!" she repeated.

Their knees touched. Once more she took the fervent

head between her hands. And again a feeling of infinite happiness possessed them, as on the eve of Roger's departure from Cornwall. Again they marveled at it. Other women had coiled their fingers around his head, his knees had brushed other women's knees. Sheer contact with these others, so infinitely less beautiful and less desirable than Albine, these others who sometimes at the very moment of the embrace, had aroused within him a feeling of repugnance, had always sharpened his bestial appetite. But nothing of the kind stirred him now; the very chastity of their touch overwhelmed him; nothing that he might obtain later could ever equal this thrill. His one violent desire was for this sweet touch to last forever, forever. . . . Other men's eyes, imploring, anxious, had lifted themselves towards this woman whose hands were clasping his head. She had then experienced the intoxication of blood and nerves, the desire to give and take, a frenzy which flings aside all modesty. By what miracle did the contact of this man, far from stirring her less worthy self, give her a feeling of purification, atonement? Both marveled at their peace, their confidence, which was neither insipid nor lifeless, but on the contrary something alive and intoxicating. And both were thinking: "Never before have I known real love. Is absolute love then this purified, spiritual desire which surpasses and consumes the vain restlessness of the flesh?"

"Albine," stammered Roger, "love me. During the days when I believed I had lost you, I regretted that you did not let me die instead of nursing me when I was wounded . . . back there."

"I love you," she answered. "I loved you from that first day; from the moment I saw you, wounded, when suffering had altered your face. . . . I realize it now. I carried within me your image and the memory of your voice. When I chanced to meet you in Paris I recognized you right away, you whom I had barely seen. . . . If my love makes you happy, ah! then be happy! How can I tell you this with words strong enough, impressive enough to convince you and dispel your anguish? No one, do you hear, no one ever won me as you did!"

She paused; then, in a lower, softer tone:

"You suffer. You suffer because of that period of my life from which you were excluded. It is not worth it. What you are jealous of—I see it now that I love you—really amounts to nothing. Do you understand me? Do you believe me?"

"I believe you," said Roger. "I understand you."

And he really did. "Yes," he thought, "all the pitiful things of my past life which I called love, all these emotions of flesh and blood were nothing but the pleasant sting of a sweet wine on tongue and palate. . . ."

Slowly she lifted his head. Her eyes searched the depths of his; in the shadows that floated about them her face seemed to attract every scattered bit of light, and to shine with the very luminousness of beauty.

"Roger . . . What I will give you of myself, no one ever had or ever will have. And yet my heart, like yours, bleeds at the thought that, in the past, other men have had of me what I might have refused them and kept for you alone. And while you were agonizing over it at Cornwall, rest assured that I, too, suffered at the recollection! Oh! why did not your mind, your sensibility, your eyes, your voice become incarnate in a youth like yourself when I was an innocent young girl? Or rather, why am I not twenty years old to-day in order to be able to tell you: There is nothing . . . nothing in my past . . . take my whole life! . . ."

"Albine!" sighed Roger, upset.

"It is not my fault that I lived so many years before I met you, so many years before you! It is not my fault. But forgive me!"

It was she now who faltered, and it was he who steadied her. To see her beaten, desperate, she whose usual attitude was dominant and fighting, she who up till now had kept a certain distance even with him, all this dissolved the last vestiges of doubt within him, at the same time firing him with an intense desire to console her, to sacrifice himself for her if need be, to shatter his own life so as to bring happiness to this other life which although still splendid was crying over past days which she could no longer bring to him as an offering.

She was sobbing softly. Then a few words broke through her sobs.

"Forgive me! Whatever life has left me I give to you. They say that I am still beautiful. I think it's true. Yes. Roger, never before, I know, was I so beautiful. Does not this console you? I will not be so always. And you will still be young when I will not be worthy of a look. Well! do not be afraid. When this time comes, I shall go."

She was speaking at random, disjointedly, disorderly. And this very confusion of words in a woman so much mistress of herself had a pathetic, irresistible appeal.

"I shall never leave you," murmured Roger. "I want to tie myself to you for life. And your wish of a moment will come true. It will be between us, as though I had met you while you were a young girl. I want nothing from you as long as we are engaged, before I am your husband."

He saw her falter. As for him, the fervor of a decision taken and formulated brought back all his strength and his insight.

"Take care!" he whispered. "They are returning."

The last guests were indeed coming back to the drawing-room with the Grand-Duchess Hilda.

Albine adjusted her hair in the shadows, and with a few quick gestures powdered her face.

"Go out in the garden and come back to the drawing-room through the stairway," she said to Roger.

He obeyed. She walked up to the grand-duchess who had not noticed her absence and who welcomed her, clamoring, to the others' ironic amusement:

"Is it not true, *chère,* that our Ramon does everything to perfection? Dancing . . . poetry . . . guitar, singing!"

"And other things she doesn't care to mention," whispered Guilloux into Saulnois' ear.

THIRD PART

I

SITTING up in bed, the lower part of her tiny body buried under a heap of scattered sheets of paper, some blank and some covered with writing, magazines, books and clippings, Berthe Lorande was writing. A soft, clinging negligé of yellow crêpe was wrapped around her bust. She sat propped up against two large white pillows. Her short, thick red hair tumbled over the mingling of yellow silk and white linen. Under the bright rays of an April sun, shining diagonally across the room and the bed, her curls glistened like those red pebbles from Auvergne which are used for beads. They hid both sides of her face; the only visible things were the pointed chin, the red lips, the sharp nose and the large eyes, which seemed dark in contrast with the bright hair. And also one saw, emerging from the wide sleeves buttoned at the wrists so as not to hamper her writing, the childish hands, one steadying a sort of small writing-pad on her knees, the other plying a gold fountain pen, a recent gift from Jean de Trévoux.

It was truly a young girl's room: light cretonne covered panels, white furniture of the same English design as the white bed with square posts. Some beautiful religious pictures of the Sienna school, three Limoges enamels upon the walls, and numerous valuable trinkets scattered about the mantel-piece, the table and other pieces of furniture, bespoke the successive impressions of an original and harmonious personality during the course of an already long life. A systematic observer would have noted the complete absence of men's, or at least young men's, photographs amidst a profusion of feminine ones, almost all autographed. Barring an old bearded bourgeois in frock coat and high hat, one hand resting against a column shaft and photographed against a background of romantic landscape—Berthe Lorande's father, the Jouy haberdasher—the male sex was represented only by a few framed prints: contemporary masters of music and literature. But on the white chiffonier near the bed a large photograph of Jean de Trévoux in lieutenant's uniform faced the head of the bed.

Through the wide open window one saw the balcony, the modern roof tops, the northern blue sky melting into gray, and through the opening vista of an adjoining street, the budding greenness of the Parc Monceau.

Berthe Lorande was writing. Earlier in the morning, she had covered six of the scattered sheets on her bed with her fine handwriting—the joy of the typographers —where each letter as clearly formed as though printed had the perfection of a drawing.

She was writing a novel for a new magazine, and of course this novel related an episode of her own life, with an almost embarrassing sincerity, interrupted at times by highly improbable happenings: the usual method of a woman writer. But just now, having finished her task and hurrying somewhat—it was past noon and Doctor Riol was expecting her at his office, Avenue Marceau, at three o'clock—she was scribbling a few letters, a writer's worst drudgery. The last one was more carefully thought out than the others, or at least before writing it she sucked for a moment the end of her gold fountain pen, her face growing dark and hostile.

Then, quickly, she wrote as follows:

No, my dear friend, I will not attend your lecture at five o'clock. I am not free. Not free to hear you and

*applaud you. What imperious necessity can prevent me
from doing so? What am I going to do? Ah, that is
just it. Deceive you, perhaps? No! You know that
I have too great an affectionate admiration for you!*

Her vivacious, charming face had already brightened.
An ironic smile spread over it. She signed, sealed the
blue envelope and addressed it:

*Monsieur Albert Saulnois, of the Institut, care of the
Union des Conférences, 113 boulevard Saint-Germain,
Paris.*

She rang. Her old nurse Clarisse, with the austere
countenance and demeanor of a nun who, having brought
Berthe up in Jouy-en-Josas had never left her, came in.
    "Clarisse, my girl, take these letters to the post-office
at once. There is a special delivery. Then come back
and help me dress."
    It was not quite three o'clock, when an automobile of
the latest modern style, the very one which would
presently take her to the Rhine on a week's visit to Jean
de Trévoux, deposited Berthe Lorande in front of Riol's
residence at the corner of avenue Marceau and rue
Goethe. She was so thickly veiled and muffled up in her
furs that she was hardly recognizable. Special instructions had evidently been given by the famous gynecologist for she was shown immediately into his private
office. There was nothing medical about it. The profusion of priceless furniture, glass cases, paintings, rare
books, betrayed a fastidious dilettante rather than a
scientist. A radiator overheated the room. Berthe
raised her veil, threw off her fur stole on the back of a
chair. A glass case with tanagra statuettes attracted her.
But catching sight of herself in a mirror, she began to

powder her face and forgot the tanagras. She made up
in her favorite fashion, in a sharp contrast of white and
red. She looked now less pretty than during the morning. Evident apprehension contracted her features, and
beneath the miraculous youthfulness of her face, her real
age suddenly showed plainly.

"Excuse me. I kept you waiting. . . ."

Riol kissed both her hands with ceremonious politeness.
Past fifty, he still remained *"le beau Riol,"* tall, with thick
black hair, a pointed beard, and so much charm and kindliness in his oriental eyes, his face, his voice, his entire
countenance and demeanor, that the world forgave him
fame, fortune, and a thing forgiven very rarely: his reputation as a Don Juan.

Standing, they exchanged a few remarks about
common social acquaintances, gossiped about certain
dinners that they had attended, alluded briefly to some
plays and an art exhibit, all this preparatory to the
serious conversation to follow and each one thinking of
one thing while saying another.

"So, you can listen to me for a while, doctor?"

"As long as you wish! To telephone callers as well
as to visitors I am out! This easy-chair suits you?
Nice, isn't it? I bought it last week in Nice, where I had
gone to confine Princess Zanthia."

He had settled comfortably in a Roman chair near his
working table. Almost doubled up in the depths of the
easy chair, Berthe began to speak in the voice of a penitent addressing the Holy Tribunal. He was staring at
her with a professional curiosity tempered by tenderness,
the tenderness of a possible lover which he extended to all
eternally wounded femininity, but which for this woman,
was heightened by admiration for her genius. Wounded,
she felt herself wrapped in his tender glance. It intensified the strong desire burning within her to conquer aim-

lessly, to conquer not a man but the desire of a man; and so the confession went on in an atmosphere both oppressing and intoxicating which brought to a paroxysm the nervous sensibility of professor and penitent. The latter's voice, that deep, sing-song voice usually so well-modulated, was breaking and bruising itself against the bitterness of her confession. It was but a breath at times, at other times almost a sob.

"You see, doctor, I must go back to my past so that you may understand the sort of young girl I was. You know my parents were very modest people. They kept a haberdashery and clothing store, something in the way of a tiny department store. Their business prospered. They sent me to college; they wanted me to become a college professor. I was a good pupil of course. During my studies all my professors either said to me brutally or gave me humbly to understand, that they loved me. . . ."

"You never discouraged any of them?" interrupted the doctor smilingly.

"Not one," she replied gravely as though the case were too serious to be smiled at. "I may even have spurred them on. I do not defend myself. I am telling you the truth. But equally true is the fact that not to a single one of them did I grant anything, do you hear, doctor? Nothing at all, not even a hand clasp. The same applies to my young men callers at home, all of whom likewise made love to me and whom I likewise encouraged. Such was my life while a young girl. A sort of ardent purity of body, a spirit fired with the hope of love, yet a total absence of love. No, not even *that*," replied Berthe in a firmer tone to Riol's silent question. "I saw *that* about me, at college, then in society. I can not understand it. I have had, and still have, some very dear women friends: Albine Anderny, Mme. de Trévoux, Camille Englemann.

But these are friendships, only.   All else sickens and also seems laughable to me."

She meditated a moment, then went on:

"Now, can you picture me as I was when I made my debut in the world?   Mme. de Trévoux who used to spend her summers at Jouy where she had a villa, was a customer of my parents; she noticed me, she found me amusing and pretty.   She gained my confidence; I showed her my first efforts.   They appealed to her.   You know what unerring taste she possesses.   It was she who introduced me into society where I read some of my work which people seemed to like."

"I remember," said Riol.   "I can still see you, so adorably pretty, your modest countenance belied by your mischievous eyes, yet so unmistakably virginal.   A specialist could see it at a glance."

"Do you think so?" asked Mme. Lorande, point-blank.

"I am certain of it."

"Take care!   I am going to put your diagnosis to a test."

"Go ahead. . . ."

"You have before you, twenty years older, the same Berthe Lorande, whom Mme. de Trévoux introduced you to the year of the exposition.   Does the specialist think she is exactly the same to-day?"

Riol thought a moment or two.   Then he said:

"You have been married."

"I lived for nineteen days with Jules Lamorinière, the son of the paper magnate, whom I married.   But what does that prove?"

"Your divorce was not granted on grounds of non-consummation, that I know of."

"No.   My husband had a mistress before he married, and he went back to her after having lived with me for nineteen days. He did not contest this charge and the degree was granted *de plano,* as the lawyers say."

"Well, then?"

"Well, Doctor," repeated Berthe, slightly impatient. "I do not ask you to give me facts based upon social conventions. I ask you to give me a physiologist's diagnosis, and you may well imagine that I do it not merely to ask you a riddle. I need this test. Suppose you had never seen me, knew nothing of my life. What would you surmise?"

Riol did not answer at once. All tender solicitude had disappeared from the glance which first prodded the depths of his patient's eyes, then traveled over each feature of her face, one by one, and the enigmatic silhouette which had arisen and stood before him. Finally he said with the serenity of a scientist establishing a fact:

"I do not know."

At once his strong hands became imprisoned in Berthe's frail ones.

"Ah!" she said. "You are a real master."

"An ignorant one, as you see. . . ."

"No," she answered, returning to her easy-chair, "a real master just because you do not know."

And lowering her head, she added:

"I myself do not know."

"Ah!" said Riol simply.

Both became engrossed in their own thoughts. Berthe's pale face, at the confession, had flushed crimson beneath her paint.

"No, truly I do not know," she continued, accentuating each syllable and so embarrassed that her audacious eyes were cast down on the pattern of the rug. "Oh! it is so painful for me to explain! How can I tell you? No, decidedly, I cannot yet. Be patient. Let me attack my story from another angle. You will understand me in the end without my having to speak words which I cannot utter."

Riol nodded in acquiescence.

"Please remember this: I entered married life like the purest young girl. I was married nineteen days. Since my husband left me my life has been as chaste as before my marriage. Do you believe me? Otherwise, it is useless that I go on."

"I do believe you."

She went on:

"You believe me, but you are almost the only one with the exception of one or two friends, Albine, Camille . . . I know what is being said about me . . . I do! Of what people basely try to convince . . . those who love me." A sob broke through her words. "They say that I am a hysterical, a maniac who craves men . . . all men. Not only my acquaintances, my friends, but mere passers-by as well. Do not protest. I have heard with my own ears Mr. de Guilloux assuring Jeanne Saulnois of it. 'All of them,' he was saying, 'all of them! The secretary of a publication bringing the proofs of an article, the electrician coming to change a fuse. . . .' In short, a Messalina. Strange Messalina, indeed, who, barring nineteen atrocious days, never had a man in her bed!"

She dabbed at her eyes nervously, with her handkerchief rolled into a ball. Tenderly Riol gathered between his strong hands the penitent's knees, which immediately drew back, and said:

"Calm yourself, Madame. No one in Paris gives credit to such infamies. People see you very popular, very courted. It does not seem to displease you; so you have the reputation of being somewhat . . . you will not be angry? . . . somewhat of a coquette, or, as they say now, somewhat . . . of an . . . exciter. . . ."

Berthe's face regained its composure as quickly as that of a child. But it remained serious while she answered:

"Exciter? No. It is a disagreeable word suggesting provocative gestures. With the exception, however, of my loathsome marriage no man ever had the slightest contact with me; no man ever held me in his arms. No one as yet. But perhaps some one will, to-morrow, and that is why I came to see you. Because I am in love at last . . ." she straightened up proudly and took a deep breath. "I know at last what desire is, after having known only the desire of desire. Do you hear me? Till now, till yesterday almost, all my love-life consisted in hoping for love, seeking it, imploring it. Not the love that was being offered me, but the love which I would feel, which I would give. In short, to make me fall in love! . . . Exciter. . . . Oh, no! . . . Rather a sala-mander, immune to the flame, and despairing of ever being burned myself. Yes. . . . To everyone I ac-knowledged my hopeless desire. I said to them all: 'Make me fall in love and I shall belong to you for life.' And to some, when they listened to me, I even dared say: 'Come back! . . . Come back on such a day. Something tells me that I am falling in love with you. . . .' I was sincere! They would go away elated, and would come back breathless. Then I had to admit: 'No . . . I was mistaken. You no longer arouse within me the desire to seek peace in you.' Some understood me and remained my friends; to those, I assure you, I am a loyal friend, a compassionate one, earnestly endeavoring to heal their wounds. Others became angry, and left my house resolving to harm me. One of these, at this very moment, is Albert Saulnois. I never promised him anything, yet he torments me and I feel that he is growing hostile. But all this is nothing," she concluded, and her mobile face became radiant once more. "All this is the

past, dead, buried! I am living in the present, Doctor.
The present which dazzles me . . . and the future is so
intoxicating that I dare not believe in it."

She bent towards him, and this time spoke in a real
confessional voice:

"I am in love, Doctor. My heart has shed its cocoon.
I am in love. There is in this world a human being
whom I think of incessantly, no longer wondering with
anguish: 'Will he, at last, teach me what love is?' but
shouting to my own self: 'I adore you, I want to be
part of you, and I am afraid lest I be unworthy of
you! . . .' And this man loves me, has faith in me.
I have told him the truth, or at least everything that can
be told to anyone but yourself, a physician. He never
doubted me for a second. He is twenty-three years old;
he knows my age and so do you, because you knew me
when I was twenty. The fifteen years between us do
not rebuff him and he implores me to be his
wife. . . . Oh! how dearly I love him!"

Tears of joy streamed down her cheeks. Riol was
staring at her with a somewhat sneering curiosity; a
vague feeling of jealousy swelled within him against
this unknown, privileged man. He replied in a less
affectionate tone:

"Congratulations, Madame, to Pygmalion and the
Statue. But I fail to see what part I am to play between
them."

Berthe highly sensitive, felt this slight drop in the
warmth of his sympathy. The caress in her eyes, her
way of suddenly offering her whole heart which, when
she so wished transfigured her face completely, easily
won back at once the physician's sympathy.

"But, Doctor, all our hopes are concentrated upon you;
mine at least, because he, poor child, has no inkling of the

uncertainty of his happiness. Within a few days, I am to join him in the Rhineland where he, an officer, is stationed with the army of occupation. Yes, you have guessed his name. Do not pronounce it, because I would not dare continue. He is shortly to have a furlough . . . and it will be our betrothal. In short, the happiness which I dreamed of all my life, is, so to speak, within reach of my hand. But it is you who will tell me whether it is not a chimera, whether I may or may not live. You do not understand? Ah! tell me you do, without the need of my speaking. . . ."

"Frankly," uttered the physician, "I do not understand. Suppositions? Yes. I can imagine. But how am I, a physician, to intervene?"

With a nervous, unexpectedly strong movement, Berthe brought her easy chair closer to the Roman chair where Riol was sitting. She moved to the very edge of her seat, covered her face with her hands, and, her voice so convulsed that it seemed almost a gasp, she whispered:

"Remember—what I told you about my marriage . . . the nineteen days . . . the eighteen nights. A nightmare which I want to forget, which often tortures me in my sleep, and from which I awaken in a cold sweat, my body aching. Remember my answer a while ago 'I do not know' . . . and bear in mind the fact that my husband had a mistress before his marriage, that he went back to her after a horrible scene when, fleeing, trapped, but fully aroused and ready to bite like a she-wolf on the defensive, I read the lust to kill in his eyes. . . ."

Riol stopped her with a gesture:

"I understand," he said.

He let her sob quite a while. Then, in a gentle, persuasive voice:

"Do not become unduly alarmed. It would really be

most extraordinary if you were right. Extraordinary,
given modern science. The celebrated mistress of
Chateaubriand was born a century too soon."

"Really!" she cried, beaming. She was on her feet at
once. Riol rose likewise.

"We shall if you don't mind step into my consultation
room . . . this way!"

He stepped aside, pointing to a double door close by.
Berthe drew back. She blushed.

"Oh," she said . . . "is it absolutely necessary? I
can speak. I will have the courage to explain; you will
get the facts just as well. But I beg of you, not in
there!"

"Come, madame," said Riol with friendly severity, "do
not be childish. Did you come here to consult a specialist,
yes or no? If you do not care to go through with it, it
is my duty not to keep the next patient waiting any
longer."

She clung to his arm.

"Do not be cruel," she murmured, "just give me one
moment. There! let's go!"

Riol's right hand had barely reached the door-knob
when Berthe Lorande's stiffened body came down heavily
on his left arm. He carried her to the easy chair, put
a bottle of smelling salts to her nostrils. She revived
slowly.

"It's over," she whispered. "Forgive me, I will not
do it again. You'll see, I will not be nervous any more.
Things always happen with me this way. The mental
picture of what I fear always upsets me far more than
the real thing. . . . I am ready."

She rose again. Riol was scrutinizing her carefully
and read determination in her eyes.

"Do you know," he said to her, smiling, "that I have
never before met with such bashfulness? Not even with

the most virtuous women, with young girls . . . not
even with nuns?

Her wonderful eyes filled with desperate resolve,
lifted towards him, Berthe replied:

"It is not sham, I assure you!"

"I know it," said Riol.

They went inside.

While the audience was pouring out through three
wide doors upon the sidewalk of the Faubourg Saint
Germain, a group of privileged characters crowded the
small reception room adjoining the auditorium where
Albert Saulnois had just finished lecturing. It was a
mundane group of special nature: the flower of intellect-
aspiring salons, "modern thought" women, a different
category from "uplift" women, the smartest members of
the Institut and contributors to serious magazines. Besides, there were at least three women to every man, a
few of them quite elegant: Mme. de Juvigny together
with "that beautiful Comtesse de Mers"; Albine Anderny with Mme de Trévoux; Camille Engelmann in a
corner with Maurice de Gilloux and Mme. de Bugey.
Guilloux was scoffing at the lecturer.

"Our brilliant master was not in good form, it seems
to me. Clever theme: *Woman's struggle against
time*. People expected to see some delicate hair splitting
done . . . splitting of gray, henna-tinted hair . . . and
instead nothing but commonplace talk . . . hackneyed
phrases. At one time he even lost the thread . . . or
rather the hair. Did you notice it? He actually
mumbled."

And whispering confidentially:

"Just before the lecture he had a special delivery letter
from Berthe Lorande, probably excusing herself from
the little oratorical party. I was there: I recognized

her handwriting. Anxiety, jealousy, confusion ensued."

A glance of Mme. de Bugey silenced him. Albert Saulnois was entering the reception room, followed by Jeanne
who was gently drying his brow with her handkerchief
rolled in a ball. He, in the meanwhile, was wiping his
gold-rimmed glasses before putting them on. He was
paler than usual and looked exceedingly tired.

"What a treat, dear master !"

"Master! One never gets tired listening to you."

"Bravo! Bravo! You were in better form than
ever !"

He shook outstretched hands, returned people's greet-
ings at times with a bow or a smile, and at times with
a spoken "thank you, dear friend," or "awfully glad I
did not bore you." But his mind was apparently elsewhere and his eyes wandered about restlessly.

"Whom is he looking for?" asked Jean de Trévoux
in a whisper of Roger Vaugrenier.

Both were patiently trying to reach him through the
swarming crowd.

"He is looking for the one who is not thinking of him,"
answered Roger.

"Mme. Lorande? She informed me she was not coming."

And, with that charming arrogance of triumphant
youth, in his case moderated by real kindness, the officer
added, looking at the celebrated lecturer:

"Poor fellow !"

Little by little only intimates remained in the small
reception room. Guilloux was congratulating Saulnois
with such persistent exaggeration that it hurt Jeanne
Saulnois who was entirely too clairvoyant where her
husband was concerned to miss feeling the unsteadiness
of the "performance" and its success. Albert was pro-
testing:

"No . . . it did not go as I wanted it to. This auditorium is a furnace. It is so hot to-day, actually suffocating. It upset me. I was on the point of stopping in the middle of the lecture and dropping it."

"Dearest," said Jeanne kissing his forehead, "furnace or no furnace, believe me you spoke as no one else in Paris could have spoken. And the newspapers will agree with me. Guilloux, please step in the offices of the *Figaro,* the *Gaulois,* the *Echo de Paris* and the *Temps.*"

"Why . . . gladly," replied the diplomat, somewhat abashed by this sudden offensive.

"Oh! it is not worth it!" feebly protested Saulnois.

"Oh yes, it is," insisted Jeanne. "Our friend over there is quite ·clever at this sort of thing. Please go at once, won't you, Maurice?"

There was coquetry, almost a promise in the sinuous glance which accompanied the command. And so naïve is man's conceit that Guilloux went immediately, determined to fulfill his duties to the best of his ability as though the ardent tenderness of her glance was really meant for him.

Roger and Trévoux were among the group of intimates who still swarmed around the speaker at the time Guilloux was sent on his errand. Roger noticed the relaxing of Saulnois' face when he saw Trévoux, his effusive hand-shake. At once he reconstructed the little inward drama being unfolded in the scientist's soul: so Trévoux was not with Berthe after all!

A few minutes later the two young men whose friendship was growing stronger all the time, walked down the boulevard towards the Seine. It was broad daylight yet, in spite of the street lamps that sparkled like livid stars between the budding green of the trees.

"That scamp Guilloux is right," Roger said. "Saulnois was not up to his usual standard, and you know why."

"Why, no," Trévoux answered sincerely. "We were mistaken, Saulnois' eyes were not searching for Mme. Lorande as we supposed. He himself told me that she informed him she could not be present."

"He made a point of letting you know that he was not being neglected without a certain decorum. And in truth, it was not Mme. Lorande whom he was trying to locate, but you. . . . Yes, you Jean! Your presence relieved him, and what made him mumble in the midst of the lecture was the mental picture which he had evolved, imagining her and you together. See Spinoza's theorem."

"I do not know myself what Mme. Lorande is doing to-day. We spoke on the telephone this morning, but I would not take the liberty of questioning her as to how she spends her time."

Instinctively they would fall into step together and purposely break away as soon as they became aware of it.

"What havoc," said Roger as though speaking to himself," is sometimes wrought in a serious life by the rustle of a skirt!"

"If it's Saulnois you have in mind," objected Trévoux laughing, "why, he spends his whole life rustling skirts."

"Saulnois is a puppet that interests me very little. The fascinating half of that household is his wife: she has such an ingenuous way of loving before the whole universe that one wonders: does she know? Or does she not? No, I was not thinking of Saulnois, or at least, my thought swerved to him accidentally. I was thinking of ourselves."

He slipped his hand under the officer's blue-clad arm, and they began to walk so slowly, that passers-by in

order to avoid them would overtake them and cross
ahead.

"I was thinking of ourselves," repeated Roger. "For
our destinies, yours and mine, are alike. We tackled life
under normal conditions, you who are a blue-blood, and
I whose future is secure, since I have a profession in
spite of my illegitimate birth and am not a fool. Marriage, children, old age, death: the usual proportion of
life's joys and sorrows awaits us. I have met Mme.
Anderny; you have met Mme. Lorande."

"I have known Berthe since childhood," protested the
officer.

"You told me yourself that only when you met her
again last year, after five years of separation, you really
saw her for the first time. What does it matter anyway?
A day came for you as well as for myself when a new,
irresistible force entered our magnetic field; since then
our trajectory has become troubled, altered. It is the
end. Neither you nor I will ever again gravitate like
common mortals."

"Are you complaining of it?"

"No. Not any more than a tiny grain of dust of the
milky way complains at being suddenly drawn beyond its
compass. One does not complain of the inevitable, one
adapts oneself to it. I feel I am the toy of an in-
exorable fate. I have fought against it as you know.
I even attempted to flee. Guilloux has done everything to
dissuade me. He told me some very accurate, detailed
incidents. He named several men whose lives were
mixed with that of the countess. Even this: before
her marriage an illegitimate daughter born to her in
Austria during her travels at the age of eighteen.
Anonymous letters repeated to me the same names with
slight variations, England instead of Austria. Nothing
matters. I burned the letters and severed my friendship

with Guilloux almost completely. Should Mme. Anderny persist in wanting it, my life is bound to hers. And you, you will share the life of Mme. Lorande, who, for different yet quite as powerful reasons, seems no more intended for you than Count Anderny's widow is for me."

Trévoux stopped and pressed Roger's hand.

"Yes, it's extraordinary. I marvel at it as you do. But what surprises me most is that such women should have cast their eyes on us, you and me who are healthy and intelligent beings, granted, but after all—we can admit it since we appreciate and like one another—we are very ordinary mortals. Your parallel was correctly drawn: we amount to just about a grain of dust of the milky way. Well then, what I admire is that such a grain of dust was chosen by one of these magnetic, irresistible forces. Roger, whatever happens to us, our fate is a great one."

"Perhaps," said Roger upon whom the blue officer's soulful words had the quieting effect of a sun-bath.

"When one loves the type of women we do," continued Trévoux, who was now pulling his friend along at a quicker gait to the swifter rhythm of his words, "do other women exist? Do they not seem to be supernumeraries, figureheads? To be sure, nothing prevented us from marrying one of these supernumeraries or figureheads and, ourselves being of average calibre, lead an average existence. And all at once, something happens to us which is similar to what war, the war you hate so, has done for the obscure jobber, the unknown scribbler; sudden opportunity, the deed accomplished, glory! No matter how hateful war appears to you, glory is a fact, like beauty, like genius. Well, we stand the same chances as these privileged ones. We were chosen accidentally, without deserving it. It is worth the suffering."

"Others had previously been chosen by them. . . ." Roger whispered, "and have subsequently returned to their nothingness. Why should we, insignificant creatures, ordinary mortals as you say, be their ultimate choice?"

"I have faith in the one love," said Trévoux simply. "Nothing will shake my belief in her."

"I, too," answered Roger as though speaking to himself. "Albine does not lie. But who can guarantee one's own heart?"

"No one, Roger. Not even you. I more so than you, perhaps. But observe this. Usually, the worry as to love's lasting tortures chiefly the hearts of women. . . . It is they who implore: it will be forever? And yet here we are, both real men with strong, masculine hearts, dangerously near imploring after the feminine fashion and almost crying: will it really be forever?"

"Yes," said Roger, struck by the remark.

"Does not that emphasize the exception in our case, our extraordinary good fortune? The right to choose, which belongs to men, we have relinquished. It is they who choose us. They are human specimens so infinitely superior to ourselves that sexual laws become abolished automatically. They demand masculine rights, freedom, the liberty of choice: we submit to it because it is right."

"The very fact that they are our seniors by a number of years accentuates this authority. As youthful as we are in physical vigor and countenance, they derive an advantage in being our seniors. I submit, I like the yoke thrust upon me."

The two friends had reached the river bank. The lights of Paris were beginning to overshadow the last vestiges of twilight. Roger thought: "Trévoux is happy. He is wise. He goes on, blissfully, towards a future which terrifies me but which I will not escape. I too cannot live without the yoke. Only, I feel it about my shoulders. . . ."

"I think this is where we part," said the officer, "Are you going to the rue Raynouard?"

"Yes."

"I have just time enough to go home and get my valise. I am leaving for Mayence on the seven-twelve."

"Without seeing her?"

"She wished it so, and I told you that I always submit. She is to join me in the Rhineland within a few days, and I live so completely wrapped in this hope that until the moment we meet once more, free and alone, ambient reality seems to me but a gloomy voyage. Good-bye, Roger!"

"Good-bye, Jean!"

A taxi whirled the officer off, while Vaugrenier continued to walk down the left river bank. Thus every day he tried to break the tension of his nerves by long walks. He watched the mirrored reflections and the white flame of the street lamps cast fading shadows on the surface of the silent waters, and he thought: "How weak-hearted I am! How I waver! Trévoux only said a few words to me, nothing but the prattle of a lover who wants his happiness in spite of everything; and I feel less worried, almost as light-hearted as he! Well! he is right! When one walks towards the inevitable it is better to stride firmly, one's eyes on the road. I shall become Albine's husband and obliterate from my memory even the suspicion of what I do not wish to know."

His soul echoed the impassioned, grief-stricken words of the one he loved. "Forgive me! What life has left me I give to you!" Could humbler words ever fall from a woman's lips. And the tears, those big tears that he had seen on her cheeks! And that woman was the

proudest among the proud. Did not such humility heal
the wound of his own pride?

The desire seized him to see her at once, without delay,
like the craving of a drug fiend. And, as an empty taxi
lazily went past along the bank, he hailed it.

III

The Grand-Duchess Hilda and her lady-in-waiting,
Mme. Lelièvre, had announced themselves for three
o'clock at Countess Anderny's home. Knowing the
scrupulous punctuality of this "royal personage," the
countess since a quarter past two sat waiting in the Louis
XVI library, a yellow-backed paper novel in her hands.
It was a new novel which was being talked about. She
was looking through it rather than reading it, skipping
pages, her wandering curiosity at times lingering upon
a dialogue, a description, a thought, at random. Once she
stopped at the following sentence:

"It is useless to deny the existence of forebodings.
Besides their mechanism is no longer a mystery now that
science has unraveled and controls telepathic phe-
nomena. . . ."

She shrugged her shoulders, closed the volume, and
put it down together with the tortoise-shell paper-cutter
on a near-by stand. She meditated. The sentence
which she had read was stupid and awkward, but its
central thought had suddenly crystallized in her vague
apprehensions which had been smoldering within her since
morning without definite cause, and which persisted in
spite of the beauty of the spring day, in spite of the
amusement that the forthcoming royal visit would afford
her, in spite of the prospective evening that she had
promised to spend with Roger.

"Foreboding?" She thought. "What a formidable word! The veil conceals the morrow, a veil gradually growing transparent, and which little by little reveals the ghastly outline of the Nemesis. To settle one's score in three lines because of such a word, to imagine that one had said everything by saying telepathy, which means nothing at all!"

> . . . *With what irreverence,*
> *This knave speaks of the gods!*

She bore the "knave" a grudge for having determined and specified the nature of her anguish by flashing the word "foreboding" before her eyes. Now there was no way of avoiding the onrush of restless thoughts. It was better to have an explanation with one's Self, to seek the Whys and Wherefores of this anguish.

Bringing her slender hands over her eyes, so as to concentrate and scrutinize their innermost recesses wherein foreboding was spreading, she tried by the method customary to her to perceive and isolate the cause of her vague anguish which had increased within her since Roger's return and which to-day was almost intolerable.

"The man I love has become submissive; the future shall be as I wished it from our first meeting. Is the apprehension of changing my mode of life causing me such anguish? Certainly not, since I am tired of society, luxury, this house, my servants, tired of being on exhibit, to be known to people whom I do not know; since I really regained my taste for life only since his advent and since I can not conceive life without him. . . .

"Am I afraid of being deceived? No! I have experienced deceptions in the past. I sought in the love of men a happiness they did not give me at all, or for a very

short time only.   But let us be sincere: upon embarking
on these adventures I instinctively knew that I was speeding towards deception in the end.   I yielded to the allure-
ment of the test, hoping, without believing, that each
would be the final one.   To-day, however, it is different.
I am certain that it is the ultimate test.   I am certain
that my life can point towards *him* only.   Though this
feature shared by both of us may hold a thousand sorrows in store, I can only go towards this future with him.
For the first time I feel the certainty of a final choice.
There is absolute accord between us.   We know that we
will be married far from Paris and that we shall make
our home abroad.   This prospect delights me.   I live
impatiently in the present; to-morrow alone matters, and
I may consider it assured.   Why then this anguish?"

She meditated with such intense attention that her lips
moved as though she were praying.   "Could it be," she
thought, "because he informed me that he would be gone
for three days to Nancy where a friend summons him on
a consultation?   On the contrary, I am rather pleased at
being able to collect my thoughts and meditate before we
take our vows.   Once more, where then does foreboding
take root?"

The noise of an automobile stopping in front of the
house interrupted her musings.   Her hands relaxed; she
strained her features, listened.   Yes, it was the grand-
duchess with her lady-in-waiting.   Albine rose to go and
meet her at the foot of the staircase.

And it was while crossing the big reception room, glad
of this diversion which cut short the thread of her
thoughts, it was then that a recollection, a name, spring-
ing from the past, flashed like lightning across her
memory. Without having either time or need for
pondering, she thought: "There . . . that's it. . . ."

Just as upon feeling a sharp pain on the right side one thinks: "Appendicitis."

"My dear, dear Albine! How nice of you to have remained at home on account of myself and Mme. Lelièvre! . . . Look, Lelièvre, *die Gräfin ist reizend*. It gives me such pleasure to see you grow more and more beautiful every day, dear countess, because we are about the same age, isn't it so? You are my senior, but only very slightly. And as I am being told— *par mes amis et ma famille, naturellement*—that I never looked better than I do now, I should like to believe it . . . and, looking at you, gives me the courage to believe it."

She began to laugh heartily as though she had just said the greatest pleasantry in the world. Mme. Lelièvre laughed louder and longer still. She was a lanky creature with greenish-gray hair who looked like a caricature of the grand-duchess. It was rumored that she was the result of a trip which the duke, Hilda's father, had made during the time of his wife's confinement. The grotesque resemblance was accentuated by the clothes, Mme. Lelièvre's wardrobe being made up of her sovereign's discarded gowns. The comic effect achieved by one of the grand-duchess' always eccentric dresses on Mme. Lelièvre's figure, surpassed all imagination.

Albine smiled.

"Madame is indeed in magnificent form," she said.

"All the men turn around to look at her Highness," quickly began Mme. Lelièvre, who spoke a correct French, but so voluble that one barely understood her. "We can no longer go *en promenade* because of it. Only yesterday, in the Bois, a group of young men followed us. Impossible to get rid of them."

"Be quiet, Lelièvre," interrupted the duchess. "Let me talk."

Albine thought: "The two of them out walking and such behavior and such clothes! Mme. Lelièvre neither invents nor exaggerates anything."

"My dear, dear countess," went on Hilda, taking one of Albine's hands in hers, "I came to enjoin you, to ask you for a little . . . a little tactful favor. We spoke of it already at Ramon's . . . at Mr. Genaz's, do you remember? The other day, at that charming party he gave us? How ravishingly pretty it was, don't you think? Yes, a marvel. The flowers . . . the sunshine . . . and he, such a gracious host. The only disparaging thing was this Vitzina, *Sie ist eine Hure—jawohl!* One does not introduce to society such a harlot, such a filthy harlot. I said so to Ramon who apologized. No, be silent, Lelièvre, or you will again prevent me from saying what I want. When you open your mouth, no one has a chance of edging a word in. Where was I? Ah! . . . there, dear Albine. You are so beautiful to-day! One forgets, looking at you, what one was going to tell you. It is concerning passports, three passports, for some friends. All I have to do is to ask for them myself, at the Foreign office, isn't that so? They will be given to me. *Mais je ne le ferai pas, comprenez-vous?* If I, a royal personage, intervene myself, at once it becomes a tremendous, formidable affair! And precisely, it concerns some good tradespeople, simple, honest people, a man and his two sisters, Mr. . . . Mr. . . . Lelièvre, what is your friend's name? Guerrier, isn't it?"

"Guernier," corrected Mme. Lelièvre, "Mr. Robert Guernier, and his sisters, the Misses Guernier. He is a jeweler who is going to America to sell pearls. A number of ladies are selling their pearls just now, especially these poor Russian noblewomen whom revolution obl. . . ."

"Be quiet, Lelièvre!" interrupted the duchess. "One hears no one but you. These Guerniers are very respectable people, in whose welfare Mme. Lelièvre is interested. They are somewhat related to her, isn't that so, Lelièvre?" The lady-in-waiting gave a slight start of astonishment. "Yes, they are your cousins, *sehr gute Leute.* So, you understand, Albine, this little family being perfectly respectable, they must obtain their passports without difficulty. Can I depend upon it?"

Albine answered:

"I will gladly make this request of Mr. Cordelier who is related to my family and who is director of the office. But I must inform Madame that my intervention is superfluous. Mme. Lelièvre's relatives certainly will not be refused passports if they simply and directly apply for them themselves."

The two visitors exchanged glances.

"Lelièvre, explain," ordered the duchess.

"It is this way, dear countess," quickly began the lady-in-waiting. "For reasons too lengthy to explain, business reasons regarding avoidance of competition, my friends," she corrected herself, "my relatives would not like to have to go to the offices in person and submit to all the formalities of establishing their identity. The matter is most important; other jewelers might interfere . . . and of course, Guernier would much prefer to have the thing done discreetly."

In spite of her natural volubility Mme. Lelièvre hesitated from time to time. The duchess grew impatient and interrupted:

"Besides, my dear countess, I may safely tell you, these relatives of Mme. Lelièvre are entrusted with a mission from me in America. I have some interests which have been neglected there . . . some real estate which is to be sold. I must have a trustworthy person. I will give you their names and descriptions. I would want the three passports confidentially. You understand?"

Albine had understood very well. "A wild prank of those two crazy women with Genaz, under a fictitious name. The grand-duke is at present cruising the north seas on his yacht; so they have three months of freedom. I will tell Cordelier the truth; let him do what he deems best. Besides, I think that the Quai d'Orsay will be quite pleased to be rid of them for some time."

"Your Highness may rest assured that I shall take the necessary steps. If I do not succeed it will be through my lack of influence. Only, Mme. Lelièvre will have to give me three slips, supplying the information requested on ordinary passports."

"Lelièvre, give it to me!" interrupted her Highness.

"You are prepared for all emergencies, countess," said Mme. Lelièvre, pulling out of her handbag a purple envelope bearing the Finsburg crest. "I had prepared it beforehand. Is it correct? Look at it, please!"

Albine glanced hurriedly at one of the slips: *Guernier* (*Robert*), *thirty-seven, dealer in jewelry, height 5 foot 8, oval face, high forehead, black hair, olive complexion. . . .*" That is Ramon all right," she thought. And aloud, replacing the slips in the envelope: "I will telephone Cordelier presently. You will have the answer to-morrow."

"Oh! I am so greatly, greatly obliged to you," replied the grand-duchess.

She embraced the countess and kissed her impetuously. With surprise Albine felt the moisture of a tear on her cheek. At the same moment a peculiar hiccough convulsed Mme. Lelièvre's throat. It was her way of sobbing. At once Hilda's emotion broke forth untrammeled. Her sobs were interrupted by words spoken into the ear of Albine to whom she still clung, incoherent words, revealing her naïve and sincere heart no longer held in check by diplomatic caution:

"What a friend you are! and how grieved I am to leave you, *chère, chère* Albine! . . . *Ach! Gott im Himmel!* Life is so terribly complicated . . . and a poor, weak woman's heart leads her as it chooses. You will think of me. You must think of me! I will write you, confide in you, because you are a most loyal woman. . . . And so infinitely sensible!"

She freed the countess from her embrace, rose and having stopped crying, yet her face still bathed in tears, she held the other's hands and looked her squarely in the eyes. At the paroxysm of her emotion, Mme. Lelièvre's hiccoughs became a tragic bark.

"Albine," said the grand-duchess, "isn't it true that love alone matters in life? You who have always been a great lover, tell me that love is everything and that one must sacrifice everything for it. Oh! you dare not answer me!"

Albine, indeed, remained silent, embarrassed by this sort of parody of her own case, the drama which was upsetting her own life. Also, the words "You have always been a great lover" touched a sore spot in her. However, the crisis through which she herself was passing, swayed her to compassion. "This woman is ridiculous, but she is really in love."

"Madame," she said at last, "things do not run alike for a royal personage like your Highness and for a mere society woman."

The grand-duchess immediately dropped Albine's hands and turning round towards the prostrated Mme. Lelièvre who was still hiccoughing, said to her severely, as though the poor lady-in-waiting were the cause of it all:

"Do you hear, Lelièvre? Do you hear the voice of wisdom, the voice of honor?"

Mme. Lelièvre was so struck that her hiccoughs stopped short.

"Well, answer, Lelièvre!" cried her Highness. "Yes or no? Is not what this dear Countess Anderny says the voice of wisdom and honor itself? Do things run alike for a royal personage and a mere society woman? Well, answer! You are forever talking when you have nothing to say, and one can not get a word out of you when it might be of some use!"

"No," mumbled Mme. Lelièvre, terrorized.

"No, what?" fumed the German woman.

"Things do not run alike for Madame and for ordinary women."

"That is the truth," concluded Hilda, turning round to Albine. "What perception in your mind, my dear friend; what intelligence! Never, not even in Germany, have I met such a noble. . . . All right. Thanks to you, I see clearly now. Come, Lelièvre, let us take our leave. I am going, feeling absolutely comforted. *Laissez-moi venir à vous quand je suis troublée, chère comtesse!* Oh, you are seeing us to the door? How gracious of you! But I excuse you from this duty, Albine. Are we not intimate friends? No? You really want to? Very well, then! Come with us as far as the elevator. So many people in Paris to-day do not even know the customs to be observed towards royal personages. All these parvenus, all these nouveaux riches!"

In front of the elevator cage, the door of which was being held open by a footman, the three women stopped. Hilda kissed Albine again, then shaking her hand:

"Thank you again, dear friend, for the beautiful profound words you said to me! Remember them, Lelièvre, and as soon as we are home, write them down on a sheet of beautiful paper; have it framed, and I shall keep it on my table, before my eyes."

Still holding Albine's hands she remained silent a moment, thinking. The struggle which was taking place in her soul contracted her mouth and the faint wrinkles of her forehead. She went on:

"Yes, beautiful, inspiring words! All the same . . ." —and in spite of her haughty manner, she cast her eyes down to the rug at the stair-head—"regarding these friends of Mme. Lelièvre, these relatives, the kindly Guernier people I spoke to you about, please arrange the necessary papers at your cousin's office. I can depend upon it, can't I, dear countess?"

"Madame can depend upon it."

"Thanks . . . thanks . . . for this and for the beautiful words. Thank you for everything. Come, Lelièvre. . . . Here, step into the elevator first to see whether it's solid. Sometimes it gives way as soon as you set your foot in it. No? It is safely fastened? Farewell, then, dear countess!"

And while the elevator was shooting down, Albine heard her Highness' shrill voice rising from the shaft. . . .

"The passports! Don't forget! To-morrow, at the very latest!"

"What a trio!" thought Albine, once more settled in the library, while the royal automobile circled noisily away from the house. "Genaz, Lelièvre, the grand duchess! It will take considerable good nature on the part of the diplomatic agents to accept them as peaceful dealers in pearls. Besides, Hilda will step out of her character in less than twenty-four hours. Still, it's their own business! I told her what it was my duty to . . ."

She tried to force herself to become interested in their

adventure. What were her Highness' real plans? A trip, incognito, in sunny climes, while the grand-duke was exploring arctic regions? Probably! But then, why this deep, genuine outburst of emotion to which both women had succumbed? One does not become so upset for a prank of a few weeks. Hilda had spoken as though she never again expected to see Albine. Was she really going to expatriate herself with this tangoing adventurer, and sacrifice her royal position to the love of romance? Once more Albine suffered in finding again a grimacing, grotesque reflection of her own sacrifice in this distorting mirror. In spite of her efforts, her apprehension, everything to-day brought her back to the examination of her own case. The name, the date which had flashed through her brain as she was going to meet her Highness, she again saw them written on the screen of her memory. Decidedly all efforts to dispel this obsessing recurrence were proving fruitless. Her lofty soul, energetic and sensible, became conscious of an inward emotion which before this she had experienced in various momentous circumstances of her life. A sort of virile resolve commanded her to be brave, to look the actual danger in the face instead of shunning it, or instead of drugging her anguish as women ordinarily strive to do, and as whatever typically feminine reactions she possessed were tempting her to do.

She rang for her maid.

"Justine, I have a slight headache. Draw my bedroom curtains and light the bed lamp only. I am going to rest. Put out my black and blue kimono and go. I shall undress myself. I'm out to everybody without exception. See that there is no noise whatever in the house. Disconnect my bedroom telephone."

A quarter of an hour later, in complete darkness, Albine, wrapped in the folds of her kimono, stretched motionless on her bed, was thinking. Hers was not the hazy, capricious dreaming which wafts thought along at random, but painstaking, fervent meditation, similar to that of a scientist who wishes that he could shut himself within his own brain and concentrate therein all his living powers in order to distinguish the better the links connecting the abstract with the concrete. The abstract, to Albine, was the menace that was being disclosed to her by an intolerable foreboding. The concrete was her own past wherefrom, she felt certain, sprang the roots of this foreboding.

A few days earlier, during one of these moments, quite frequent now, of perfect understanding with Roger, she had told him:

"I know your whole life, and you know mine chiefly through the venomous comments of my enemies. We are about to cast our lives together. The past must not poison the future. I feel vague grudges, hostile conjectures coiling back of this brow which I love. Out with it now! Question me! I shall answer."

Roger had hung his head. Then he had taken Albine's hands and whispered:

"I can not."

Albine had not insisted; but she had made a resolution. She must establish at any cost Roger's creed regarding this critical past. And now was the time to do it. For now Roger was able to hear everything. Albine felt that he was attached to her like the most trusting fiancé to the most virginal bride-to-be. Besides, were it the very image of truth, to him this confession would reveal nothing that the wickedness of Guilloux had not already disclosed. The painful operation performed, Roger would champion the cause of the beloved woman; he would defend, exonerate her by the same arguments which, in order to defend and exonerate herself, Albine was using.

Without further raising the question with Roger, she had started that very day a written confession. Would she surrender it to Roger? She did not in the least know at the time of writing. But writing down beforehand something that will be difficult to say—she had experienced it many a time—proved an infallible safeguard against imprudent words to be avoided. She had begun her task with the will to tell the truth; and, indeed, truth, the entire truth, impregnated the opening pages relating the story of her family, her childhood, education, the blossoming forth of adolescence. But she was too far-sighted, too sincere to delude herself. "It is not my girlhood that matters. I want to tell the truth of my life as a woman." And jumping over a period of ten years, she had started, with a sort of vehement generosity, the recital of her affair in Rome with the Chevalier Bellinconi, a discreet affair, as they always were with Albine, devoid of either notoriety or scandal. But all society had known of it and cloaked it with this unhealthy protection for which it avenges itself later by publicit; and calumny. Albine had related it in a style rather like that of Chateaubriand when he related his affair, which too, had happened in Rome, with Pauline de Beaumont. It had lasted two and a half years and had ended amicably through mutual boredom. Bellinconi had since married a Borgese princess. Thirty months during which Albine had said to herself: "I was true to him. . . ." And yet, in relating the history of that period, she made her first compromise with truth. She did not write the full truth. There was, during that period of thirty months, a fortnight spent in Paris which she omitted. She could not, no, she could not relate an incredible faltering, suffered on a certain afternoon in her own apartment among the canvas-covered furniture and the gauze-wrapped paintings and chandeliers, a faint golden-hued ray of light dimly filtering through the closed shutters. . . . A man of the world? No. An artist, a painter, not even a famous one, summoned to complete arrangements about a portrait to be copied. She had never seen him again, and no one had ever known. Must she inflict an additional suffering upon Roger, and a useless one at that? "Really I did not consent . . . in this empty apartment I was compelled." Thus she had suppressed the avowal before starting it.

Without chronological order, guided only by memory and inspiration, she wrote about the important periods of her youth and maturity. In tacit agreement with herself, incidents similar to the one with the Parisian painter were not mentioned. However, it is only fair to say that in the course of the twenty-five years which she was examining such incidents were the exception.

Women possess the faculty of truly forgetting whatever has embarrassed or humiliated them in the past. It is as though their memory can like a stomach reject, before assimilating, such nourishment as becomes distasteful to it immediately following its absorption. Albine's confession, contrary to her original, generous plan, thus pointed toward a brief exposé of what Roger either knew already or might chance to learn: and this exposé unconsciously took on the nature of an apology. What a pathetic controversy! To be one's own tormentor, and like the wretched victim submitting to the third degree, confess as little as possible, just enough to bring the torture to an end.

To-day while Albine, swathed in black and blue crêpe, was meditating in the silence and darkness of her bedroom the painful report was almost finished. The written sheets were locked in the safe near the bed, together with her most precious jewels and her most intimate papers. To an un-forewarned reader their contents would have brought to mind the memoirs of a noblewoman of the XVIIth or XVIIIth century, relating with womanly reserve and dignity the story of a life interwoven with the lives of other great personages whom she designated by initials only without naming any. There were three besides the Roman adventure; the son of a Hungarian prince, and two Parisian aristocrats. The writer had dwelt at full length upon the history of her marriage. She related in detail how, in the year 1898—she was then eighteen and travelling through Europe chaperoned by the famous woman painter Henriquette Dupont whose pupil she was—Count Anderny, an eccentric middle-aged multimillionaire, had asked for her hand after meeting her twice, had married her, and bestowed upon her a dowry of two millions. The memorandum laid particular stress upon the conjugal faithfulness which the young wife had rigidly observed until a day when, after the couple had made their home in Paris living there on a sumptuous scale, the count had made a public exhibition of his affair with an actress of the Théâtre Français, had openly established her in a villa, and had so to speak taken up his residence with her. With the advent of divorce, followed by widowhood fifteen months later, Countess Anderny had deemed herself a free woman. She said so in appropriate terms. Her life, according to the document, divided itself into a daring yet virtuous adolescence—Albine did not deny the fact that she had been as the English say a little "fast"—an honest marriage to whose vows she had blamelessly lived up; an adventurous womanhood for which the husband's unworthiness was responsible. . . .

Even in its present state she thought the report too bitter to be shown to Roger, and several times daily, occasionally quite late at night, she would retouch it, bringing into play all the resources of her mind and her heart so that one sentence may heal the wound which the preceding one perhaps chanced to inflict, that each word be an antidote to the poison it held. So, gradually, the confession had become the most ardent impassioned pleading. The only thing that remained to be written in order to complete it was the beginning of the trip undertaken with Henriquette Dupont, at the age of eighteen. A period covering less than a year's time, and stretching from the finish of her education in Paris to her Hungarian marriage.

Albine's orders to keep the house silent had been carried out to the letter. It was as still as in the dead of night. The silence was suddenly broken by five crystal-like peals which startled the motionless form on the bed. It came from the little clock on the writing desk. Albine got up, switched on the light, and carried the clock into the adjoining dressing room. The sunlight streaming into this spacious, white-tiled room hurt her eyes, blinding her. She hastened back into her tightly-shut bedroom where only the bedside lamp shaded in red was lit. But before returning to her bed she stopped in front of the safe, set the combination, opened it, took out the manuscript, stood perusing it for a moment, and went to lay down taking about one-third of it along.

Stretched out, propped on one elbow, leaning towards the soft light, she re-read the whole beginning. The absolute sincerity of it pleased her and comforted her:

"Both of my parents were French," said the first few lines, "and on my father's side I belong to a fine family of the Dordogne. The Mestrots were elevated to the rank of nobility by Louis the XVth. The senior branch of the family retains the title of count; a Count Alexis de Mestrot, bachelor, is still alive to-day, and resides in the family's country-seat.

"His younger brother, Pierre de Mestrot, being fond of painting, came to Paris in 1877. He was not without talent: but his state of health was a precarious one. He soon became tubercular, and after vegetating a few years died in 1885. He left a widow, a former model, very beautiful, whom he had married and by whom he had had a daughter, then five years old: myself.

"My mother had been a faithful companion to her husband. Widowed, her resources quickly dwindled. But my father's legal executor, a rather rich bachelor uncle of his—André Vériau—became enamored of her during the winding-up of affairs and married her as soon as legal delays had expired.

"My mother had acquired worldly manners through her first marriage. She acquitted herself very creditably of her new social duties. She had no children by Vériau; the couple's entire affection was lavished upon me: I was extremely spoiled. From the standpoint of culture I was brought up like a society girl: English governess, the most fashionable schools, Henriquette Dupont as teacher of painting. But my education was nil. My step-father was a dyspeptic concerned with his own health above all else; my mother nursed him; no young French girl at that time was freer than I have been from my fifteenth year. I inaugurated customs which to-day no longer shock anybody, but which then aroused sharp criticism; going out alone, attending parties with young men, entertaining in my studio like a grown woman. I add that at sixteen I looked twenty and that—it has been said and even written often enough for me to be convinced—I was very beautiful. Naturally, I was credited with numerous adventures. I brought this upon myself

by the absolute freedom and unconventionality of my
ways. The truth of the matter is that my girlhood was
that of a young English or American girl. . . ."

The rest of the page on which these lines were written
remained blank. The next sheet began thus:
"After two months' stay in London and a leisurely trip
through Germany and Austria, Henriquette and I reached
Salzburg in July 1898. . . ."
Followed the story of her marriage. Albine did not
go on with her reading. She put the folded manuscript
on the small table near the bed, switched off the light and,
once more settled among the cushions, resumed her
musings.
Examining herself with the sternness of a questioning
magistrate, she could not accuse herself of having purposely left this gap in her confession. Like all the others
—for there were other gaps, insignificant ones, relating
to other periods—this one was entirely unpremeditated.
Albine had written under the impetus of reminiscence,
without following chronological order. Inspiration to
her was, when she found a clever way, a favorable manner of depicting some crisis or other difficult to relate.
She would at such times run to the safe and write a few
lines or a few more pages. But the secret motives of our
omissions as well as our actions generate within ourselves; Albine was perfectly aware of this. If there
remained in her confession, written frankly and so far
for her own self, only *one* important hiatus; if, upon a
period of about five months her narrative remained silent,
it was because Albine had not as yet found the desired
form of presentation for the events that took place within
these five months.
"Or rather," she said to herself, "I have not yet de-

cided whether I must, whether I can or can not reveal
this period of my life to Roger.

"Let me not delude myself. I began this confession
with the desire to tell everything. My efforts were to
be concentrated only upon the best way of saying it.

"From the very start I found out that the undertaking
was impracticable. I felt that I did not have the
right, through a mystical love for sincerity, to inflict
needless torture on the man I love.

"On the contrary: I understood that the kindly object of this confession was, while clearing the situation
before marriage, to heal as best I could the wounds
caused by the hints, revelations and lies which my enemies
tell about me. It must palliate the effect of what he
knows, what he may learn. It must on no account
mention that which he does not know and which he will
never know. Such is my object.

"Thus, I instinctively and resolutely omitted certain
facts. At the time I did so, I did not even stop to
introspect.

"Then why haven't I instinctively remained silent
about the five months from the time of my departure
from Paris at the age of eighteen with Henriquette Dupont to our arrival in Salzburg where I met Anderny?"

"What happened during these five months, neither
Roger nor anyone else will ever know. The only two
witnesses who know, Jules Perdigant and Henriquette
Dupont, died, he sixteen years ago, she six. Were they
alive to-day, they would no more breathe a word of it
ever, than they did during their lifetime.

"Yet a sort of mysterious impulse commanded me to
leave the place of the avowal blank: an avowal which
would merely serve to upset Roger.

"And a while ago, when I was crossing the big reception room to greet those two crazy women, I saw, as in a flash of lightning that the foreboding which developed a few days ago and grew intolerable this morning, originates in this period of my youth, in the six months which I could not make up my mind to either *relate or omit*—in the blank pages.

"Come, it is useless to play the ostrich. I have the foreboding of danger, and I know what a real menace foreboding is. My hesitation to confess this incident, hesitation which I could not settle one way or the other, is another form of this same foreboding. The danger lies here, or rather in the continuation, in the consequences of what occurred here, in this blank page.

"And yet, in spite of the fact that I now look this danger in the face instead of shunning it as I decided to only this morning, I can not conceive how it could have any bearing on my marriage with Roger Vaugrenier.

"But as I wish to rid myself of both danger and foreboding, I shall tell Roger everything. It will certainly hurt him: but, just as certainly, he will not stop loving me because of it, and our plans will remain unaltered by it.

"That is settled! He is going to spend this evening with me. To-night then, he will learn the first crisis of my sentimental life. He will leave for Nancy to-morrow morning, taking these confessions away with him. He will have three days of solitude in which to think. God's will be done!"

As always, the decision to face one's destiny instead of passively submitting to it brings solace to the tortured soul. Albine, her decision made, could no longer remain motionless and inactive. She switched on the lights again, locked the manuscript in the safe, rang for her maid. While she pressed the amethyst button set in malachite she saw the reflection of her face in a mirror. Her lengthy inward struggle which had resulted in her present decision had invested her features and especially her eyes with such mingled fire and pathos that she herself was moved by it.

"I am beautiful," she thought. "God grant that I be as beautiful to-night when I shall speak to him!"

The maid came in.

"Justine, draw the curtains, open the blinds, and dress me. My grey jersey dress."

"Madame la comtesse is feeling better?"

"Yes. Very well."

"Madame la comtesse has rested?"

"A little, I believe. Open quickly. This darkness annoys me."

Once more daylight streamed into the room. Justine turned off the lamp, a bleak, red point in the suffused, white light.

"Mme. Englemann telephoned," she said. "Just when madame la comtesse had lain down."

"Ah! What did she want?"

"She wished to see madame la comtesse. She simply said that it was about the house; that madame la comtesse would understand."

"Yes, I understand. Where did she want to see me? Here?"

"At the time Mme. Englemann phoned she wanted to come and see madame la comtesse here. But she said that after four o'clock she would no longer be able to leave the bank."

"Telephone her and say that I shall go to the bank. I need fresh air, to be in the open. The car will accompany me, but I shall walk a little. Instead of my grey jersey dress I will wear my Redfern suit, the newest one."

"Dear friend, you came just in time. I signed my last letter a moment ago. But why did you disturb yourself? There was no hurry. Only an answer pertaining to the sale of your mansion. And I wanted to avail myself of this opportunity to have a chat with you. It's a century since I have seen you."

"Well," said Albine, sitting down, "it was friendly telepathy. I, too, when Justine told me you had telephoned, wished to see you; I had the blues to-day."

"I thought everything was going well?"

Albine made a wry face. Her intimacy with Camille Englemann was neither as close as with Berthe Lorande, nor yet as close as the latter's intimacy with Camille. Berthe had been the hyphen between her two friends. Certain masculine habits of Camille's shocked Albine who, throughout her untramelled life, had always remained very much a woman, concerned with her behavior and appearances, while Camille Englemann put her theories openly into practice. On the other hand Camille, flooded with work, went very little into society, while Albine hardly ever ventured outside the social circle where she continued to be welcome. All told, the two women saw each other chiefly at Berthe's home, or at least in Berthe's presence. But each valued the other's intelligence, and they consulted each other with absolute confidence in delicate cases, sure of one another's discretion as well as of enlightening and profitable advice. For the rather delicate financial transactions necessitated by the change in her mode of life decided upon by Albine, she had of course sought Camille Englemann's assistance.

"I have a buyer for your house in the rue Raynouard, all furnished and appointed as it is," went on Camille. You will be able to keep for yourself whatever furnishings you wish, up to the amount of one hundred thousand francs. The price you are asking has not been named

as yet. But I am convinced that it will be very shortly.
When will it be vacant?"

"In about two months, if there are no obstacles to my
plans."

"Do you foresee any?"

Albine answered, after a moment's hesitation:
"Nothing definite. But a trifling incident, a mere word
can upset everything in an arrangement of this kind."

"It is true," said Camille.

They were sitting side by side on the sofa framed by
the bookcases. For a moment they stared at each other
silently. Albine's face still shone with the glow of her
impassioned resolution, a glow which she had admired
on her own features a while ago. Camille also thought:
"She is very beautiful!" And painfully came back to
her own self: "Ah! What wouldn't I sacrifice, brain,
position, wealth, everything, in order to bring so much
beauty in offering to the man I love!" Albine, on the
other hand, thought: "Her eyes are still magnificent
and there is a sort of Asiatic nobility about the shape, the
lines of her face. Besides, she looks much better than
she did when I saw her last. And yet, what a change
since her wounds and her illness! What waste! What
emaciation!" A profound pity surged within her heart;
she drew close to the smoldering, sorrowful Jewess.

"You, Camille," she said to her, "have more than
beauty. You have the irresistible magnetism of your
eyes. I know none that can compare with yours. It
imposes your will. No one could withstand it."

Camille was at a period of her life when, like the dried
earth instantly absorbing the drop of water, the tortured
heart devours anything that soothes its fiery longing.

"Really?" she said. "You do not think me too thin,
too aged? You know I'm barely thirty-seven!"

"I know it; you look much younger!"

"Thirty-seven! To many women of to-day it is still the bloom of life! Can't the glance of a man nearing forty linger upon me? I think so! On the street, in the stores, at the theatre of late I once more begin to attract masculine attention. I am sure of it. I convinced myself. Yesterday, as I was coming back here, at twilight, a well-groomed young man, evidently wellborn, accosted me. I did not try to escape. I allowed him to walk along with me. He said commonplace trite things, naturally, what men usually say under the circumstances. And men are so mediocre! But I was drinking his words because they betrayed real desire, even eagerness. 'It is dark, I thought, and he does not see me as I really am. . . . So I brought him before the windows of a perfumery shop, ablaze with lights, and looked straight at him. Well! he became still more pressing."

"I should think so!" said Albine, smiling. "With those eyes fastened on him!"

"I had the greatest trouble getting rid of him; I was obliged to make a fictitious appointment with him. Ah! how happy I was! Not because of this possible adventure, nor of any others, good Heavens! Just now one being only matters to me! Ah! to win him over!"

The two women had loosened their embrace, but their hands still clung to each other. The fever of Camille's fingers communicated itself to Albine. How tragic, this feminine confusion with beauty fading and the woman's desire to wrestle from destiny's grasp enough beauty for another conquest, just one more, the last one! Albine's generous heart was deeply moved. Yet deep down within herself mingled with compassion rose the victorious, triumphant chant: "*I* am beautiful! *I* am sure!"

"It took," went on Camille, "this crisis, the wound,

illness, physical decay, to teach me what love is . . . as other women love. Before that I used to love rather after the fashion of men. I would choose, certain that nothing would hinder my choice, without troubling about my partner's moral worth. What such experiences have taught me about men is not to their credit. But no matter! To-day, it is I who crave to be chosen, I who humbly beseech the other one's love! This is what I have come to. . . ."

She remained silent for a moment and then, in a low, trembling voice:

"You know him, don't you?"

"I believe I do . . . by sight. Was he not in your box at the Opera last Monday? Tall, distinguished, very young-looking in spite of his greying hair?"

"Yes. His greying hair," exclaimed Camille, "is perhaps what I love best in him. I wish it were white, all white. In spite of the fact that it was turning grey, he does not look his thirty-nine years. Yes! He was in my box. He is manager of our bond department. Intelligence, honesty, devotion itself. My future business partner! And while observing the most absolute regard, he is the most attentive, reliable friend. The day before yesterday he chastised publicly, English fashion, you know, two blows and a knockout, an employee who took the liberty of slandering me in his presence."

"So he loves you?"

"I do not know. He appreciates my qualities, intelligence, energy. He admires, oh! passionately, my former war work. He is a competent judge in the matter, inasmuch as he himself has three honorary mentions. I feel he is grateful, tenderly so, for the marked interest that I have taken in him. His solicitude, his kindness, hover about me all the time."

"Well, then? . . ."

"All this . . . and never a word of love, never a hint of betraying desire. One thing, though, is certain: he is content to be near me, he never tires of seeing me."

"Why, but that is love, Camille! The surest sign of love."

And, while saying these words, Albine thought: "There goes another distorted image of my own love. Roger did tell me he loved me, I felt the fire of his jealousy. But what strange lovers we are, whose lips have never touched! Are these passionate ascetics the forerunners of a new race of men?"

For the first time she felt the sting of anxiety: the mystery in the absolute chastity of their mutual fascination. "I," she thought, "am so agitated when I am near him . . . and yet pure! As for him, his attitude towards me reminds me of that of some fathers in whom the presence of men near their daughters provokes real physical jealousy. . . ."

Thus the two friends, prompted by the irresistible force of sentimental egoism, reverted each back to her own fate. From that moment a conversation on this to them all absorbing subject could only continue in the guise of most intimate revelations; but their intimacy was not close enough to permit this. They allowed their talk to wander off into less intimate realms. They spoke of other people's affairs: Berthe Lorande between Trévoux and Saulnois; Maurice de Guilloux endeavoring to take advantage of Saulnois' infatuation with Mme. Lorande.

"You know," said Camille, "the poor academician is losing his mind. Berthe was obliged to forbid him entrance to her home and she is really worried about it."

"She can rest at peace," answered the countess, laughing. "Professor Saulnois is far from being an Anthony,

and his charming Jeanne, his guardian angel, will not
let him stray."

"Unless she herself were to heed the tempter."

"Jeanne Saulnois? No fear. She is a one-man
woman. People are born that way."

They ended by talking clothes and, anyone hearing
them wax enthusiastic over a certainy Reverdy model, or
the blended shades of Spanish shawls—in vogue then and
bringing fabulous prices for handsome specimens—would
have refused to believe that a genuine, great passion in
which their lives were at stake tortured both these
frivolous prattlers. They also talked trinkets, Chinese
and Japanese baubles, sold at recent auctions. Carried
away by the game of feminine gossip they forgot their
worries, as well as the hour. Albine who was dining
alone at home and was to receive Vaugrenier afterwards
—and for what a dreadful interview!—left just early
enough to have time, on reaching home, to change from
her afternoon frock into evening dress.

But as soon as she found herself alone in her car, the
soothing magic of feminine gossip wore off. It even
seemed to her that the blackness in her heart was greater
than before her visit to Camille. By an effort of will
she took herself in hand, looked straight at the causes of
the anguish which she knew so well. First, the ordeal
to be gone through that very evening; it would be painful,
granted, but "that would pass," she felt sure. Then the
foreboding! But wasn't it precisely the anguish preceding the confession which she was determined upon
making? The confession made, this anguish would
vanish. But there was still another black shadow in the
recesses of her heart. . . . What was it? Ah! the sudden anxiety aroused by Camille's confidences: Roger's
strange chastity, his manner of treating her as a father,

irreproachable but jealous, would treat his guilty daughter. How could this fierce reserve, coming from that brooding heart, surprise her? Had he not declared to Albine over and over again that he wanted nothing from her until he had taken her away from her home, her world, and carried her off for himself, his own possession, his mate?

"No telephone calls in my absence, Justine?"

"No, madame la comtesse. But there are two letters."

Albine started so violently that the maid who was unfastening the belt of her skirt, tore off a hook.

"Give them . . . give them to me!"

They had been placed as usual on a lacquer tray near the bed. Justine brought them. Albine, somewhat ashamed of her show of temper, had already regained her poise; she opened both envelopes with deliberate slowness. One contained the address of a manufacturer of steamer trunks which Mme. de Trévoux had promised her. The other one, signed Blanche Villain, and recommended by Albert Saulnois, solicited secretarial work.

"It is the last mail," thought Albine. "The unexpected can no longer happen to-day!"

And she went on with her dressing, paying as much attention to her gown and her beauty as though she were going to her first tryst.

Like most society women of our day, she had almost entirely done away with the evening meal, when she did not dine out. As soon as she was ready, she ordered brought to her room a light broth and some stewed fruits which constituted her whole supper. Neither bread nor beverage of any kind. It was but one of a thousand abstinences imposed upon her by her will to triumph over age, to remain young, slender, blooming and desirable beyond the limits allowed by time to the

majority of women. An abstinence more rigid than that
of a nun: inspired by a faith that would have opened the
gates of heaven to a devout person. Albine enjoyed its
reward in the incredible persistency of her beauty. The
havoc wrought by time is irreparable indeed; but,
through intense ascetism a woman can escape it.

"In a half-hour Roger will be here. I will receive
him in the library. I will give him a honeyed cigarette
and before he has finished smoking it I shall speak. . . ."

Now she desired this meeting, as a patient desires the
painful operation which will bring him relief.

"Madame la comtesse does not wish any more fruit?"

"No. Bring me my linden-tea and go. Let me know
only when Mr. Vaugrenier arrives."

The maid carried out the tray on which the frugal
meal had been served. A few minutes later she came
back with a smaller tray and the linden-tea. Albine was
dreaming, wide-eyed.

"There is a special delivery letter on the tray," said
Justine on the threshold and left.

Albine's eyes fastened on the small blue rectangle.

It lay aslant the silver edge near the teapot; the heat
of the metal had slightly curled one of its corners. Albine had a sinking feeling, similar to the one experienced
in an elevator speeding downward. "Ah!" she thought,
remembering that the insignificance of the two letters
received a while ago had dispelled her fears, "I wonder
what . . ." So great was her agitation that she did not
at once reach out for the message. And when she had
grown calmer she forced herself to wait a few more moments in order to regain control of her nerves thoroughly.
"I recognize no longer my own self," she thought.
"Is the most trivial incident going to upset me now?
There are a thousand chances against one that this special
is as devoid of interest as the two earlier letters."

She took it between her hands which were cold but trembled no longer. The writing of the address? Totally unfamiliar. Rather English in appearance. But to-day this is not an indication of the writer's nationality. Albine tore open the envelope and unfolded the letter with deliberate slowness. At once the meaning of the twenty black lines written there saturated her mind, as the innermost thoughts of a man are sometimes revealed to one by a mere glimpse of his face. A violent reaction brought the blood back to her cheeks and her fingers. She felt on the defensive, ready to fight. . . .

The text of the note was as follows:

> *Hotel Bradford,*
> *rue Cambon, 23.*

Madame,

My name is known to you according to what M. Roger Vaugrenier, my ward and godson, writes me. It is in the double capacity of guardian and godfather that I solicit the honor of an interview with you as soon as possible. I hope it may be to-morrow. I will come to your house at whatever hour you will appoint, informing me of it by telephone, if you will.

Before our interview takes place I most earnestly entreat you not to disclose to Roger my presence in Paris, which fact you alone know and must be alone to know.

Roger, who has spoken on the subject, very vaguely only, during his recent stay with me, wrote me the day before yesterday, announcing his forthcoming marriage to you. I started on my journey at once. This, madame, will tell you what the object of my visit will be, and how urgent I felt the need of it.

Please accept, madame, the expression of my grea respect.

> *Doctor S. G. Hobson.*

Albine replaced the blue slip on the tray. She remained standing. As usual the imminence of danger had gathered all her strength. She felt slightly feverish, but uncannily lucid.

"Well. What of it?" . . . she thought. "This man is evidently displeased and will try to spoke my wheels.

"He says that Roger has written him. Quite true. Roger did not conceal the fact to me. Without having seen the letter I can guess its contents: the truth, except whatever caused suffering to Roger himself. But my age, my wealth, my past and present position . . . all of this and more. This old puritan of a Hobson, as his godson described him to me, could not be pleased by such a marriage. Besides, he picked his own candidate for Roger, and even introduced her to him.

"To be sure, it's annoying. But no more than that. It's not a catastrophe. Hobson's attitude is hostile. He is going to ask me to renounce my plans; if I refuse, he will appeal to Roger. Let him! I dare him to win his appeal. All the arguments he will put forth, Roger has already discussed with his own self and refuted."

Our thoughts sometimes intersect each other at a given point. Albine's meditation was crossed by the recollection of another worry:

"Roger will be here in about ten minutes. I have just been upset . . . and I must be beautiful."

This new worry at once became stronger than the other one. Seated before her dressing-table, scrutinizing her eyes, her lids, her complexion and the corners of her mouth, she truly forgot for a few moments Doctor Hobson and his plans. She alone knew the parts of her face jeopardized by age; she perceived in them the menace, as yet imperceptible, of ravages. She re-touched such spots with minute care, plying her cosmetics with consummate art but also with wise parsimony, like a woman

who wishes to remain beautiful not only one more evening, but months and years to come.

As usual, the skillful restoring completed, it brought
her a feeling of warmth and comfort. "Yes," she
thought, "I am beautiful. At no period of my life, I
think, was I more beautiful. There is in this face which
I have contemplated so many years, a new beauty, something fiery, mystic, and—how shall I say?—final. Perhaps it is this desperate will to attract of which the poor
Engelmann spoke so tragically this afternoon."

She took up once more the blue note and re-read carefully, weighing each word. More so than at the first
reading, she was struck by its seriousness and the impatience betrayed by the wording.

"Well! He is quite the curt man Roger described
him to be. . . ." She foresaw that she would find no
common ground with him. Roger would have to choose
between herself and Hobson. "He will choose me, I
know it . . . even if this Hobson is to Roger more than
a guardian. . . ."

Hobson, not guardian and godfather, but father: it
was not the first time since Roger's revelations concerning his illegitimacy that Albine felt haunted by such
suspicions.

"Roger does not believe so. That is certain. He is
convinced that he is the illegitimate son of Sir Charles
Bosden who seduced Mlle. Vaugrenier, the governess of
the little Bosden girl. Everything that he has told me
confirms this belief. It is true that I can not say to
Roger: Mlle. Vaugrenier may have had two lovers, Sir
Charles and Doctor Hobson, a childhood friend and Ox-
ford classmate of the baronet. And Doctor Hobson
may have good reasons to believe himself Roger's father.
Reasons, perhaps even proofs. . . ."

All this was possible. But likewise all this did not

alter her conjectures in the least. If Hobson, Roger's father, should want to lay stress upon his authority, it would take Albine no time to reply: "Since you reserve for yourself the right to make use of your paternal influence, why didn't you marry the mother or at least recognize the child?" And she felt certain that in this strife Roger would be on her side.

"There are great indications that my suppositions are correct and that events will shape themselves accordingly," thought Albine sitting down at her writing-desk.

She had completely regained her poise when she started to write her answer:

Sir,

You will find me at home to-morrow, Thursday, in the forenoon, from ten-thirty on.

She raised her pen, thought of adding:

I shall comply with your request for secrecy concerning your ward.

But, on second thought, she ended her note with the first sentence and signed: *Countess Anderny.*

She addressed the envelope and rang for Justine.

"Have this note delivered at once. Mr. Vaugrenier is not here yet?"

"Not yet, Madame. But I believe the bell just rang!"

The massive house door was closing. "It is he!" thought Albine. And it was only then that she remembered her carefully built and lengthy plan of relating this very evening to the man she was going to marry the first weakness of her life.

She observed that, since she had received Doctor Hobson's note, this resolution had suddenly broken within her. It astonished her.

"There is absolutely no connection whatever between the outburst of this old maniac and the confession I deemed necessary!"

Doubtless: but the very source of the avowal she felt was as though walled in within herself. But she was too firm a believer in the infallibility of instinct to counteract its injunctions.

"Sufficient unto the day is the evil thereof," she thought. "Let us first settle the Hobson matter which is urgent. The rest can wait!"

Her ear caught beyond the empty drawing-rooms the sound of Roger's step in the library. She put the special delivery letter in the safe. She gave a last, surveying glance to the reflection of her face in the three-panelled mirror of the dressing-room. Then, without waiting for the servant to announce him, she hastened towards Roger.

FOURTH PART

O N the eve of their departure for America—the state-rooms had been reserved ahead of time on the "Guyenne" in the name of "Mr. Guernier, Mrs. Guernier, his wife, and Miss Legrand, his sister-in-law," the "Guyenne" sailed from Havre four days hence—Ramon Genaz became the prey of scruples wherein the grand-duchess admired once more the nobility of that flaming soul.

He arrived at her home at the usual hour, near five o'clock. She saw that his attitude was reserved, his appearance, downcast. The rings around his beautiful eyes seemed deeper and darker. The heart of the enamored woman contracted: from now on nothing mattered to her except her "dear subject," as she called him. To the happiness of running away with him, uniting her life to his, she was resolutely sacrificing husband, children, title, wealth.

"—What is the trouble, beloved friend?" she anxiously inquired while he brushed her wrist with a kiss.

He raised his hands to his forehead as though to hold in check the turmoil of his worries. Then, with a cold and calculated gesture, he corrected his pose: he stood motionless, his gaze lowered, respectful, silent.

"—Why don't you speak, Ramon?" insisted her Highness." Are there any difficulties? My husband? The government? Are we betrayed? . . ."

He shook his head.

"—Sit down near me and speak. I command you to!"

"—My queen," he finally said, sitting very close to her,

"there are no material obstacles. Everything is ready for our departure, and our incognito is in no danger of being discovered."

"—Then what? Speak! Ah, you are torturing me!"

"—Well! I have no right . . . no, I have no right to accept your sacrifice. Do not be angry with me, my beloved queen." He seized her left hand and went on speaking, his lips brushing her skin, so that his words were caresses. "Be merciful and pity me!"

Hilda snatched her hand away from the dancer's lips.

"—I command you to explain yourself," she uttered with dignity. *"Dast ist wirklich unrecht!* What you have just said is incomprehensible. I am perfectly aware of the fact that I am sacrificing myself. But then I am perfectly free to do so if I please."

"—I shall explain," said Genaz, and at once his attitude became so respectful and so dignified that the grandduchess in spite of her displeasure could not help mumbling between her lips: *"Ach! wie reizend!"* meaning: "Ah! how charming!"

"—My queen," he said, "knows that I was born rich, of one of the oldest and wealthiest families of the Spanish Estramadura."

"—I know, Ramon."

"—At the age of twenty-five the death of my parents left me in possession of a fortune of three million pesetas which is—well—comfortable for a bachelor. But I was very impetuous, I loved luxury and pleasure. A rich young nobleman is exposed to many temptations"—her Highness' brow became clouded—"till the moment he meets the ideal mate who is to shape his life—"a smile relaxed the naïve face of the enamored woman—"Besides, Madame is witness that even now I can not reckon in the matter of expenditures. I prefer ruining myself like a nobleman to hoarding like a middle-class shopkeeper!"

"—That is true," exclaimed the grand-duchess. "You are so generous! Only yesterday—that steamer bag you sent me! You are a spendthrift, Ramon, and I forbid you, in the future, to . . ."

She took his hand and, with a gesture symbolizing the reversing of roles, she kissed it. With perfect tact, Ramon seemed not to have noticed this faltering which a moment later brought a furious blush to her Highness' cheeks.

"—My duty," he went on, "before undertaking our great voyage was to convert into cash whatever belongings I still had in my dear fatherland, to convert everything into transferable securities and, for the first time in my life to reckon, to establish a balance, as the trades-people say. I did it."

"—Dear, dear Ramon!" exclaimed her Highness, admiringly. "You did that! Accounts! like a tradesman! A balance! You who are always doing things on a large scale! I am deeply moved!"

"—I have balanced my accounts. And that is why I am so worried."

"—*Gott in Himmel!* Are you ruined?"

"—No. I am not ruined. Far from it. I am even better situated than I supposed, thanks to the exchange which is quite favorable to my country at present. A single peseta is worth over two francs."

"—Thank heaven!" said Hilda.

"—I have here"—he tapped his coat at the place of the heart—"drafts on the Banque de Rio de la Plata amounting to one million seven hundred thousand francs."

And he drew from his pocket a check-book, untouched, similar to all other check-books, but which in the eyes of the bewitched Royal Highness took on a documentary value as authentic as though she herself had counted the seventeen hundred banknotes claimed by Ramon.

"—Nearly two millions!" she said. "It is a big sum."
Ramon smiled disdainfully.

"—It is more than I need, madame, and even if I
did not have it, if I had nothing at all, what does it
matter? A gentleman has a right to be poor. If I am
prohibited from besmirching my family name, nothing
prevents my earning a living under a fictitious
name. . . ."

"—With your voice! Your talent for dancing! You
would earn a fortune, Ramon."

"—I believe so. Therefore, concerning my own self,
I have no worries. But," he rose to the full height of
his small figure, so well proportioned that it did not seem
small; and his voice grew serious, "I have no right to
drag into poverty the being whom I respect and adore,
especially when this adored being is a royal personage
whose glance has condescended to linger on me. . . . Well—
two million francs is poverty for Her Royal Highness
Hilda, the niece of an emperor. . . . I spent the day with
an attorney in order to establish a budget of expenditures and income, things of which I know as little as
Your Highness herself. I have at my disposal about two
hundred and fifty francs per day: one half of the amount
necessary to provide with decent food M. and Mme.
Guernier and Mme. Lelièvre."

He became silent. Her Highness' face looked pitiful.
She had never concerned herself about her lovers' financial resources. As Guilloux had some time ago related
at Albine's, she had ruined a few of them with absolute
unconcern: the thought of giving them money never entered her mind. The Grand-Duke Otto supplied her with
a monthly allowance of ten thousand francs; if at the end
of the month she was short of money to settle a bill, she
sent the bill to him and he paid it. All this, by the way,
taken from her dowry, which was dwindling little by

little. She had therefore never known financial worries. And so it was because of money that her enchanted dream threatened to vanish into smoke! She had to admit it: Ramon, who so advantageously substituted the Grand Duke Otto in a number of conjugal functions, could not replace him in all of them.

He was, at this moment, watching the face of his queen whom the meditative effort did not exactly embellish. He felt that he had reached the critical moment in his enterprise. At such times he thought in Spanish: a language rich in invectives which it often borrows from animals or parts of animals. A few of these powerful syllables moved the tangoist's silent lips.

"—But," remarked her Highness looking up, "my dowry is my own?"

"—There is little left of it!" replied Ramon with involuntary brutality.

He quickly resumed his tone of tender regard:

"—The claiming of your dowry will involve formalities, annoyances, which I want to cause you at no price. From the moment madame will set foot on the Guyenne, madame must rely upon no one but her humble subject. Everything I have belongs to madame, but I have so very little, even by adding to it the price of a few jewels— for instance, this pearl which is worth about thirty thousand francs, since pearls are priceless."

His finger pointed to the magnificent pink pearl nestling in his tie. Hilda who has followed this gesture, straightened up and motioned him to silence. An idea had struck her.

"—Wait!"

She rose, left the drawing room and disappeared into her bedroom. She remained there about five minutes during which in spite of his poise, the Spaniard, left alone, was obliged to sit down to relax his nerves for a

moment and to rally his audacity.   His olive complexion
was just now totally devoid of its brown tinges; a livid
tragic green alone remained.   At the noise of the opening
door, he rose, and at once the warmth of blood restored
life to his cheeks.   Hilda came back, holding between her
lean fingers her necklace consisting of one hundred and
fifty-six matched pearls of the purest sheen.   The ardor
of the decision that she had just made shone in her
eyes and her protruding cheek bones.

"—If your tie pearl is worth thirty thousand francs,"
she said, "how much can this necklace be worth?"

Ramon managed to say with perfect unconcern:

"—Madame, I do not know.   I know the price of my
pink pearl because my jeweler wants to buy it.   But I
know nothing about it.   Perhaps close to a million."

"—Oh! surely a million!   The Marquise de Bergues
paid more for hers, and mine is much longer.   Well! I
ask you to sell this necklace which is my property."

Ramon took two steps backward.

"—I do not care to think," he said in a low, tense
voice, "that madame means to offer me . . ."

"—I am not offering you a thing," interrupted Hilda.
"Nor do I want to suppose that my subject permits himself to prescribe his queen's actions?"

Ramon bowed:

"—Certainly not.   But then I implore Your Highness
not to entrust me . . ."

"—And whom would I entrust with it then?   I would
be taken advantage of by the tradespeople as royalty
always is."

"—Mme. Lelièvre," suggested Ramon.

"—Lelièvre is a goose," impatiently exclaimed Hilda.
"She loses all her pitiful belongings in drawing rooms,
in theatre boxes, at department stores and in taxis, and

you want me to put a million's worth of pearls into her hands? Ramon, it is a command: sell this necklace!"

For a while yet these two noble souls clashed. But the conflict ended, as could be foreseen, with Ramon's submission. On the following day the necklace was sold. Ramon brought the Duchess four checks, drawn at intervals of two months each, on the *London and River Plate Bank*; they were made out to him and signed by one of the biggest dealers in pearls of Paris. Each one was for the amount of four hundred and twenty thousand francs; all told, one million six hundred thousand and eighty francs, nearly the amount named by Ramon the day before as constituting his own fortune. Hilda admired Providence's ingenious stroke; also, the profitable bargain delighted her; it was well sold. In her presence Ramon indorsed the four checks; then he proffered them to her. She took them up, perplexed.

"—What must I do with these papers?" she asked.

"—Guard them carefully and have them cashed when they fall due. It is exactly like four banknotes, the sole difference being that they are redeemable only on the date stated."

Her Highness looked worried.

"—Would you keep them for me? I sometimes lose papers. Too, Lelièvre rummages through my drawers and messes everything up. I would feel easier if they remained in your care."

But on this score Ramon was obdurate: he would not take into his keeping as large a sum which did not belong to him. The grand-duchess was obliged to give in:

"—I will have Lelièvre sew them in her belt, in a little bag," she mumbled. "She wears an abdominal belt which she never takes off, even at night. That way, she will not be able to lose them."

The end of that last day in Paris shone brightly with hope and love. Genaz was leaving for Havre that very evening ahead of time, in order to reserve a suite of rooms at the Hotel Plaisance where the two travelers would join him twenty-four hours later. "M. and Mme. Guernier." would spend the night and also the following day, until sailing time, in these rooms. In spite of the free life which she led, Hilda had so far never spent a night at a hotel with Ramon. Besides, she felt that Ramon would unwillingly lend himself to it, and she admired the care which he took of a royal reputation. The prospect of this night, this day, spent in intimacy, incognito, brought her fiery enraptured Highness to the paroxysm of emotion. Later on, there would be intimacy, on board ship; but she always felt quite sick at sea and she remembered, rather bitterly, the enforced abstinence inflicted upon her three years earlier during a certain yachting cruise started upon under auspices of love. In short, the Hotel Plaisance appeared to her a heavenly halt before the trials of the journey across the water. Genaz's words during that last day which he had spent with her in Paris, contributed largely to the kindling of her passion. Upon taking leave of her, after a thousand vows and caresses, he had whispered in her ear:

"Till to-morrow! In order not to attract attention I shall not come to meet you at the station, but will await you at the hotel instead. . . . O, my queen, it will truly be our wedding night!"

The following evening at the same hour her Highness and her lady-in-waiting took the Havre train towards seven o'clock. It was still daylight; the ebbing of a spring day, refreshing, aglow with yellow splendor, fragrant with the new bloom of earth; just what was needed to intoxicate completely a forty-year old enamored woman and divest her of all reasoning power, about to plunge into the abyss of happiness. The two travelers were so carefully and so grotesquely veiled that everyone stared at them; but Ramon had reserved a compartment for them; they immediately locked themselves in, and never left it during the entire trip, looking out of the window only when the train was going full speed and pulling the shades over the windows at stations. These precautions, superfluous since there was nothing compromising in their railway journey, easily kept them busy until Mantes. When the train headed for Rouen Hilda became hungry. Mme. Lelièvre pulled out of her bag some ham sandwiches which her Highness devoured, and some port wine of which she drank considerably. She had the appetite of a German cavalryman.

"—What, Lelièvre, you only had eight of these prepared? Eight sandwiches for us both? Why it's hardly enough for one of us!"

"—I thought," said the attendant, "that it would last us until ten o'clock. Was it not agreed that M. Genaz was to order supper at the hotel?"

"—M. Guernier," corrected Hilda severely. "How can you be so forgetful, Lelièvre? You will have us arrested through your lack of caution. Of course, we will have supper at the hotel and I am sure, Ramon— M. Guernier will have done things on a large scale. But we will not sit down to table before eleven o'clock, and from now till then, your eight sandwiches. . . ."

Already there remained but two, and Mme. Lelièvre had not touched any.

"—Go on, eat, Lelièvre," said Hilda. "Eat. . . . I will deprive myself, that's all."

"—I assure Madame that I have no appetite whatsoever, and I beg madame to eat the rest. Travelling kills my appetite."

"—Then it's different," said Hilda, biting into her seventh sandwich. . . . "If it's because of your stomach then you are right to be cautious, because your stomach is in rather poor shape. I, on the contrary, if not well-fed while travelling, get cramps. Here, we'll share the last one; it can not harm you."

Mme. Lelièvre had scarcely finished swallowing her half-sandwich when her Highness screamed:

"—Lelièvre!"

"—Madame?"

"—The checks? Where are they? I am sure you forgot them."

"—Oh, no, madame! They are sewn to my corset, as Your Highness instructed me to."

"—I did not tell you to sew them to your corset. I told you to sew them to your belt, the one you never take off, even at night."

Mme. Lelièvre disliked the duchess to speak of her belt. She flushed and mumbled:

"—I did what Madame told me to."

"—And you are sure it is well fastened?"

"—Oh, absolutely sure."

"—Verify it all the same. I am worried."

Mme. Lelièvre obeyed. She walked to the other end of the compartment and, chastely turning her back on her queen, lifted her skirts up in front and examined the intimate hiding-place.

"—Everything is in good shape," she said, resuming her seat opposite Hilda.

"—All right! That relieves my mind greatly. As soon as we will have joined M. Guernier"—she emphasized the name, and Mme. Lelièvre smiled knowingly —"I shall demand that he rid us of these papers. Oh, it will be difficult, and I shall have to command him to do so. He had such a sensitive soul! Yesterday when I wanted him to take them back, I thought he was going to swoon. He drew back, his handsome face became stony. . . ."

For the fourth time since the previous day the lady-in-waiting was made to listen to the story of Ramon's refusal to take the checks into his keeping. This time it slightly irritated her; anyway, she bore the dancer a grudge for being the direct cause why her belt was being abusively spoken of.

"There was a very simple way of satisfying madame," she made bold to say. "He had but to sign over to Madame a check for one million sixteen hundred and eighty thousand francs."

"You understand nothing in such matters, Lelièvre. Mr. Ramon does not sign receipts like a tradesman. His word is sufficient."

They became silent. The fertile Norman country was bathed in darkness. Through the half-open window of the near-by carriage door a fragrant breeze drifted in gently; it floated through the compartment, vanished, reappeared; the purring of the train was conducive to dreaming. Mme. Lelièvre dozed off. Hilda did not sleep. Her sturdy temperament was now concentrated upon the need of seeing again her splendid lover, the hope of the promised night. On the day when this incredible elopement had finally been decided upon, the astute Spaniard had had the inspiration to say to his queen: "Until the moment when we meet free and alone, I immolate my desire to my respect for the one who has consented to unite her life to mine. This interval of communion with ourselves shall be our betrothal. . . ." And Hilda, on the spur of the moment, had accepted enthusiastically. In practice she found this idealistic abstinence unbearable. But Ramon, more tender, more attentive than ever and, rebelling against the martyrdom inflicted upon him by this abstinence, did not disabuse her; which made the enamored woman completely lose her head and shortened the delay. . . . At last, at last the long hoped for meeting was close at hand. Through the fragrant shadows, the train sped towards supreme felicity; each one of the engine's staccato gasps in the night marked one second less of longing. The city betrayed itself by numerous lights scattered here and there, and a red halo coloring the sky towards the west.

The emotion gripping Hilda's soul rose to her lips.

"Ramon!" she whispered as though he were there, "I never loved anyone but you!"

These words, spoken in an undertone, startled Mme. Lelièvre out of her sleep.

"What does madame wish?" she mumbled, sitting up.

Hilda, whose ecstasy was slowly vanishing, answered with a gentleness to which the attendant was unaccustomed:

"We are arriving, my dear. But do not hurry, we have time."

At the railroad station they took a cab and drove to the Hotel Plaisance, a rich and discreet house, patronized by local society and with a reputation for comfort. As Hilda had foreseen it was nearly eleven when they reached there. The lobby was empty. Hilda thanked Providence to which she frequently appealed in her amorous adventures. At the desk they gave the names inscribed on their passports.

"Show these ladies to suite 24, 25, 26," said the clerk to the chambermaid, "and have their baggage brought up."

Her Highness could not refrain from asking:

"Has Mr. Guernier arrived?"

"Yes, madame. He arrived last night and is expecting the ladies for supper."

She admired his caution in not showing himself, but she experienced a slight twitching at the heart, as though all at once she were alone, lost in the wide world.

"Let us go up!"

The elevator brought them to the first floor. As soon as they entered the apartment, Hilda recognized Ramon's black felt hat and narrow-waisted overcoat hanging on the hall-rack. Her heart melted. Another chambermaid appeared. The first one said:

"These are the ladies Mr. Guernier is expecting."

"Will the ladies please come this way" said the second one, taking charge of the travelers. "Everything is ready."

And she added smilingly:

"Mr. Guernier certainly went to a great deal of trouble today to arrange everything!"

It was a sumptuous apartment, in the style of Belloir; gold and crimson damask furnishings. But the profusion of flowers scattered everywhere by Ramon livened this commonplace setting with the bloom of spring. Each room boasted a different scheme of decoration. Roses in the sitting room, rare geraniums in the dining-room, amidst the silverware, on the tablecloth; and in the bedroom—where the grand-duchess at first saw only the bed, likewise gold and crimson damask—an immense bridal bouquet of white freesias. The cautious Spaniard had felt that he could not attempt lilies. Even Mme. Lelièvre's room was not forgotten. A sheaf of early carnations beamed from a long crystal vase on a stand. In a corner of this same room the travelers noticed two used steamer trunks, one on top of the other, marked with the initials R. G.

"Mr. Guernier apologizes for having put these trunks in the room of one of these ladies," said the chambermaid. "It was in order not to obstruct the big dressing-room. If the ladies wish to have them removed I shall have to call a porter because they are heavy."

"But," said the grand-duchess, somewhat timidly, "where is Mr. Guernier?"

"He was here a while ago, madame, and he will be back any moment. He went to the main post-office to send a telegram, a telegram which he remembered suddenly. He and I were busy setting the table. He is very meticulous as the ladies know, but so kindly. All of a sudden he said: 'Ah, a telegram I forgot to send! Josephine, till what time is the office open?' 'The main office remains open till midnight, sir.' 'Well,' he said, 'I'll go there. Should the ladies arrive during my absence, Josephine, ask them to excuse me, and say I'll be back shortly.'"

Her Highness' slight disappointment was compensated by coquettish satisfaction; before Ramon's return she had time to perform her ablutions, repair the damages to her face and hair, change her gown.

"Quick, Lelièvre, come and undress me. Prepare enough hot water in the tub for a sponge bath. Take my green spangled dress out of the trunk, the dress from Priolet."

The bedroom and bathroom were barricaded to prevent Ramon from inadvertently dropping in on these intimate preparations. Never did a young bride plan with such loving care the attire which the groom himself will remove later on. Mme. Lelièvre was rushing back and forth.

"Lelièvre, not this shirt. Not this one either. . . . You are stupid. . . . The one with the embroidered top. Yes . . . yes . . . that one! Lelièvre, my hair does not stay combed to-night. Take the curling irons and wave the strand over the ears. . . . Shine my nails, Lelièvre. . . ."

Now her Highness was wishing Ramon would not come

back too soon, so as to give her time to appear in all her glory. A door opened and shut rather noisily in the adjoining room.

"It is he," said Hilda. "Hurry, Lelièvre, hurry!"

But when they re-entered the dining-room, they only found Josephine setting bottles of sparkling wine and a very appetizing platter of oysters on the table.

"Has Monsieur returned?"

"Not yet, Madame, but he will surely be back very soon."

Hilda had to be satisfied with this encouragement. She went into the crimson and gold sitting room, sat down at the center table and began to peruse an old copy of the *Graphic* magazine.

"Will Madame allow me to go and likewise dress up a bit?" asked the attendant timorously.

Hilda answered:

"Go to the devil!"

Which Mme. Lelièvre interpreted as acquiescence.

The grand-duchess remained alone in the sitting room ablaze with lights, reading her *Graphic*.

A mysterious anguish was smoldering within her, but she persisted in refusing to feel its bitter tang in her heart. On the contrary, her mind clung to all the indications, the proofs of her felicity; the apartment selected, adorned by Ramon; the set table, the platter with oysters, the wine sparkling in the decanters. To this she added, without acknowledging that she thereby attested to a beginning of doubt, the overcoat and the felt hat on the hall rack; the trunks in Mme. Lelièvre's room. She caught herself thinking: "The four checks are sewn in Lelièvre's belt." But she discarded at once this thought without "admitting it" as say father-confessors. The clock on the yellow marble mantelpiece pointed to five minutes past midnight. Her Highness suddenly became terrified at the possibility of an accident. She imagined a side-slipping taxi, crashing into a wall.

"Josephine!"

"Madame?"

"Exactly what time was it that Mr. Genaz went out?"

The maid repeated, staring:

"Mr. Genaz?"

"I mean Mr. Guernier. What time was it when he went to telegraph?"

"Shortly before the ladies arrived. It might have been fifteen or ten minutes to eleven."

"Did he start out on foot?"

"No. He took advantage of a cab that had just brought some guests here."

"But then, it's extraordinary that he has not returned yet?"

"It's true, it is over an hour," said the girl, "But sometimes when there is a steamer leaving the following day, it takes a long time to telegraph at night because there is only one office open."

Another half hour went by. Mme. Lelièvre reappeared in a sleeveless, low-cut, black velvet evening gown.

"You are crazy!" said the grand-duchess. "For whose benefit are you exhibiting all this mass of flesh?"

"Madame told me to dress," mumbled the attendant.

Hilda shrugged her shoulders.

"I am hungry," she said drily. "Let us eat."

The meal proceeded gloomily. But to robust constitutions like Hilda von Finsburg's, food is a moral bracer. Following the oysters, a chicken wing and three glasses of sparkling wine, her face brightened. Mme. Lelièvre noticed it and intervened immediately. This ludicrous person, clumsy in problems of every-day life, was endowed with a stupendous imagination, both daring and coördinate: this was one of the qualities which rendered her invaluable to her Highness who could grasp nothing beyond present actualities.

"As far as I am concerned," suggested Mme. Lelièvre after the maid had left them alone with the cakes and fruits, "here is what probably happened. Mr. Genaz must have noticed that either he or Your Highness and I were being followed. Madame remembers what the girl said: a cab drove up here with some travelers shortly before our arrival. These people were either emissaries instructed to warn Don Ramon or else spies whom he spotted. At any rate, he understood that he must leave the hotel."

"And why so?"

"Because Your Highness is in no way compromised by remaining here alone with me, but would be should Mr. Genaz spend the night here."

"After all, it's possible."

"It is quite certain, Madame; rest assured that early to-morrow Your Highness will receive a message explaining everything."

"But do you think we will be able to sail just the same?" said the grand-duchess in the plaintive, anxious voice of a child afraid of being deprived of jam.

"Why not? Mr. Genaz probably went to spend the night in his cabin on the Guyenne."

"We could send someone to the steamer to investigate."

"We must do nothing of the kind, Madame. It would be frustrating Don Ramon's caution! Trust me. Let us wait patiently till morning; it is but an annoying mishap which will in no way alter the course of events. If Your Highness takes my advice she will simply go to bed. I shall help you undress. I take it upon myself to inform the maid that the understanding between Mr. Guernier and ourselves was that after midnight we would no longer wait for him."

Everything was carried out according to this schedule. Mme. Lelièvre's romantic zeal was impelled by the desire not to spend a sleepless night. Having had to pack trunks and attend to all the minute details of the trip, she was drooping from fatigue. Unfortunately, after Hilda was stretched out in the big bed and the attendant had bidden her good night, her Highness had a fit of hysterics, cried and became frightened.

"Lelièvre, my dear, I implore you, do not leave me. . . . I feel that I am going to die here. To-morrow morning you will find me as cold as ice."

"Well, then, I am going to settle in that armchair and sit up with madame."

"No! Undress quickly and come to bed with me. I have chills, I am shivering, I need to be warmed!"

The lady-in-waiting had to obey. Towards three o'clock in the morning, the two women at last were lying side by side. Mme. Lelièvre fell at once into a heavy sleep. Her Highness' feverish slumber was disturbed by nightmares and insommia. Whenever she woke up she would try to rouse Mme. Lelièvre; but although she called and shook her, the only response she ever got from her was a wail; worn out with fatigue, perhaps, also, somewhat intoxicated by the sparkling wine, the poor woman seemed to be dead to the world. Hilda would then feel her companion's abdominal belt and derive a slight comfort from the knowledge that the bag with the checks was fastened to it. . . . The checks, the black felt hat, the overcoat, the two heavy trunks, initialed R. G.: these were the only tangible things left to sustain the dream of

free love which had enthralled her until to-night. The
magic of Mme. Lelièvre's fanciful prattle having worn
off, the grand-duchess fell back to her natural realism.
"In order to be able to expatriate himself, Ramon dis-
posed of everything that bound him to Paris. He has
even given up his apartment there. These last three days
he has been living in a hotel. He is free. . . ." She
recollected that La Vitzina had left Paris during the preceding week. "Oh! the monster . . . could he have
joined that slut?" She began to weep: *"Ramon! mein
Schatz!* Ramon, my treasure!" She tried to loosen the
little bag that held the checks from the belt, but Mme.
Lelièvre's inertia proved an unyielding obstacle. With
an impatient fist blow, she finally pushed the inert body
against the wall. She recalled to her memory the four
precious pink papers. The buyer's signature, *Durandy
et Cie,* graved itself on her mind. She knew nothing
about the business mechanism of checks, but with that
feeling for the positive existing beneath her seeming romanticism, she thought; "Yesterday, I had a pearl necklace costing over a million; to-day, I have four pink papers
instead." At the height of nervousness and on the point
of rising in order to flee the onrush of hostile thoughts,
she too sank suddenly into an abyss of torpor, bereft of
dreams and nightmare.

She did not open her eyes again until a pale dawn
strained through the curtains, striking the ceiling. Mme.
Lelièvre was softly snoring, her face to the wall, exactly
where her Highness' blow had landed her. The ringing
of a few bells marked the awaking of the hotel.

So ended the wedding night.

II

In the offices of the Crédit Général Englemann, or as it was more familiarly called: the C. G. E., no one, from directors down to stenographers and office boys, doubted the fact that Mr. Laurent Sixte, Dutrier's successor as director of the bond department, had equally succeeded him in the employer's good graces. The staff commented upon it freely, gaily, sometimes brutally, but never bitterly. As much as it is possible to-day for an executive to be liked by those who serve him and under whose command they are, Camille Englemann was liked by her employees. She possessed the three qualities essential to it: an unbending authority, always coldly polite in its terms of expression; a scrupulous fairness in the observance of everyone's rights; and a sincere generosity grown of the conviction that money is more usefully spent in paying people than in paying for things. Even the women employees, inclined to dislike the Great Catherine type, had let up since a horrible war wound had partly disfigured her. Only when referring to the favored one, they whispered:

"Poor fellow! What taste!"

The male employees whose duties took them near *her* or *him* related countless anecdotes of their intimacy. "She cannot be one hour without sending for him. His eyes devour her. They hold hands forever when they say good-bye. . . ." All this was nearly correct. Others vowed that they had caught her sitting in the lap of the director of the bond department, that they had interrupted a kiss. They lied. Four months after his advent at the bank, a close and tender intimacy had sprung up between Laurent and her; but the exact boundary separating friendship from love had never been crossed, not even in words. It was through no fault of Camille's, who was consumed with desire.

"And yet he loves me," she thought. She felt that she had won him over so completely, that he was so totally her creation! Intelligent but lacking that genius for business which is a form of imagination, she had re-created, or rather she had within a few weeks' time re-shaped his brain. With amorous joy she now recognized in Laurent's ideas in the solutions which he suggested, in his way of thinking, even in his words and his de-meanor, a mysterious offspring of her own brain. On the other hand, while it seemed as though he felt the desire to be near her, to watch, serve, devote himself to her, he did not feel the essential emotion, the craving for passionate kisses and bodily surrender. . . .

"He is too dignified to force the issue" . . . thought Camille. At last a man with scruples! I am his chief, his career depends on me, and that prevents him from speaking of his feelings; but after all, I can not be the aggressor! . . ."

During the course of her sentimental career she had at times by a sudden advance overcome the shyness of a partner; but she felt that with Laurent Sixte similar tactics would spoil, kill everything. Alas! she sometimes wondered whether the obstacle between them was not pre-cisely the part of provoker which she had played in love during the course of her own life, known to all.

A formidable question, an unforeseen crisis. When the Don Juane ceases to be an instinctive provoker, when she views love after the fashion of other women as the surrender of self and not as a conquest of the male, she is astonished and becomes frightened. And, as Guilloux had said, the statue of the commander in the opera rises before her in the shape of the ancient law of morality, the old idol of stone, which, since the biblical days, stands between the sexes. Camille Englemann, endowed with a superior intelligence and trained to think, was following all the phases of the crisis, analyzing, discussing them.

"The majority of really superior human beings," she thought, "establish their own moral standard, as do societies and peoples. They fashion it according to their temperament and interests. I, too, have built my own moral code and have rigidly lived up to it for twenty years. It is based on courage, kindliness, respect for the given word, manly honesty. As for feminine honesty, that of the so-called 'righteous women,' I think it a mere convention and a delusion. A convention because worldly hypocrisy, while observing it theoretically, eludes it in practice. A delusion since woman sacrifices to this hypocritical convention her most precious right and her greatest chance for happiness: to be loved, to love.

"According to this code fashioned to suit my own self I have lived for the past twenty-five years in perfect harmony between body and soul, at peace with my conscience. The manner in which I have regulated my life does not arouse any misgivings within me. I have done no one any harm. In fact I have done several people good.

"But, of a sudden, this past which I absolve, of which I approve, embarrasses me in front of this man although he knows it. To a man like Dutrier I not only admitted this past, I almost boasted of it. But to Laurent Sixte I fear that I seem a sort of moral monstrosity. Ah! if he only knew, on the contrary, what a pure heart I bring to his love! I have known girls who, virgins physically, had given themselves in mind to a dozen imaginary fiancées. . . . Will he understand that I have never really given myself to anyone, and that he is the first man to whom I desire to give myself?"

In spite of this deep worry, in spite of the restlessness

of the flesh and the anguish caused by the obstacle which
she felt, this new love, so different from the others, was
altering her life considerably. Everyone about her noticed her renewed youth, a return to her vigorous activi-
ties of the days prior to wounds and illness. Little by
little her appearance and even her face regained that
power of fascination which for a long time had made her
irresistible. Once more men, aroused by the fire of her
golden stare, would turn when she passed, follow her.
Once she was happy for an entire afternoon because a
sign-painter having watched her go by his ladder and
pail, yelled loudly to his assistant: "Say, Poucot?
Who do you think is going to do without women when
there are such bed-fellows around?" Laurent himself,
so guarded, so respectful in his manner of speech, pre-
sumed to compliment her upon her evident return to
health, her appearance, the radiance emanating from her.

They met almost every day outside of business con-
ferences. She engineered these meetings with as much
ingenuity as though they were business deals, careful not
to appear aggressive, unable to live without seeing the
man whom she loved, but at the same time to speak to him
freely. At first it was theatres, receptions, art exhibits.
She began calling him "Laurent"; he dared call her "dear
chief." Then she grew bolder; she suggested dinners
and box parties for two, trips to the country. He brought
to this relationship a tender regard, a frankly proud joy
at being selected as partner and Knight, while she, in the
guise of a patronizing comradeship, brought to it the
most fiery temptations. Ah! to seize his charming head,
hold it clasped between her hands, kiss the smooth forehead, the clear cheeks where the blood flowed so richly
beneath the skin, the thick, greying, chestnut colored
hair, the red curve of the lips! She would have risked
it, had he seemed to understand ever so little; but she felt

intuitively that whatever initiative she might take would break the spell. This loyal, blameless man who to everybody's knowledge had no mistress, whose only friends, besides the social acquaintances which she had gained for him in order to be able to meet him, were modest middle-class people—she had made investigations—this puritan would become frightened, lose the respect, so annoying and yet so comforting, which he showed to her! Should he give in—he was human after all!—it would only be an added conquest, a Don Juane triumph similar to her past ones; cold, barren pleasures which now left in her memory an after-taste of soot and ashes. . . .

Quite accidentally the provocation came from Sixte himself.

He had requested a three days' leave of absence from her, in order to go and settle some family matters in Burgundy, his native province. From there, she received the following note:

"*Madame,*

Distance lends me courage. I ask you to see me as soon as I come back and not at the office if you will. It is true that I have the good fortune of seeing you every day; but on being granted this special audience I hope to overcome my timidity and force myself to speak. Do you know that I stand in great awe of my dear chief? I implore her to help me a little, as I want to confide to her certain intimate matters which I wanted to tell her long ago, but did not dare. . . ."

She replied by telegram, inviting him to dinner on the evening of his return, namely the following day. Impossible to delay, to wait any longer. A triumphant impatience devoured her; Venus was tightening the hold on

her prey. At last, at last, he had made up his mind!
"What a child"! she thought, . . . "and how much time
wasted already! Ah! this time, since he asks me to help
him, I shall take everything into my own hands! And
he will not have to go to the trouble of explaining!"
Twenty times she imagined, mentally staged the interview.
He and she facing each other; a pause; the silent message of his eyes; then his ardent yet shy approach; still
respectful. Then words, bits of sentences crossing in
mid-air while their hands clasped with feverish awkwardness. "So it is true, you really love me?" Then happiness, and peace.

In reality, events occurred altogether differently.
Alone with her, Laurent Sixte was as usual tender and
gay, thanked her for granting him the desired interview
and in his friendly manner described his trip and his visit.
When Camille finally asked: "You have certain things
to tell me. . . . I am most anxious to hear them," he
replied: "Oh! when we are alone in your small sitting
room, do you mind?"
She reconciled herself to this further delay, but she
had no doubts as to the outcome of the interview. She
deemed herself fascinating to-night, her mask of oriental
Jewess animated by desire and hope. Encouraged by an
expert and devoted maid who had said to her: "Madame's shoulders are completely restored, just as they
were previously," she had dared attire herself in a dark
red velvet gown, its décolletage baring the entire upper
part of her bust, without even a pearl necklace. She
knew that her amber-colored skin, somewhat dry in the
daylight, took on a soft sheen under electric lights. On
seeing her thus, the man had duly shown the astonishment which she expected; she ascribed this astonishment
to admiration. What finally comforted her was that

Laurent seemed happy; the air of a man who is going to
reveal a precious, joyful secret, yet knows that the woman
knows this secret even before he reveals it.

In spite of all this her heart was beating very wildly,
when, the butler having placed the coffee on a taboret and
closed the door of the sitting room, she found herself alone
with her guest. While filling the two cups she scolded
herself inwardly! "I am mad. . . . Even if I am mistaken in him, have I not become desirable again? There
are other people in the world besides this stripling!"
But at once she felt the pangs of remorse as though she
had committed blasphemy! "Ah! no, no! . . . I am lying, lying! Without him I could no longer live!"

"My dear chief," began Laurent, "what I want to say
to you is not easy. But it affords me great happiness to
tell it to you, all the same."

He was seated in an armchair facing the sofa on which
Camille was leaning against some cushions. He was
holding in his hand the saucer and coffee cup. Mechani-
cally he stirred the sugar with his spoon, then put the
cup on a near-by table without even tasting his coffee.

"Speak!" Camille whispered.

She was bending, straining towards him, offering herself. But, his eyes on a corner of the rug, he did not
look at her.

He spoke gravely:

"I found in you so much kindness, so much affection,
that, although not forgetting the distance which separates
us, it no longer arouses within me either fear or
constraint. . . ."

Camille, moved as though it were the tenderest avowal,
took one of Laurent's hands and drew it towards her,
thus compelling him to turn round and face her.

"Yes," she whispered, "I am indeed your friend.
Never mind our business relations. We are equals,

Laurent. And if I have contributed ever so little happiness to your life, rest assured that you have given mine its reason for existence."

Their hands had now clasped; and the tamed Don Juane felt a sensuous pleasure which no expert caress had ever given her. And she thought: "I love you! I love you! Speak! Go on."

As though he had read her mind, he continued:

"Nothing in the world could either lessen or abolish the sentiments which I entertain towards you. That part of my heart which is yours belongs to you for life. You believe me, don't you? You feel quite certain of it?"

"Of course, my friend, of course!"

And, although in the heat of protest his hands raised their clasp on hers above the waist, she felt, under her left breast, a sudden icy current which left her breathless for the moment.

"Our dear intimacy, this life wherein work becomes easy through the pleasure of doing it together; our walks; the joy of listening to you, admiring you . . . tell me that nothing can ever change all that?"

"The strange boy," she thought, "He believes in the old bromide that love destroys friendship."

And, her voice trembling with passion, she mumbled:

"My most fervent wish is but to give you more."

Had Laurent Sixte understood what was then taking place in her soul, such words would have dumfounded him. However, intent upon his effort to express what he had to say, he scarcely heard them. This loyal man was not naïve enough to have noticed Camille's growing liking for him. Besides, quite often, he noticed allusions, smiles around them. But, conscious of having remained within the strict bounds of respect, he merely returned that protective comradeship, which Camille herself had never overstepped towards him. He thought: "She has

been slandered. She has had adventures, but has sobered
up and grown wiser. The years, the trials of war . . .
illness." It was his basic ignorance of the feminine soul
which persuaded him to say to himself: "In spite of
what I am going to say she will remain my dear chief."

After numerous hesitations he took the plunge,
suddenly.

"I wanted you to be the very first to learn of my forthcoming marriage."

There was nothing abrupt in the gesture with which
Camille drew her hands away from Laurent's. Her
voice did not even tremble when she answered:

"Ah! You are going to marry! Whom?"

"A young girl who is distantly related to me and for
whom I secured, last year, a position as Italian interpreter
at the Banque des Vosges. Like myself, she comes from
Burgundy. And it was in order to look after some matters for her that I had to . . ."

"How old is she?" she interrupted.

"Past twenty . . ."

"What is her name?"

"Mlle. Migier. Marie Migier."

"Have you her picture with you? Show it to me!"

For a while the conversation went on in short and
natural sentences. Camille displayed not the remotest
embarrassment; only there was a slight chill in her manner. But Laurent was losing ground more and more;
though she had said nothing definite, he understood at
last. His kindly heart grieved to humiliate, to bring
suffering to a woman whom he admired and to whom he
had pledged undying gratitude and devotion. Yet he
showed her a photograph of his fiancée. Camille saw
a young girl, well-built, an intelligent face without
genuine beauty, but as appetizingly fresh as a springtime
peach.

"She is charming," she said.

How could they continue an interview of this sort? It was Laurent who, his head afire, rose first to take his leave, pleading the fatigue of the journey, a head-ache. . . .

"And then," said Camille accompanying him to the door of the small sitting room, "I trust you will not consider the day complete without paying your respects to Mlle. Migier?"

The door of the small sitting room has closed behind Laurent Sixte. She is alone. For a moment she stands in front of this door which slammed shut upon her dead dream like a lid upon a coffin. Big tears stream down her cheeks, but she does not sob. She is motionless. Suddenly the tears cease. She goes to the high mirror hanging above a stand between two windows. A tall vase filled with languishing roses partly obstructs the reflecting surface; she moves it aside. She now sees herself from her hair down to her knees. She looks at herself, appraises herself. She takes off the tiara which covers the glorious scar on her brow. There she is, offering herself to her own criticism. With venomous eagerness she notes the hair growing sparse about the temples, the withering eyelids and sockets, and the lines around the too fiery, too beautiful eyes whose striking youthfulness, by contrast, outlines still more bluntly the decrepitude of her face. Why has she never noticed nor wanted to notice the two long furrows which follow the curve of the cheek bones, dividing each cheek into two protuberant parts, one straining towards the nostrils, the other towards the ears? Since her illness she had formed the habit, whenever she happened to glance into her mirror, of moving her jaws in a certain way, so as to conceal the base of these two furrows where they were at their deepest, namely to right and left of her mouth. This time she relaxes her muscles purposely: the skeleton's head seems to protrude under the mask of the skin; it becomes suddenly terrifying because of the very fire of her eyes. She also stops straining her chin forward and the flabby dewlap, crumpled like the skin of an over-ripe fruit, sinks from the lower jaw down to the Adam's apple. It is not enough. Her right hand endeavors to unfasten the shoulder strap of the velvet bodice; she wants to see, see closely everything she meant to offer to the new lover. And as the strap does not give way and her nervous fingers can not find the hook, she becomes irritated and furiously tears off the shoulder strap together with one whole side of the red bodice; the mirror reflects half of her bare bosom, the fleshless collar-bone, the naked sagging, pouch-like breast, the curve of the ribs. . . .

There. . . . This is Camille Englemann . . . who used to be Dutrier's mistress, who wished to become Sixte's mistress.

She greets this hideous phantom with a sinister chuckle. . . . She yells out to it loudly, drawing very close to it, as though the image could hear:

"Why, he is right, perfectly right, do you hear? What do you expect with such a face?"

And, suddenly terrified, as though the phantom had really hurled these words at her from behind the mirror, she darts away; she flees from the sitting room, half dressed as she is, rushes into the dining-room where the butler, putting away some glasses into a cupboard, stares dumfounded at this sinister semi-nakedness which leaps past him and disappears, trailing some red velvet rags in her wake.

III

In spite of Albine's efforts to control herself—it was the last evening which Roger spent with her before going to Nancy on a consultation—the young man found her in a rather tense nervous condition. She had spontaneously explained its cause by saying: "I feel my neuralgia coming on. . . ." Roger therefore was not unduly surprised when, having called on the day of his return to Paris, he was told by the maid:

"Mme. la comtesse begs monsieur to excuse her. Right after monsieur's departure madame suffered an attack of neuralgia. Monsieur knows in what condition madame is at such times: huddled up in her bed, in the dark, without eating, almost without speaking. That is why monsieur received only a telegram in Nancy and even that was written by me."

All Albine's intimates, including Roger, knew the violent fits of headache and prostration which tormented her almost every month, sometimes for hours and sometimes for days at a stretch. And this was not the first time that Roger was confronted by the unrelenting orders of a woman who, having made her beauty the object of her life, consented to be seen only when beautiful.

Besides, Justine insisted upon reassuring him:

"Mme. la comtesse particularly instructed me to tell monsieur not to worry. It's a neuralgia just like all the others; monsieur knows. I will telephone monsieur and let him know how madame is getting on. And as soon as she is able to get up, perhaps to-morrow, Mme. la comtesse will receive monsieur."

Roger went home, no longer worried but vexed and slightly irritated. His impassioned feeling towards Albine was not of the kind which a physical failing, a defect of face, havoc wrought by illness, could diminish: on the contrary, there were moments when Roger hated Albine's commanding beauty equally as much as her wealth, her luxury, her worldly manners . . . Ah! he thought, by what aberration of coquetry to-day, did she forbid him access to the agonizing shadows where he imagined her lying ill, with clammy brow, feverish hands and panting breath? How tenderly he would have embraced her, rocked her, how he would have adored her, so purified, become sublime through suffering, freed for one moment from that which had aroused nothing but the desires of men straining towards her beauty.

Justine had not exaggerated her mistress' pitiful condition. There actually was, as she had said, at times on the bed, again on the cushions of the lounge, a woman torn by pain, who moaned in the night.

Ever since Hobson's visit she has been in this condition, prone, overcome, eyes shut, her hands covering eyes and forehead, feeling, as though in a recurrent nightmare, the sensation of being closed in by a wall against which she must hurl herself in order to go beyond it, to tear it down with her weak muscles strained to the breaking point. For go beyond she must. Vainly she strives to divert her mind, vainly she keeps on swallowing sleeping powders. Sleep to her is but a sudden sinking into oblivion, then a few minutes later the atrocious awakening when she lives over and over again, beat by beat and with perception tenfold intensified, Hobson's visit.

It had been neither lengthy nor dramatic. Justine had announced: "Madame, the English gentleman!"

He came in, stocky, pink-cheeked, his white hair closely cropped, a short, straight, still blond mustache on his upper lip. And no sooner had he started to speak, than Albine glimpsed the truth, like Jocasta at the first words of the Theban shepherd.

Hobson said:

"Madame, in the south of London, at South Croydon, there has existed for over fifty years a sanitarium of a special nature, devoted to clandestine confinements. Secluded small houses in a park; reliable physicians; close-mouthed nurses. In May of the year 1898 a young Frenchwoman was brought there one evening by a French gentleman of about thirty who for the last two months had been secretary of the Embassy at Albert House, having previously been attached to the Quai d' Orsay in Paris: Mr. Jules Perdigant.

"Having given birth to a boy the mother left the clandestine sanitarium as soon as possible after the confinement. The father, who was married and therefore unable to right his wrong, undertook to have the child brought up.

"All this, madame, is known to you.

"What you do not know is that after the young woman's departure Mr. Perdigant became acquainted at the sanitarium with a physician from Cornwall who found himself in similar circumstances. He also was married. His mistress, a French teacher, had been confined the same day. That physician, madame, I confess it, was I.

"Our child died twelve days after his birth. Do not expect anything romantic; a most natural thing occurred. My mistress grieved violently over her baby's death and her grief worried me. I suggested to her, with the father's consent, the legitimizing and adopting of the other little French boy, born almost at the same time. She consented, somewhat guardedly in the beginning, then passionately. Like most women in similar cases she wanted the adopted one to be her real son, to know nothing. This satisfied everyone concerned, myself as well as Mr. Perdigant, who by the way turned over to the adoptive mother a sufficiently large sum of money to educate and later endow the child.

"There you are. . . ."

Albine had listened to these few sentences without the slightest show of emotion, as though this commonplace tale about a legitimized child had concerned not herself but someone else. Only she was absolutely motionless, almost inhumanly so; even her eyes and lashes did not flicker. Hobson finally grew alarmed. She seemed so like a lifeless statue.

"I am hurting you, madame. Believe me that only imminent necessity forced me to. . . ."

She became alive and mobile once more, as though awakening from a trance.

"You could not act otherwise, monsieur. Do not apologize. And now spare me the necessity of hearing what you wish to hear. It will be done, by myself. Go back to Cornwall. Roger is away now. He is in Nancy, on a consultation. Had he informed you of this trip?"

"No."

"Then stop at his home, as though you thought he were here. Leave him a note explaining in a plausible way your presence in Paris, a few lines that will not worry him. On the contrary, tell him . . . that you received his letter . . . that you will come back in a few days to talk over his plans with him. What must be avoided at any cost is his learning that you made a stay in Paris without making an attempt to see him. As he anticipates your opposition he would immediately suspect that you came straight to me."

Hobson assented and took his leave; they had nothing

else to say to one another. The interview had lasted
less than half an hour.

Left alone, Albine had just enough strength to reach
her bedroom and sink into the nearest chair. The
crisis at first was physical; incoherent thoughts kept
whirling through her brain.

"Oh," cried Justine, finding her prostrate, "Madame
la comtesse has her neuralgia again!"

It was indeed "her neuralgia," intensified tenfold.
After seemingly endless hours the physical torture
lessened, her thoughts became coherent once more.
Then came the obsession, the forever recurring nightmare, of Hobson's visit, his story, his departure, sudden
lapses into brief unconsciousness, then the nightmare
anew, and again the feeling that she must hurl herself
against a wall, pitch all the strength of her body against
it: for she must tear it down, she must go beyond it,
she must!

"If I do not succeed in falling asleep for a few hours,"
she thought during a lucid moment," I shall go
insane. . . ."

She increased the dose of veronal and finally sank into
a semi-lethargy, disturbed by hazy awakenings in which
her rambling thoughts mingled with dreams. All no-
tion of time was abolished. She learned later on from
Justine that she had thus lived one whole night followed
by one whole day and another night. At dawn of the
second day when she re-opened her eyes the dim light of
a night lamp outlined flickering circles on the dark
shadow of the ceiling. Justine, asleep in an armchair
near the bed, was softly snoring. . . .

"I am better," thought Albine; "I am worn out.
But I can think."

In truth her thoughts, in spite of the drug which she had taken, floated as though purified, entirely apart from her body. Thus detached from her own self, Albine felt as though she had *returned,* like a spirit, to the ruins of a previously populated world now destroyed. She marvelled at the feeling of peace which she was experiencing in that desert. The mysterious anguish whose prey she had become ever since she met Roger, anguish which, two days ago and yesterday, had become unbearable, well! this very anguish had disappeared, destroyed by the catastrophe itself.

"Perhaps it will kill me. Yet I am saved. . . ." And, at the start, this feeling of being rescued predominated and, doubtless, like a violent reaction, saved her from insanity while leaving her physically broken. She realized this and, obstinately setting aside the worry as to what would follow, the anguish of breaking through this wall which, during her nightmares, barred her way, she lingered, she basked in this feeling of relief. For the first time in her life she was humble and resigned. For the first time this proud woman felt: "I am punished. But I deserve it." For the first time the thought that she had erred, sinned, crept into her mind. She took herself to task; she weighed this *Don-Juanisme,* this law based on whims and caprices, which she had substituted, in the handling of her love affairs, to the old traditional law, so mysterious, so condemnable and which, all the same, is ever present, which gains in strength and obtrudes itself again and again following the failure of all social or individual attempts to denounce it. The title of the book which Roger was preparing came to her memory: *'Against the morality of the sexes.'* Yesterday she would have subscribed to its doctrines. Yet if this book were right, if there existed no morals of the sexes, why did she, Albine Anderny, broken as she was by so formidable a disaster that she did not know whether she would live until to-morrow, why did she, to-day, feel that she had escaped a hideous peril? If there is no sex morality, then there is no morality at all: it is like eating, drinking, walking, and within the happy, carefree province of animaldom which, in truth, knows nothing of such anguish or scruples. There is neither a Jocasta nor an Oedipus in the life of animals. . . . Then, the thought it *does* differ from that of men and women, and the gesture of love is wrought with good and evil in its own self as well as in its consequences? How? Why? . . . Mystery! Cosmic secret. Divine secret. Why is a poison a poison? Was it not the occult virtue of this law that from the very beginning, robbed Roger's attraction for her of all sensuality and vice-versa?

Albine no longer analyzes the problem; she bows her head, she turns away, terrified at what might have happened; the intense horror of it fills to the very brim and overflows the present, reaches to her remotest past: and this whole past irritates and disgusts her. She wishes that she could wipe it from her memory and from time itself. She hates it.

She hates it to such an extent that she no longer understands it. She can not comprehend how she could have acted as she did. She became a mother and she fled from her child as one flees from a danger.

She tries to exonerate herself: "I was so young . . . eighteen! . . . I was very badly advised . . . Henriquette Dupont . . . Julien . . . a drug fiend and a fast man. . . ."

She abandoned her child; she was satisfied with the assurance that he would be brought up by others, that he would not suffer from poverty. She not only fled him, but his memory as well, and she succeeded in forgetting him.

It is wonderful how one's moral scruples can be lulled by the pastimes that life offers. She who never harmed anyone, she who even showed pity, charity, devotion to others, she did this without the slightest feeling of remorse because, had she not stifled that remorse, she could not have gone on living as she wanted to live. . . . Father confessors, hearing avowals under the pressure of death, know in how many human lives, righteous and sometimes even kindly ones, thus lies hidden one single but essential crime,—without which the entire life would have been upset, could not have been.

"Now I am punished. It is just! How happy," she thought, "are those who, bowed beneath destiny, are able to make thus, like people sentenced to death in older days, honorable amends before that enormous fate which, by the same stroke, chastises them and relieves them of life's burden!"

To die! If she only could! . . . To die! Pay her debt, to put it in the language of the law, pay her debt in full settlement for the miserable price of life! That would be too beautiful! Too easy.

Alas! In spite of her actual distress she feels that the magnificent vitality of her blood, her nerves, her muscles, is not shattered. Life will once more take possession of her, for years and years to come. What desperate irony! Werther's words flashed through her memory: "There lies the key to thy prison. . . ." It is true: the pulling of a trigger, a drop of liquid on the tongue, and one has escaped. But, then, the traditional social code has suddenly reclaimed this unfortunate woman, has brought close to her consciousness, everything in which, at their country-seat in Périgord, her

ancestors believed as they knelt in prayer before the
Holy Virgin, or avowed their creed, in the black jails
during the Terror. . . . She rebels no longer against
Providence's mysterious and unfathomable decrees!
Submission! Submission, she thought, which guides
you in spite of yourself and supplants your ignorance
by age-old experience! Werther lied. One has no right
to put an end to a human life, not even one's own;
such is humanity's instinct, and sophist argument can
prevail against it no more than with Oedipus and Jocasta.

Albine will bear the burden of the years to come as
long as destiny sees fit: she will not violate the traditional law. Besides, she has another reason for wanting to live, a more intimate, personal one: she is no
longer alone in the world. Some one has a claim upon
her, an older, heavier, more imperious claim than he himself supposes. To evade this claim by death or flight
would be to commit anew the crime of South Croydon
and to sin more deeply in doing so since the life of the
child was made secure. Yet would this grown man,
forsaken, consent to go on living?

Again the wall of her nightmare looms up before
her. Again she strains to either tear it down or leap
across it. Behind this obstacle may be a possibility of
life, for him and for her. Her mind dwells on it. Why
think of it? It cannot be. There are no human means
of passing from the present state to the reëstablishment
of things as they might have grown in their natural
sequence. It is not humanly possible to say to Roger:
"The woman I was, the woman who did what I did,
is your mother." Nor is there a way of keeping him
in the dark.

So the wall is there to stay, insurmountable, and impenetrable.

"Time flies! It will soon be forty-eight hours since

Roger's return to Paris. He will telephone shortly
after daybreak. He will insist . . . and if he imagines
that I do not want to see him, he will do something
rash. . . ."

Albine tries to visualize their meeting, she succeeds in
composing a few sentences: but as soon as she reaches
the main fact, the essential one, again her head hits
the wall. Tears of despair stream from her eyes; sobbing, she implores the hidden ordainer of these mysterious powers, the legislator of these peculiar laws, the
foundation of which remains unfathomable to the mind.
Has she become a believer? She herself knows nothing of it. She gropes, seeking an issue.

Daylight, in spite of closed blinds and drawn curtains,
slowly invades the room. The floating, shadowy circles
have disappeared from the ceiling. The yellow night
lamp, steeped in a pool of white light, is barely noticeable.
Justine, worn out with fatigue, seems a broken doll,
thrown partly in and partly out of the arm-chair. Albine is no longer praying. Her mind drifts, somewhat
hazily. Is she falling asleep? She feels at peace.
Without knowing how it happened, she finds herself
beyond the wall; a quiet hallucination shows her Roger
near her, Roger aware of the truth, accepting and loving
her! It is a mother with her son: everything is clear,
natural, sincere and sane from now on. And, from the
depths of her security, she wants to say the word which
rose to her lips the day before, when she was so desperate: "my son! . . ." But the syllables refuse to shape
themselves on her tongue; sound refuses to burst from
her throat; her lips will not articulate. And these two
words impossible to utter, choke her, strangle her. . . .
She moans, she tosses about.

"Madame! . . . Madame! . . ."

Justine wakes her, shakes her by the shoulders.

"What? What is it?" Albine mumbles.

"Madame la comtesse had a nightmare. . . . She was screaming. . . . Then I spoke to her. . . . But madame kept on screaming. . . . She seemed to be suffering so! So I shook her a little."

"You were right, Justine. Besides, I do not wish to stay in bed any longer. Prepare my bath, I am going to get up."

She rises, she strives to accomplish minutely the intricate rites of dressing. The bath. The pumicing of feet and hands. The dressing of her hair. The underclothes. The dressing-gown. But she goes through the ceremony as though she were a stranger to it. The vanity of it all does not even irritate her: it amazes and discourages her. "This has been my life! This and people's admiration for the results! This and a few thrills, the same ones that Justine experiences, without all these preparations, when she meets Camille Englemann's chauffeur!" Nine o'clock already. Roger will certainly telephone very soon. She will be able to put him off until after noon at the very latest. But the day will not pass without his coming here and facing her.

"I will say nothing. I will let him speak. . . . No! I will say that my head aches too much, that I can neither utter a word, nor listen. . . . No! I will say that I am compelled to go away to Hungary to settle some business matters. Ah! All this is absurd!"

All this is absurd, indeed. But, through all these absurdities something definite begins to take shape in the penitent's mind.

The truth must not, cannot be revealed to Roger: he must never know of his mother's unworthiness. The final break between them must take place very soon; to-day if possible. Finally, the break cannot be accomplished by a mere letter and a hasty departure:

She might as well put a gun in the hands of the unfortunate man saying: "Vanish!" The break must
come from him. He must leave her, resolved never to
see her again.

"Why, what is the matter with madame? Madame
feels ill?"

Justine bringing the dressing gown, quickly draws
up a chair, Albine sits down, rigid, stiff. Justine slaps
her hands, holds a bottle of smelling salts to her pinched
nostrils.

"Thank you, Justine. It is nothing."

It is, indeed. The blood begins to circulate once more,
and the muscles are again at play. It is nothing. Only
it is worse than death. In a flash of lucidity Albine has
seen the way of putting her ghastly plan into action: not
to tell Roger what he can not be told, and yet, having
seen him once more, drive him from her for life without
his ever wanting to see her again. Yes, it is possible. It
can be done. Only, will she be able to go on living afterwards? Ah! the telephone! There is the dreaded call.
She will have to appoint the hour of supreme expiation.

Albine watches Justine lift the receiver. She listens.

"Hello! That is right. Yes. . . . It is Justine
speaking, madame."

"So! It is not Roger." Then it does not matter.
Albine no longer listens.

"Hello! You see, Madame la comtesse is not feeling
well, madame, I do not believe she can see anyone. . . ."

"No! No! . . ." Albine motions to her.

"I am going to ask Madame la comtesse just the
same. Mme. Lorande needs to see Mme. la comtesse
at once, without delay," adds Justine turning towards
her mistress.

Albine repeats the gesture of her right hand: "No!
No!"

"Madame la comtesse is extremely sorry, she cannot see any . . ."

But Albine, having changed her mind, has leaped from her chair and taken the receiver from her maid's hands.

"Hello! Is it you, Berthe?"

"Yes. I beg you. I must see you!"

"Come. I will expect you."

It is better to speak, to lose herself until the approaching hour when her martyrdom will begin.

IV

When a quarter of an hour later she entered Albine's bedroom, Berthe Lorande's first words were totally unexpected. But they were characteristically feminine.

"Why," she exclaimed, "what have you done to your hair?"

"My hair? Nothing."

"Look at it."

Albine had seen it a moment ago in the mirror of her dressing table while Justine was combing and dressing it. Neither of them had noticed anything. Albine went over to the window and examined herself in a hand mirror. It was true: something had changed the shade of the sumptuous chestnut coils. But to notice this change it required the artist's keen eye, an eye which shape, coloring and sound impress like a contact, this exceptional faculty which continues to act instinctively even when the artist is harassed with worry. Berthe already regretted her imprudent question.

"No, I was mistaken," she said. "It is the reflected sheen of the draperies."

"No, no, you are right," answered Albine. "It is a bit, a wee bit, lusterless and paler."

And with absolute unconcern she replaced the mirror on her dresser.

"Send Justine away," said Berthe in a low voice.

"Justine, leave us. . . ."

They are alone, seated opposite one another, in their favorite attitude when they talk intimately so close that their knees almost touch and that they can stare deeply into each other's eyes. Only then Albine, whose perceptive powers are still dulled by the veronal, notices that Berthe also is dressed in a kimona and bedroom slippers. Berthe tears off abruptly the hat jammed in a devil-may-care way on her russet curls: her disheveled hair, carelessly caught up with a large tortoise-shell hairpin, tumbles halfway down to her shoulders. Albine stares at the bloodless face, the color of fading camelia petals, and the unrecognizable eyes, tortured, suffering, robbed of all sparkle and beauty.

"Good heavens! What happened to you, dearest?"

"Yes . . . you wonder, hey? I received a blow, I can feel it yet! I did not dare look at myself after this ghastly night. It seems to me that I have put on thirty more years. . . . Albine! Albine! I am lost! Everything is gone!"

She nestles in the arms of her friend; from the russet hair tumbling upon the blue Chinese silk emanates a sharp scent which rises to Albine's nostrils and which would be unbearable to her if her sense of smell as well as her eyesight and her other faculties were not dulled. On the contrary, Albine feels a strange relief in soothing this sorrow which she at first allows to pour itself out in silent weeping. She rocks the feverish head, the slim, shuddering waist. She says; "Cry, darling, relieve yourself . . . Do not talk."

Indeed what is the use of talking? Has not Albine un-

derstood? This pitiful bundle of femininity trembling
in her arms, Albine knows very well that she is a cast-
away of the same shipwreck as herself, and that she
clings to her not so much in the hope of being rescued
as in order not to sink alone.

At last Berthe lifts up her head, throws back the russet curls, gathers upon the double points of her still
childish breasts the folds of her kimono which have become loosened during her stormy weeping. She settles
in an arm-chair; she thinks, speaks.

"There . . . what a night I spent . . . there are no
words to depict such hours . . . and should there exist
any I could not possibly find them. When dawn came
I wanted to kill myself. But I do not know how it can
be done. It seems that to-day everybody owns a pistol.
I do not . . . and should one be put into my hands I
would not know how to use it. Poison? I fingered the
vials of a first-aid kit which I had bought on the previous day. You know I was going away. What did
those vials contain? Doubtless enough poison to cure
or soothe . . . but probably not enough to kill. And
besides how does it kill you? I do not want to suffer
too much. I do not want to be a horrible-looking corpse.
But at last I found a way: my balcony. . . . You know?
The one opening perpendicularly from my bedroom on
the street. I ran to it. I looked down. Not a single
cab. A man walking along rapidly turned around the
corner, vanished. A small wagon, no larger than a
baby-carriage, filled with milk bottles appeared; a young
girl with a blue linen dress and light hair was pushing
it along easily; and it looked so small from up there,
small and flat: an ant pushing a seed. She stopped
near the curb, right beneath my window. Heavens!
how high up it was! Surely one has time to think while
falling, and how dreadful it must be! . . . what a

lengthy horror! I bent a little further down. I understood that I was too small to swing myself over the balcony. But with a footstool I could manage. From the corner of my left eye, in spite of myself, I was looking, staring at the footstool, through the window which had remained open. It was the yellow silk one; a folded newspaper was thrown across it. I wanted to go and fetch it. I resisted this desire, but I felt an outside will penetrating me, substituting itself for my own will, almost dominating me . . . Would you believe it, Albine? At that moment I had forgotten everything. I did not even remember why I wanted to kill myself. The only thing that mattered was to ascertain whether I would fetch the footstool or not. I reëntered the room. I walked up to the footstool and snatched it. At that moment my poor faithful Clarisse who, unseen by me, had entered the room while I was out on the balcony said to me: 'Does madame wish anything?' . . . It broke the horrible spell. And suddenly I became dreadfully afraid of going back to the balcony, climbing on the footstool, falling, taking this long, ghastly journey . . . till I would reach the small milk wagon . . . collapsing on it, dying. I took a coat and a hat, which Clarisse was holding and put them on, at random. Clarisse was watching me, dumfounded. I told her to telephone you, and as soon as I got your answer, I fled as though the house were on fire. . . ."

Albine's fingers seized her wrists, clutched them instinctively as though to hold her back.

"Dearest! Dearest! What you tell me upsets me. So, you almost . . . ?"

"Yes . . . I believe so. Perhaps at the last moment I would have resisted! Well, no! It drew me too much . . . And if I should go home again, it seems to me that I would once more find temptation hovering about the room, watching me."

"Remain here! Stay! I will not allow you to go until you are rid of this haunting thought. You must not, little Berthe. We have no right to. There is the other who needs us. One cannot drop everything thus, thinking: 'Happen what may! As for me, I am going to escape!' I say this to you because I too had thoughts of escaping."

"You? What, are you too unhappy? And I sit here and bore you with my troubles!"

"Let us not talk about myself. But whatever your sorrow may be, rest assured that I would selfishly exchange it for mine. No. Do not ask any questions. To-day I can confide nothing to you. But I can still be of service to you, and it relieves me. You have quieted down a good deal. Explain to me . . ."

"Yes, I am going to tell you. Only let me pin up my hair. It annoys me. And I should like to bathe my poor eyes with warm water."

When, having repaired the disorder of her hair and soothed her eyes, she assumed her seat opposite Albine, she spoke with deliberate slowness and precision.

"Have you seen Riol lately?"

"I dined with him Saturday at the Pellet-Maurices."

"Did you speak to him?"

"Yes, quite a while, after dinner."

"He did not mention me to you?"

"He told me that you had been at his office three times lately for a slight unimportant treatment, the same one I underwent last year."

"Yes. Professional discretion. Saturday? It was just on that day, that he pronounced my fate. And he was able afterwards to dine out? He was able to eat, drink, gossip, flirt with you! Well! On that very day, a few hours before he had sentenced me to death. Oh! the hangman! the hangman!"

"What," exclaimed Albine, "is your condition grave?"

"It is not a question of my health. I have the arteries of a twenty-year old; Riol himself says so! Only—" and she bent nearer to her friend so as to speak to her very close, in a low voice—"these youthful arteries . . . and the adolescence of my whole body . . . my hair which keeps on growing . . . and this feeling which I have of forever going towards fulfillment, of being the unfinished outline of what I will become some day, of being a child on the road to womanhood, of growing instead of maturing: well! Albine, it is not an illusion. It is my real self. Yes. Nearing forty, I am still twenty. In two years from now I shall still be twenty! The good, good fairies, bending over my crib, made me this extraordinary gift. Only there was the evil fairy who added, snickering: 'Only you shall never be a woman.'"

"I do not understand."

"I will never be a human being like yourself, like Jeanne Saulnois, like Camille. I can never be a mother, never be loved. It seems that it is the rarest phenomenon, that the modern art of a Riol can conquer all cases, except mine. Can you conceive of a physician saying this to an infatuated woman, dreaming of completely surrendering herself for the first time in her life, can you conceive of a physician who, after three agonizing sessions, informs me of a thing like that without realizing that he is sentencing me to death? Well! . . . Riol was smiling. He tried to jest . . ."

Albine was going to reply, but Berthe did not allow her time to do so. She was in a hurry to talk about herself, and already the relief afforded her by her con-

fession showed in her relaxed features, in her less fever-
sh gestures.

"Now," she said, suddenly grown pensive, "I understand that peculiar sentimental life which I have led.
I have been accused of coquetry. I was labeled with
the nasty nickname of 'exciter.' Some men who had
once adored me hated me. Albert Saulnois, I am told,
is sinking into deathly neurasthenia. I thought at one
time that I could love him, . . . love *them,* and then,
nothing. It is not my fault! It is not fair that I should
be detested. . . . I sought, without as yet knowing the
real cause of my anxiety, the magician who would utter
the *Sesame* . . . I did not find him, I could not find
him. There was neither magician, nor *Sesame!* Even
the man whom I at last feel certain of loving, the man
I desire—do you hear, Albine?—because I do desire
him, physically, as men have desired me . . . not even
this man can utter the *Sesame.* There . . . Tell me,
Albine, is there a more wretched creature on this earth
than I?"

"There is one," said Albine. "It is I. Do not question me!" she added, throwing her hands forward in a
forbidding gesture. "The proof that my sorrow is
greater than yours is that you could tell me yours. I cannot tell you mine."

And drawing very close, her deep voice ringing like a
broken crystal:

"Understand that I envy you. Yes, I envy you. As
the damned may envy the souls in purgatory. Well!
Tell me what you have done with the man you love,
after you were told. . . . If you drove him to despair,
you are unpardonable. Go on!"

"How you speak to me!" mumbled Berthe.

"Go on."

"Well—after leaving Riol's office I went home resolved, you do not doubt it, to abandon the proposed trip to the Rhineland. Even face to face with Riol I felt so atrociously humiliated that now I hate him. I wish he were dead with what he knows of me. So, you understand, Jean. . . . the youthful, ardent, trusting being who admires me unreservedly, whose entire hope of happiness rests with me . . . it was impossible . . . it was all over. I telegraphed that I would not come, that I was ill."

"And he came to Paris the very same day."

"You saw him? No? Well! your guess is correct. At six o'clock yesterday evening, he forced his way into my house; he faced me. He had understood; in my commonplace telegram he had sensed the catastrophe, the end."

For a moment her mouth became parched and she was obliged to stop.

"Go on!" said Albine, almost rudely.

She thought: "One more distorted image of my disaster. Could it be then a ghastly law, a relentless Nemesis mercilessly destroying us all?"

Berthe went on: "I was strong. Oh! I could not foresee that I would have so much strength. As soon as I saw him I felt my whole body straining against him. Not to give way. Not to betray my secret. I played my scene well. A horrible scene. A scene which was not new to me. I had played it so often with others who had implored, cried, threatened . . . and ended by insulting me, hurling their bitterness at me in vulgar language. As for him, poor child! All despair, but not a single low, ugly gesture. At bottom the fury of the others had amused me, like a parade of broken puppets. But he, towards the end, I wanted to throw myself at his feet, to tell him: 'I love you! I love you! trample upon me, kill me. I want to be yours, I swear

it!' Alas! This was exactly what I could not tell
him! With death in my heart I was obliged once
more to be this Berthe Lorande whom others have
known on the fatal day when, weary of their desire, I
drove them away. Guilloux, Saulnois, all. I only had
to let my lips speak from memory. They uttered the
words required to frustrate hope, to try to kill love,
because I do not want anyone to suffer. I laid the
blame upon my own nature, my fickle heart. Once
more I said: 'Do not bear me any grudge! I thought
I felt the spark . . . and then . . . it died out.' And
while I was saying it the fire was consuming me."

Albine, horrified, was thinking: "Why, it is I . . .
it is I . . . it is the part which I, too, will have to
play. . . ." Aloud she said: "And he? What about
him?"

"He was so hurt, but so dignified, so beautiful, that
had he remained a few moments longer, I would not
have given in, no! That I cannot do. But I would
have cried out to him: 'It is not true! What I told
you is not true! I still am the same Berthe. I still
belong to you, as I did yesterday. You are the reason
for my existence! You are my divinity! Spare me,
do not demand anything from me, neither my body, nor
my mind. I can not! But do not hate me! Do not
leave me!' Yes, I was going to cry this out in my sobs
when, after having for a moment looked at me in silence,
a look which still burns my eyes, he said very simply:
'Farewell! Have no fear. You will never see me
again.' And he left."

"And then, what?" said Albine.

"Then? why . . . nothing. All my strength abandoned me as soon as I was alone again. I told you what
a night I had spent. I wanted to die. I was afraid. I
sought refuge in you . . . Albine! Do not look at me

so! You seem no longer to like me, no longer to want to protect me, console me. . . ."

Albine had risen and was studying the strange, captivating, ambiguous little being, neither woman nor girl, who was staring at her with frightened eyes. She seized the frail shoulders with both hands.

"Berthe," she said, "do you not realize that you are a criminal?"

"But . . . "

"I am speaking of your morals, of your heart. Do not answer! Do not defend yourself! Listen! You told me of your anguish, your suffering, your temptation of putting an end to it. And the ghastly thing about it is that you told me all this without for a moment forgetting your own self. You spoke of him only to tell me how *you* suffered from hurting him. You wept over your loneliness: you forgot his. You wanted to kill yourself: and he, how about him? How do you know, you wretched creature, whether he is still alive at this very minute?"

"Albine!"

"Unfortunate, wretched creature! It is a fact that in spite of your beauty, your charm, your genius, nature left you uncompleted. And that is why I pity you, proud, unfeeling, wicked as you are!"

"Be quiet, Albine, be quiet," sobbed the guilty woman. "Do not hurt me any more. I will do . . . I will do . . . whatever you tell me."

"What?" continued Albine, "the thing which separates you from the man whom you love and who adores you is only an admission which hurts your pride, and you drive him away? You would rather see him carry away a monstrous image of your heart than have him know that you are wounded, crippled, in body? Oh! child-woman! How little you know these men whom

you played with as a child plays with dolls. Go at once
to this unhappy man and tell him: 'I lied to you. My
most fervent wish is to belong to you. This is the
pitiful thing I am. Do you want me? If you deem that
by giving myself to you, such as I am, I do not fulfil
your expectations . . . well! you will discard me, cast
me in the dust, you will seek others more perfect. I, at
least, will have refused you nothing.' "

In Berthe's widening eyes, fear was gradually giving
way to vibrant ecstasy.

"Yes . . . ," she murmured. . . . "Yes . . . that's
it. Go on speaking, Albine, go on!"

Albine, broken with the emotion of her divine wrath,
sank back on the couch, head bent, her hands stretched
between her knees. Berthe was staring at her; her first
impression was confirming itself:

"Oh! she is a different woman! Still, how beautiful
she is! But she is a different woman! . . . "

"We traveled the wrong road, you and I," went on
Albine. "If you find me harsh with you, rest assured
that I am much more so with my own self. We both
traveled the wrong road. We boldly upset a certain
sequence of things which is inexplicable, which can not
be proven by argumentative logic, it is true, but which is
the law of all living nature and likewise, the law of all
mankind since the beginning of the ages. There are two
sexes that complete each other, but it is an idle dream
to want to reverse their respective rôles in the love game;
it is as mad as wanting to reverse the rôle of the seed
which goes in search of soil and, that of the soil which
awaits and receives it. We have wanted to wrest from
man his privilege of choice, of offensive in love. This
in itself was a mistake. And, at once, we carried this
doctrine to its extreme. We were not content with
being Romeo, we wanted to be Don Juan! The finish

of Don Juan awaits us: that wily fox of a Guilloux was
right. What he calls 'the old idol of stone' looms up
before us on the day when, conquered by love, we once
more want to assume our feminine rôle, to be chosen
instead of choosing, to give ourselves instead of taking.
The statue looms up before us and crushes us. So
much the worse for us!"

She brushed her hand across her eyes, as though to
stop the tears about to flow.

"As for myself, it is all over," she said in a broken
voice. "I am crushed, dead; do not ask me anything,
I do not want to be consoled. My entire problem consists in finding out how I will succeed in dying. Because
I will not kill myself. For you, there is still a ray of
hope: after all, it is nothing but fair, and fate owes it to
you. You are the least guilty. You are only a child.
Let me see. Have you any idea as to what became of
Jean after he left you?"

"No. But," she added in a whisper, like a guilty person trying to apologize, "he will not kill himself, either."

"Are you sure of it?"

"Jean is a believer."

"And what if sorrow should destroy everything, including faith?"

"Could it be possible? Ah! you are right! I am a
criminal! Let me go away, run away. . . ."

She had sprung to her feet and was going to rush out
dressed as she was, without even stopping to cover her
russet hair. Albine detained her.

"Wait! Not aimlessly. After a shock of such nature where would a man like Jean de Trevoux go? To
a priest, it seems to me. You told me that he has a
father confessor in Paris?"

"Yes, Father Pilliart of the Saint-Clotilde Church.

He was, of course, opposed to our plans. He was fighting me."

"Never mind. As a final step, if you find no trace of Jean elsewhere, you will have to steel yourself and go to Sainte-Clotilde. Besides this priest, whom else could Jean have sought refuge with?"

"At his home, perhaps. With his mother, in the residence of the rue du Pré-aux-Clercs. But you know Mme. de Trévoux is away."

"Yes. She will not be back from Italy before next week. Stop at the house just the same. In fact you must go there first. The janitor may know something. And then what?"

"Jean is very fond of Roger."

Albine hesitated, thought for a moment.

"Roger is the last person to whom Jean would tell of a scene where you played such a part."

"There is Jeanne Saulnois. He trusts her implicitly."

"Jeanne Saulnois sees no one. Her husband is dangerously ill. She does not leave his bedside and closes her door to everyone. No one is even allowed into the house. Still, try anyway. Run home and dress. Well? What are you waiting for?"

"I don't want to go home," mumbled Berthe casting down her eyes.

"Why?"

"I am afraid! I am afraid of the balcony! I am afraid of the yellow footstool!"

"Then come. I will lend you shoes, clothes, anything. Justine will dress you. But hurry, hurry!"

FIFTH PART

I

THE seed sown by Albine in Berthe's fertile imagination, that Jean de Trévoux, in despair, might disregard his religious precepts and kill himself—this idea, dismissed at first, had suddenly sprouted, developed roots and branches and cast its shadow over her mind, like those shrubs of the tropics which burst from seed into blossom within one day, in the spring. The red taxicab in which she had come was still waiting at Albine's door; Berthe got into it and gave Trévoux's address. It was quite far: in the heart of the faubourg Saint-Germain, rue du Pré-aux-Clercs. The chauffeur complained of having waited a long time, spoke of the scarcity of gasoline.

"You will get twenty francs an hour. But do not grumble, and hurry!"

Tossing, bumping, clanking with all the parts of its short-winded motor and its dilapidated body, the red taxicab began to move, gathering speed. Berthe Lorande, sitting on the edge of the fallen-in seat, was bending forward, panting, imagining that she could spur on the car by her own impatience. She recalled Jean's attitude, his face, his voice, at the moment when he was leaving her; she tried to infer from it what he might do afterwards. "He did not threaten. Not a word of reproach, not a gesture of anger. But what suffering and also what amazement in his stare! It was as though he had discovered me as I am. . . ." And she sobbed; "Jean, I am not that woman. . . . I am truly the one you loved and who belongs to you body and soul. . . ."

The taxicab stopped in front of the Trévoux residence, a narrow, smoky, plaster façade, with high windows and closed blinds. Mme. de Trévoux had not yet returned from Italy. Only the grated bay window to the left of the entrance-gate, that of the janitor's lodgings, was open and adorned with curtains. Berthe knew the janitor and his wife well, an old peasant couple who, for the past twenty years had become acclimated to the capital. The woman, plump and neat, answered:

"Monsieur Jean left his valise here yesterday afternoon, towards five o'clock. He said not to trouble and bring it up to his room, that he would probably leave in the evening. Only, he did not come back for it."

"But then, where did he spend the night?"

"Oh! that, madame, I don't know!" replied the woman without the least show of anxiety. "It is not the first time M. Jean spends the night away from home, especially when Mme. la baronne is away. And this time, I was out in the neighborhood and M. Jean spoke to my husband; and as my husband is a bit deaf perhaps he did not understand right, althought he always makes believe he does . . . out of pride. . . ."

Berthe, whose parched tongue and lips could not utter a word, went back to the taxicab. The janitress followed her:

"If M. Jean comes in shall I give a message from Mlle. Lorande?"

"Yes." She managed to utter: "let him telephone me . . . at once."

And as soon as the woman had left her: "To police headquarters!" she flung at the driver.

Now she doubted no longer that Jean had killed himself. Her imagination, unrestrained yet clear at the

same time, was reconstruing events: the blue clad officer
walking down the stairs, reaching the street, wandering
for a time through the wide alleys of Parc Monceau, then
coming to a decision . . . running towards the fortifi-
cations . . . cutting through the boulevard Malesherbes
nearby. Berthe saw him as distinctly as though she were
witnessing the tragedy; tumbling—into the ditch, down
the side of the slopes, falling into the ruins and there . . .

She knocked on the pane. The taxicab stopped.

"Go first to the police station of the boulevard
Malesherbes," she ordered.

But the chauffeur did not obey. He stopped the
machine, got out and came to the door with a friendly
and confidential countenance. The twenty francs an
hour had made him amiable.

"Is it an accident that's worrying you?" he said.

"Yes . . . an accident which must have occurred in
the vicinity of the Parc Monceau . . . at the fortifica-
tions, probably."

"That's it. I thought so. Somebody that didn't
come home last night, and you're afraid that something's
happened to him? The police station for that precinct
is rue Jouffroy. But I'll tell you something. The best
thing to do is to continue on our way to headquarters.
There, by this time they have all the reports of the night
on hand . . . absolutely everything, accidents as well as
thefts and murders."

"All right! . . . let us go to headquarters first," consented Berthe.

The police commissioner's assistant ushered her into
a small reception room furnished in a crude green; green
wall-paper, green velvet chairs, green cloth on the table.
An important looking man, displaying the red rosette on
his coat and the red rosette on his summer overcoat left
unbuttoned, was pacing up and down the room impa-

tiently. In order to see neither the green reception room nor the agitated visitor, Berthe stared out of the window that overlooked a tradesman's backyard. But in her mind this quiet, lonely backyard was being supplanted by inclosure ditches, slopes crumbling into ruins, and a body falling. . . .

Suddenly, voices behind her . . . The door of the chief's office opened. The commissioner was speaking from the threshold:

"Your Highness can rest at peace. Absolute discretion. My respects . . . Come in, my dear president."

Involuntarily, Berthe had turned round.

She saw the "dear president" disappear in the commissioner's private office. The two women who had just stepped out of it, the Grand-Duchess Hilda and Mme. Lelièvre, recognized her.

"What, dearest lady, you here?" exclaimed her Highness, running toward her. "You came to see this charming commissioner *ein feiner Herr,* and discretion itself. Was anything stolen from you, too? Me, it's my necklace . . . my big pearl necklace . . . worth nearly two million francs. And you would never guess who . . . Lelièvre, I may say it to Mme. Lorande who writes such beautiful novels, so that she may write a book against that bandit? . . . I will give you all the details, *Ach! Schade!* . . . a man whom I loaded with kindnesses . . . Say his name, Lelièvre. I swore that I would never pronounce it again."

"Ramon Genaz," piteously mumbled the lady-in-waiting. "He abused madame's confidence. He sold her pearl necklace, stole the money, and ran off abroad."

"Where he is living with La Vitzina as his mistress, I am sure of it," stormed the German woman. "Because the commissioner tells me that this harlot can not be found in Paris either! But truly, why did you come here, you, my dear, great authoress?"

Berthe concocted a story about a valuable purse lost in a theatre. Besides, the duchess, who was hardly listening to her at all, suddenly cut in with:

"Let us hurry, Lelièvre. The commissioner said that the minister of the interior is expecting us. Goodbye, charming authoress. Write at once your novel about this thief and his harlot! Begin to-day. I will supply you with all the details. Without disclosing the names, of course!"

She was already on the stairs, dragging along Mme. Lelièvre, who was trying to correct with bows and smiles the impertinence of that leave-taking. But the door of the commissioner's office had re-opened:

"Settled, dear president. Tuesday, at eight. Settled! . . . Madame?"

He received Berthe courteously, wondering. He showed her into his office, bade her to be seated.

"Barring the fact that I have read all your novels, madame," he said, "I take the liberty of reminding you that we have met at the Inter-Allied Club, on the evening of the reception for that American general . . ."

She interrupted him, told him of her plight. The reports of the different police stations were brought to the commissioner.

"The night has been unusually quiet," he declared, perusing the reports. "A sudden death in a saloon at Vaugirard . . . a laborer of sixty-two. A brawl at the place d'Anvers . . . a woman named Leboucq, seriously wounded . . . A neurasthenic named Perginard, a rentner, fifty-two, rue des Saules, hanged himself . . . That is all, I see in the way of serious cases. Do you want me to have additional inquiries made at the various stations?"

"Oh! yes! . . . I beg of you!"

She gave all the information required, with a complete disregard of how she was compromising herself: the time of Jean's visit to her home on the previous day, their discussion, the break, the officer's departure, the fact that he had left his valise in the rue du Pré-aux-Clercs and had not been there since.

"M. de Trévoux," questioned the commissioner, "is not . . . how shall I say? In short, he is a rational man? He is not impulsive?"

"No. But he is a very impassioned man, very decisive."

"Well, madame, I do not think that there is any cause for worry. You will probably see him at your house to-day. Besides, I will telephone you at once should further investigation disclose anything new. It is very improbable. Still, there is in Paris an accomplice of those in despair, an accomplice who sometimes keeps her secret for a long time."

"And who is this accomplice?"

"Why . . . the Seine, madame."

In spite of this vague threat Berthe left headquarters feeling calmer. She refused to picture lieutenant Jean de Trévoux climbing over the parapet of a bridge like a shop girl deserted by her lover. She gave the driver the address of the Saulnois: 29 rue d'Assas. As the taxi was crossing the Châtelet bridge the panorama of the city unfurled itself before her entranced stare: the imposing nave, tossed about by endless centuries without ever sinking, loomed up, symbolically, as though anchored in its harbors. To-day a most radiant, fragrant spring shed an ecstatic joy over the city. The jet-colored river, streaked with gold, rippled softly. No, it did not guard the secret of Jean's disappearance, Berthe felt certain. Fired with a strange hope, the infatuated woman was no longer in doubt. She would find the right road, overtake the fugitive, see him, seize him . . . perhaps presently when this jerky taxicab would pass the second bridge, cross the wharfs, the boulevard Saint-Germain, reach the Luxembourg. . . .

But, at the Saulnois residence, as Albine predicted, she was not permitted to enter.

"It is useless for madame to disturb herself. The door-bell, the telephone have been disconnected. The physician in attendance was given a key. M. Saulnois is very ill; the least noise brings about a crisis. He is going to be moved to Valmont and kept in a dark room for several months without seeing anyone . . . will madame write?"

In spite of her usual audacity Berthe did not dare force her way in. Was she not responsible for the suffering that lay like a pall over this house? Besides, if no one could enter, Jean must have encountered the same obstacle. She asked if a young lieutenant in blue uniform had called. No, no officer either young or old, had called. No one at all.

This failure, although foreseen, shattered the energy which had sustained Berthe until then. Reëntering the red taxicab she gave the driver her own address, rue de Logelbach. Crumpled on the creaking seat she did not even dare to glance at the glittering surface of the water when the car crossed the Concorde bridge. "There is in Paris an accomplice of those in despair, an accomplice who sometimes keeps her secret for a long time. . . ." The sentence stuck in her memory like a poisoned arrow. She nearly knocked on the window to tell the driver to go to the morgue. But her muscles refused to move; she had just enough strength left to return to her home, a pitiful, broken animal whose only thought was of the dark warmth of its lair. The trip seemed endless to

her.   Her spirits rose somewhat when finally she got out
of the hateful red taxicab.   The elevator was busy.   She
walked up the five flights of stairs, suddenly spurred on
by the hope that Jean had come back perhaps, or that he
had telephoned, or that the police commissioner had telephoned as he had promised.

No one had telephoned except Albine, to comfort
Clarisse, her old maid.

The latter, who in her childhood had been employed
at the dry goods store in Jouy-en-Josas, admired her mistress blindly.   Pious and chaste herself, she resolutely
exonerated all Berthe's actions of any guilt.   The frequent visits of Thévoux whom she had known when a
little boy, did not shock her more than many other masculine presences in the house.   She knew quite well that
"madame did not sin."   Her only sorrow was Berthe's
absolute paganism; she spent all of her wages on candles,
which she burnt to Saint Anthony of Padua and to Sainte
Claire, so as to obtain from God the precious conversion.
This time after Clarisse had, as best she could, bathed,
sponged, rubbed, and soothed her mistress without questioning her, since she possessed marvelous tact and never
hurt this delicate sensitiveness, after she had succeeded
in making her swallow a cup of tea and munch a biscuit,
Berthe suddenly said to her:

"Clarisse, teach me how to say a prayer."

Overwhelmed with happiness the old servant obeyed.
Berthe lay on her bed, one elbow propped up on the bol-
ster.   Clarisse, kneeling, her knotty hands clasped on the
comforter near the head of the bed, was saying the fervent words.   Berthe stared with a passionate curiosity at
the tanned, worn, wrinkled face, already speckled and
stamped with age, but which a life of austerity and ab-
negation had invested with dignity, even a certain nobility; something rigid, final, intangible.   The somewhat

filmy, dull blue eyeballs lifted towards the ceiling, straining towards the invisible with superhuman trust. The
chapped, pallid lips uttered as well as they could the
words of prayer, mingling a broken Latin and French.
What did it matter? If there really existed a mysterious
dictator beyond these very material appearances, could so
strong and so sincere an appeal fail to reach him, to move
him? "How happy Clarisse is," thought Berthe,
"even if her faith is a delusion!" And already her mind
hesitated between the faith of her maid and her own un-
belief. "All our active powers strive instinctively to
reach their goal, their real goal. Can this woman's absolute faith travel by its own self towards the goal?"
With the docility recommended by Pascal to novices of
faith she began from the very beginning like an ignorant
schoolgirl.

"Go slowly, Clarisse, that I may hear you well! . . ."
And after her she repeated inwardly the syllables which
the old mouth uttered, mispronouncing them. But Berthe
was not enough accustomed to praying to concentrate her
thoughts, and, while she was repeating the words
prompted by Clarisse, her mind wandered. She thought
of all the churches that she had visited, seeking in them
only the emotion of artistic curiosity: truly a pagan, her
only religion was a sort of pantheist cult for nature,
spring, sunshine, the beauty of things and of people. . . .
Oh! yes! . . . Once, though, she had felt, seeing another
being in prayer, an emotion similar to the one which
Clarisse's faith inspired in her to-day. It was during
the trip to Corsica taken with Albine six or seven years
ago. In the chapel of a Bernardine convent, at the peak
of the Corsican Cape, in Maorta, one day during Easter
week when the Holy Sacrament shone, bathed in gold,
in front of the tabernacle. The nave was empty, except for two nuns kneeling to the right and left of the

choir. The head of one was downcast, and her features were hardly visible. But the other one, still young and beautiful as much as one could judge from a distance and in the semi-darkness of the choir, was lifting towards the shining Host her face transfigured by such passion that the two travelers felt the burn of its flame on leaving the chapel: they spoke of it for a long while. Albine had said: "While looking at this woman in prayer I felt the faint rustle of angel wings. Usually the setting of a church rather antagonizes me: I like them only when they are empty. Should life ever disappoint me I will come back here to seek the faint rustle of angel wings." . . . "God in Heaven," Clarisse was saying, "I deeply regret having offended you, for love of you, because you are infinitely kind, infinitely amiable, and sin is distasteful to you!"

"Ask that Jean come back here. . . ." Berthe interrupted her: "soon . . . to-day . . . presently."

The old woman, dumfounded, suddenly brought from heaven down to earth, mumbled: "How can I ask that?"

Then, very definitely, she said: "We are going to say a *Sub tuum* together!"

This time Berthe compelled her mind to adhere closely to Clarisse's words. Quick at mental gymnastics, she had scarcely finished her prayer when she already felt invigorated. "No," she thought, "Jean did not kill himself. He suffered, he prayed. He too, believes. Would Clarisse kill herself because of a sorrow?"

The old chambermaid, seeing her grown calmer and drowsy, tiptoed softly to the window and pulled down the curtains. Worn out with fatigue Berthe Lorande fell asleep. Clarisse at her bedside was saying her rosary. After every ten beads she would add, trustingly: "Dear God, Holy Mother of God, let Mr. Jean come back here before my Berthe awakens. . . ."

Alas! When Berthe did awaken towards four o'clock Jean had not returned. Berthe had a violent fit of nerves and tears which Clarisse soothed to the best of her ability. But she could not dissuade her mistress from getting up and hurriedly putting on her street clothes.

"Is the car downstairs?"

"Yes, as usual."

"I am going out then. Back in a little while. I am going to Sainte-Clotilde to see Father Pilliart. He is Jean's friend as well as his father confessor."

At the door of the apartment she kissed the old woman's tanned cheeks, whispering in her ear:

"Pray for me! Pray all the time!"

At Sainte-Clotilde she did not find Father Pilliart. He was suffering from rheumatism in the arm, she was told, and was confined to his room; but the sexton, amiable and talkative, disclosed the fact that he did not deny himself to his penitents at 23 rue de Martignac across the street. It was a house inhabited by clergymen exclusively and adjoined the church. There was a chapel with two confessionals. Berthe walked over to it. She was ushered in at once, but was obliged to wait over a quarter of an hour in a small, provincial-looking reception room where a few valuable knicknacks in excellent taste, doubtless presents from mundane parishioners, contrasted sharply with the bourgeois background of the setting. Father Pilliart finally opened the door of his office, adjoining the reception room. Berthe saw a man of about forty with a bilious face in which shone two very small eyes of a yellowish brown. His coarse hair was turning gray. He looked remote and bored. His left hand and wrist were bandaged.

He made Berthe Lorande sit down in a somewhat faded red armchair beside the bare walnut table which he used in lieu of a desk. Immediately she directed

against him the flow of her fiery eloquence, convinced
that in this priest was embodied her last chance of ever
finding and joining Trévoux; also, it must be admitted,
she was actuated by the uncontrollable desire to conquer,
to bend a man's will to her fancy. Without realizing
that she was lying, or even inventing, she drew for the
priest, an entirely transfigured image of herself, a mystic,
exalted Berthe Lorande, who had granted Jean nothing
beyond an ardent yet chaste friendship. She told, with
such heart-breaking words that the avowal sounded
chaste, of the obstacle which stood between them. She
was disclosing it to the father confessor. But did she
not have the right to keep it a secret from as youthful
and sensitive a being as the man she loved?

At this juncture the priest, whose attentive face had
not moved under this elaborate bombardment of words,
interrupted her:

"Madame, I beg you, let us not confuse things. Holy
penitence is one, the conversation we are having now is
another . . . You have so far not spoken of confession
to me."

Berthe had the sensation of having struck against a
barrier. The entire structure of her eloquence suddenly
crumbled. She read in the priest's small yellowish eyes
his contemptuous judgment of her. She burst into tears.

"Ah!" she cried. "I knew it. I understood . . .
from some of Jean's words . . . I understood that you
were my foe. . . . Yet, I do not deserve it . . . I . . .
I . . ."

The priest did not seem affected in the least.

"Madame," he said, "I am the foe of moral confusion
only. My former pupil, Jean de Trévoux, is in your
hands: whatever the nature of your relations—and I
want to know nothing of it beyond what you just said to

me—I deem such relations dangerous for his future. . . ."

"Dangerous? Why?"

"Because you are much older than he. Because you belong to an unconventional, artistic circle which is totally unsuited to him. Finally, because you are an unbeliever while he is a believer. Neither you nor he can be happy together: therefore your duty is, in my opinion, not to detract him from his real path."

Each word uttered in an even voice and as though he were reciting them, fell on the wretched woman's heart like a drop of burning sulphur. In spite of her suffering she felt that the priest was speaking of Jean as a being whose future mattered more than the present. Jean, therefore was alive.

"Have you seen him . . . since?" she asked.

The priest hesitated a moment.

"Yes; I saw him. He came here last night, after leaving you."

"Ah!" she exclaimed. "He is alive! Where is he?"

She had already risen. The priest's icy stare made her sink back into the armchair.

"I promise you," she mumbled, "not to go to him, not to seek him. But . . . he is well, isn't he? He is not unhappy?"

"There is no reason for me to conceal this from you; Jean de Trévoux came to Paris on a four days' furlough and will on my advice spend these four days in retirement, in a house that I indicated to him."

"Will you see him?"

"I will. . . ."

"Ah! tell him that I lied to him yesterday . . . that I dismissed him with breaking heart. I think of him only . . . I . . ."

Again she experienced the sensation of having hurled herself against a barrier. The words which she started to say died on her lips; she despised this man in black, standing between herself and her lover. She despised him: yet she could not break away from him. It seemed to her that were she to leave him, the last tie linking her to Trévoux would break, and that, through this priest alone, even if she were never to see Trévoux again, would Jean learn that she was not unworthy. Suddenly she felt cold. Her teeth chattered.

"Do not dismiss me, Father!" she implored.

The priest whose eyes had never for a moment left her face, answered in a voice in which Berthe's acutely sensitive ear perceived a somewhat less severe intonation.

"Why, madame, I was not thinking of dismissing you."

He let her cry silently to her heart's content. It was as though he knew beforehand how the crisis would end and was awaiting the outcome with patient certainty, like a chemist who watches a precipitate settle in the test tube.

At last Berthe wiped her tear-stained eyes. All her eloquence, all her confidence in her own power, were shattered. The black-frocked man, neither handsome nor distinguished, nor even very intelligent, had broken her resistance with two or three mysterious gestures like the Japanese wrestlers who with one jerk, completely disable a giant.

"Would you consent . . . to hear me?" she murmured.

She did not dare to pronounce the word. It was the priest who uttered it.

"In confession? Now?"

"Yes."

"If you wish it. But there is someone whom I must see before."

He was the first one to rise; she followed him to the office door which he opened out into the hall.

"Valerie! . . . Valerie!"

At the second call a slender woman, clad in gray like a convert and wearing a black bonnet, appeared.

"Show madame to the chapel," he said to her. And to Berthe: "In about ten minutes I will be free to hear you. Until then, meditate."

Berthe followed the gray-clad convert. A spotlessly waxed hallway, lit by an old-fashioned gas jet whose weak flame flickered feebly, smelled of polish and benzoin. "It is the end," Berthe thought. "I am caught. Still, I can run away if I want to. . . ." But she followed the convert's gray back.

About an hour later her machine brought her back to the rue de Logelbach. She was calm and sad. Still introspective in spite of her depression, she diagnosed this condition by saying: "I am spent. . . ." A chain of events and conflicting emotions was driving her into a new order of things. To resist would have required strength, and all strength was broken within her. "Jean is alive!" She repeated to herself from time to time to avoid sinking into a sort of lethargy. But these three words no longer had the same intoxicating meaning for her.

It was in this state of depression, indifference to life, a frequent symptom of beginning conversion, that she reached home. Clarisse was watching for her in the hallway. When she saw the old servant Berthe had a brief moment of lucidity; their conversation of a while ago, so unusual, now appeared to her as the initial step on the road on which she felt herself committed for the rest of her life. She burst into tears. Clarisse was holding her in her arms, mingling in her speech names of yesteryear and to-day:

"Madame . . . my little girl . . . you aren't ill? You have not had bad news?"

"No, Clarisse," said Berthe, wiping her eyes, "On the contrary."

"Mr. Jean?"

"Mr. Jean is well."

Vainly she sponged her eyes. The endless flow of tears continued to run down her cheeks without her knowing what she was crying about: Jean, the broken love, her own self. Rather her own self.

Clarisse led her into her bedroom, and while Berthe was taking off her hat and coat, she said:

"There is a lady waiting to see madame in the drawing room. She did not want to go away, although I said that perhaps madame would not come home for dinner. Nor was there a way of making her tell her name. But it is a lady whom madame knows."

"Who is it?"

"I don't know. My memory is no longer good enough to remember people's names or the places where I see them. I don't think this blonde lady has ever been here before. But I must have gone to her home to deliver a message. Or perhaps, she was at Mme. de Trévoux's country place while we were there."

"I will see who it is," said Berthe.

She straightened her dress a little without a trace of coquetry, then went to the drawing-room. It was absolutely indifferent to her whom she was going to find waiting. Nothing mattered any longer.

In the drawing-room Clarisse, economically, had lit only one of the lamps on the mantelpiece.

Berthe recognized the visitor when she came quite close.

"Hello! Jeanne!"

It was Jeanne Saulnois. Having regained the somewhat sleepy calm which she had brought from the priest's house, Berthe noticed that Jeanne was looking thin and worn.

"I made you wait, forgive me," she said. "What is the matter?"

"You came to our house this morning," Jeanne answered, her lips trembling:

"Yes. Around eleven o'clock."

"What for?"

Jeanne noticed Berthe's hesitation before she answered.

"Why. I came to inquire about the professor."

"No, Berthe," replied Jeanne quickly, "You insisted to be allowed to go upstairs. But it was not me, whom you wanted to see, isn't that so? You care very little about me. You wanted to see Albert. After weeks have passed since you completely cast him out of your life, it pleased your fancy to re-capture him. Unless it was the morbid curiosity of seeing the harm that you have done him . . ."

Her parched tongue was uttering the words with difficulty. She was obliged to stop. Berthe listened, very calmly, wondering at her own calm. What distance had she traveled during this memorable day, that all this should seem to her so futile, so remote?

"Berthe," went on Jeanne, "I—" she was going to say "I forbid you!" but the words would not come.— "I . . . ask you to leave my husband in peace. He was, he still is, very ill. However, the doctors say he will recover, but through complete isolation. I myself "—there was a sob in her voice—" am going to be separated from him for weeks. You . . . you . . . it

would mean a relapse. Let him alone. Let us
alone. . . ."

She sank upon a seat and sobbed, pressing her handkerchief to her mouth. Berthe heard nothing but these
words which she kept on repeating obstinately: "Let
us alone! Let us alone!" But even that did not soften
her heart. She thought: "Jeanne annoys me, that is
all. She must go as quickly as possible. . . ." And it
was in a somewhat impatient voice that she answered:

"You can rest at peace, Jeanne. I have not the slightest desire of seeing your husband again. And, since you
wish it, I will even abstain from manifestations of ordinary politeness."

It was said so clearly, so calmly, that Jeanne could
not doubt its sincerity. But this very calmness offended
her; in a mysterious recess of her heart she felt hurt
that her husband should be so easily sacrificed. The
satisfaction of touching the rival's sore spot, a satisfaction which no woman can withstand, made her reply:

"Very well. I shall depend on it. Besides, you have
something better!"

She rose and wanted to break the interview right
there and then. Berthe placed her hand on Jeanne's
forearm:

"Jeanne, you want to hurt me. What benefit will you
derive from it? But like all exemplary women you
entertain a somewhat vindictive bitterness against . . .
others. I am what I am, but I bear malice to no one,
not even to you. And I am going to prove it to you."

Jeanne, nonplussed, mumbled:

"I do not understand."

"Exactly, you understand nothing of your husband's
ailment. Albert does not love me, he does not suffer
because of my absence. He is simply jealous. He
thinks I belong to Jean de Trévoux, I who refused my-

self to him, Albert. Well! I will give you the means
of curing him. In the first place, tell him that I be-
longed to Jean de Trévoux no more than I did to him.
Also tell him that I will never see Jean de Trévoux again.
It is the truth. You know that I am not lying. Go!
Go and tell this to your husband."

Jeanne's emotion was so intense that she seized
Berthe's hands and put so much strength in that grasp
that Berthe did not know whether it was violence or
gratitude. She freed herself gently.

"Now," she said, "I do not want to be annoyed with
all this any longer. I belong to no one, never did, and
never will. All this bores me. Go!"

Together both women reached the door of the hallway which Berthe opened:

"Farewell, Jeanne. You are not to be pitied, believe
me."

For a moment they stared at each other trying to
find the vestiges of their former friendship. But the
break with the past was too deep.

"Good-by, Berthe! . . ." Jeanne said simply.

II

"My dear Laurent, I have waited before writing you
this until the whole house had gone to sleep, this big
house which I love because I created it, because it is
the Camille Englemann concern, and also because it is
here, amidst its feverish turmoil, that I really came to
know you, and that my heart became filled to the brim
with the thought of you. Yes, Laurent. Away from
you I have the courage to say what I did not succeed in
making you understand, nor dared confess. Besides,
things have taken a new turn altogether. You have con-
fided in me that you love a young girl whom you are

going to marry. Therefore my humble avowal no longer matters, though granted that it may hold an introspective sort of interest for you. I know that you profess sincere devotion to the 'chief,' that you scorn neither her nature nor her mind. It can not possibly be indifferent to you that she loves you, that she loves you foolishly, after the manner of any shopgirl.

"What was I going to say? My thoughts are somewhat confused and refuse to become orderly. You will soon understand why. What was I going to say? Oh yes. I was saying that at this moment the silence of night is at its deepest. I am seated at the table where we worked together so often. Opposite me is the armchair in which you sat every morning during our serious conversations. How I would stare at you while you spoke! So much so that at times I did not listen to what you were saying. You were obliged to repeat. And you did not notice anything! You believed that I had only the Jugoslav loan or the Galician prospects in mind! Men are naïve! Imagine that I am writing on the brief case made of a seventeenth century binding. You can see it, can't you? So often you bent over it with me when we were examining a document together. At such moments I was possessed with a mad desire to kiss you. Do not laugh, Laurent! Anyway, I am quite certain that you are not laughing; it grieved you, I saw it quite well when you left me after having shown me Mlle. Migier's photograph. The fact that I love you does not make you laugh; it dismays you. You realize that in this encounter someone must be sacrificed: Mlle. Migier, you, or I. You are terribly sorry, that it should be I: yet you consent to it because in spite of being kindness itself, you are cruelly selfish regarding your love. It is quite natural.

"I lost the thread of my thoughts once more. The

'chief' certainly must be thoroughly upset to lose thus the thread twice within two pages, don't you think so, my friend? All this, leaving disgressions aside, was to ask you to make an effort of imagination. You are quite unimaginative; but try to picture the exact hour and place from which I am writing to you. It is gratifying for me to think that you will have 'seen' me at this fateful hour of my life. I mean to say that it is a slight consolation to me.

"For my sorrow is quite deep. I am filled with spite against life, my own life. I did not deserve this sordid finish. I worked so much, Laurent! And my work was of use to people who either lived at all or lived more happily because of me and my efforts! Vainly I try to fathom my conscience. I do not remember ever having wilfully done harm to anyone. Even in business, with my competitors I have always played fair. I deserve no praise for it, because my conscience is my tyrant. I had to obey it; otherwise my life would have been poisoned. For instance when the war broke out nothing compelled me, responsible for such momentous financial affairs, to enroll as a nurse, and having become a nurse to be stationed on duty at the most dangerous spot. Well! Yes, Laurent! I had to. I could not escape. An irresistible power drove me where I had not the slightest desire of going. When I removed my wounded men under the barrage of the Fokkers at Serrigny, I was not exalted, not heroic. I thought: 'How stupid to risk what I am risking, when one can dispense with it and so many people actually do.' But I went on exposing myself to the fire. I could not do otherwise.

"It was absurd. I realize it to-day when this life tyrannized by conscience has reached a climax of such complete failure that it seems like one of destiny's grim jests.

"I, who have more imagination than you, Laurent, can see you very clearly as you read my letter. And I can see you, having read the few lines which I have just finished, putting away the sheet of paper and assuming your thoughtful air, sitting back, thrusting your head slightly forward, half closing your dear gray eyes and wrinkling your nose, so funnily! How many times, again, I felt like kissing you while you were thus meditating! You will meditate while reading the preceding lines, and you will think: 'Yes, the chief has the conscience of a righteous man, a loyal, generous, brave man. It is a pity that . . .' And you feel so tender and kind towards me that perhaps you will not finish your thought to the bitter end. Well! I am going to formulate it for you: 'It's a pity,' you will think, 'that this loyal and kindly woman valued so lightly woman's most essential virtue, a virtue which I, Laurent Sixte, value above all others, which I feel is potent and strong in my fiancée, and which my fiancée will of course continue to respect after she has become Mme. Sixte.' Laurent, as a matter of fact you are right! During the course of my life I have practiced important virtues, rather rare in a woman. I did not practice what, in a woman, is called *virtue*. While a young girl, and imbued with no moral traditions whatever, since I have never known my mother and since my father was a man of lax morals, I looked squarely at this feminine virtue. I deemed it a convention based upon the jealous egotism of the male and his concern as to the transfer of his worldly goods to children actually conceived by him: in short, a simple law ruled by material interest, respectable, like a customhouse tariff, no more nor less. I grew up. I looked about me, watched the lives of the working classes as well as that of the wealthy. I saw that this famous law, respected by all in theory, was being violated by many of

its supporters in practice; history taught me that it had
always been so. Men or women, the only beings who
really abided by this so-called essential rule, were those
who temperamentally were not inclined to transgression.
Are you one of them, my friend? Mme. Laurent Sixte
will, I am certain, have a considerate husband who will
give her complete satisfaction. But you are more affectionate than passionate; desire does not haunt you. I
envy you. For nature has created me altogether different. Continence weighs heavily upon me; the torments
of Phaedra are not unknown to me. This probably in-
fluenced my outlook upon these things. I was sincere
in deeming that my untrammeled love life, more like
a man's than a woman's, was never an outrage to the
real morale. And if I led this life openly it was not
through ostentation but because of my conscience. I
abhor hypocrisy. I want the private as well as the public
responsibility for any and every act which I commit.

"I have thus shocked many people who lead the same
life, but secretly. For these I have the greatest contempt. Unfortunately I have, likewise, shocked the
'real believers'—you for instance. But, Laurent, I want
you to know that since I have known you my life has
been perfectly pure, taking purity as you interpret it.
If I had been your wife, Laurent, which after all was not
in the least abnormal, you would have found me as
faithful as Mlle. Migier. I give you my word for it,
and you know the true worth of your 'chief's' word.

"Why this change? Because I loved you as I never
loved anyone, and in order to attract you my instinct
bade me to be altogether different from what I had been
hitherto. This new instinct altered my idea of love
immediately. My Don Juanism, ah! how it embarrassed
me before you! I would have liked to wipe it out of my
life. It filled me with bitterness. I was beginning to

detest it. Not knowing Mlle. Migier, it was Jeanne
Saulnois whom I envied. How happy she was whose entire life was devoted to one single love! People admire
her, respect her; she is looked up to as a type of virtuous
wife, yet not prudish; loyal comrade, loyal partner.
People say: 'See, she even withstood Guilloux, a professional seducer!' Easy, this sort of virtue! What
woman would not have practiced it in her place? She
had the advantage of a traditional education in an old
provincial family; at twenty she met a man made for her,
she loved him; she married him; he was charming, refined, witty; he soon became famous; some flirtatious
society women fought over his favors, and if he succumbed occasionally Jeanne knew quite well that she had
a firm hold on the best part of him. Of the ones whom
Guilloux calls Don Juanes, is there one among us that
would not gladly exchange her own fate for that of
Jeanne Saulnois? I too, with this one favor of destiny
—to meet at twenty the man you will love—I would not
have become a Don Juane, I would have been a most
ardent but faithful wife.

"Laurent, I assure you I am not contemptible. More
sincere than the Commander's Guest in the opera of Don
Juan, my efforts strained towards an ideal. At the
very moment I meet that ideal, the stone statue rises
between him and myself; the old idol, the deceitful, traditional figure of feminine virtue. Very well, for me as
well as for the Guest, in the opera, the hour has struck!

"But why tell you all this, anyway? I am trying to
exonerate my past before you, as though your condemna-
tion of this past were the real obstacle between us.

"You, perhaps, think so. But you are entirely
mistaken.

"The real obstacle lies not in the past, but in the

present. It is not a moral one, but physical and material.

"If instead of becoming my collaborator in 1920 you had been it in 1912, Laurent Sixte, when I possessed this power of attraction which no man could withstand, you would not have withstood it either. You would have forsworn the cult of the old stone idol: divine passion would have driven you into my arms, and once mine, as I would have been a most faithful comrade, your morals, like all morals, would have conformed themselves to the unyielding demands of your instinct.

"Laurent, it is this delay, this whim of fate, that I can not become reconciled to. To think that I might have met you when my eyes still retained their brilliance, when my hair was fragrant with youth, when my mouth was so sensuous that sometimes men would turn their eyes away from it for fear of losing their minds, when the contours of my face and the lines of my body still retained their firm purity, when I still possessed the legs and breasts of a Diana! I shall never become reconciled to this sly trick of fate, which, having given me the power of conquering all men, brought into my life the only man whom I could really love, and then delighted in bringing about the meeting after robbing me of this power. Laurent! Laurent! You did not know the real Camille, and that is why you did not love her! You have known a pitiful cripple who suffered and moaned for months, her stomach sewn together, on a hospital bed, who was able to live again, but only a wreck of what she once had been!

"But I have spoken entirely too much of my disaster. And it is not merely in the way of idle talk that I write you.

"Dear Laurent, I especially wanted to assure you that I am leaving you without bearing you the least grudge. You have been the fairest, most loyal friend. You could

not possibly have told me: 'Chief, take care not to fall
in love with me. My heart is not free.' The more
so, you big, naïve child, since you suspected nothing.
You were doubly blinded, by the love of your fiancée and
by my physical decrepitude. Carelessly you trampled
on my heart. I bear you no malice for it. On the
contrary, I am grateful to you for the loyal and strong
affection which you gave me. I had never known anything to approach it. What a fine man you are! So
sincere, so upright, so clean . . . and, also, so good-
looking! How I love your eyes, the color of your skin,
your grayish hair which only emphasizes your youth,
your big, fine hands, the calculated slowness of your gestures. And this trusting, somewhat naïve countenance,
so attractive! The thought that I will never again see
it all breaks my heart.

"For I shall not see you again, my friend. Neither
you nor anybody else. The life which I have led heretofore has become a burden, and you have made me realize
that I can live no other. The more or less interested
attentions of the subordinates for their 'chief' have now
become nauseating to her. And as in spite of appearances she remains young in temperament, she sees no
other solution to the problem but a discreet disappearance. Besides, life without you would seem very empty:
and I would not have the necessary strength of soul to
keep up, with the fiancée or husband of Mlle. Migier, the
relations of tender comradeship which meant so much to
me.

"I am going. It is my wish that no one suspect the
real reasons for my departure. In addition to this
letter which will reach you early to-morrow morning—
I arranged that in advance—I am leaving, together with
my testament, a short and concise statement, explaining
that I can no longer endure the suffering due to my

wound and the operation which I underwent. In fact
I am not lying. Had I not been wounded, operated on,
maimed, I would still be beautiful and you would have
loved me. Isn't it unjust? I have acted like a courageous man; and because I am not a man I am punished
for my courage. Truly, I am dying of my wound, and
my letter tells the truth.

"Together with this 'official' letter will be found my
testament. I ask you to be the executor of my wishes:
you will not refuse me this last proof of devotion. My
wealth is quite considerable. I am willing three quarters
of it to the institutions which I founded and kept up.
The remaining quarter will be divided between Mlle.
Migier and yourself. In this way no one will be able
to suspect anything. I implore you to keep it an absolute secret, even from your fiancée. Tell her that you
had spoken to me of your plans, that I encouraged
them, and that, in spite of the sudden neurasthenic attack which precipitated my end, I have not forgotten to
help a bit towards feathering your young nest.

"I am also leaving you most of the things which surround me in my office; the brief case is one of them,
our brief case which you used several times in my presence. Finally I am giving you a large portrait of myself, painted by Laslow in 1913. I never showed it
to you because I dreaded the comparison between my past
and my present. I ask you to hang it in your home, in
the room in which you work: thus, the real Camille
Englemann, the young, pretty one, the Camille as she
was before the catastrophe, will little by little substitute her image to the devastating image that you have
known."

"Finally I am notifying the president of our adminis-
trative council that I am leaving everything in order, so
that my voluntary death does not complicate matters

at the bank.   And I am appointing you to the council as
my eventual successor.   I wish my suggestions to be carried out.   At any rate I go, happy in the knowledge that
your future is secure.

"There!   All business matters are settled at last.
Now good-by, Laurent.   I am going to escape from life.
In a very few moments I will no longer be either young,
old, beautiful or ugly.   I will be nothing.   No one will
be able ever to hurt me.   You will not be able to hurt
me any more, bad boy!   Do you know that I am experiencing a feeling of limitless power, a feeling of joy
almost at throwing this challenge in destiny's face?   You
will be powerless against me now.   Powerless . . . if
everything ends with life.   Oh!   I know that it is a
very simple hypothesis that can no more be proven
than the hypothesis of after-life.   Sensible people do
not pretend to be able to see clearly in the dark.   The
hypothesis that presently Camille Englemann will be
nothing at all is the one best adapted to my reasoning, my
experience, my instinct.   That is all.   Should I be mistaken, I cannot believe that the improbable after-life will
bring me before a judge of the Inquisition.   When the
unhappy Camille with her wretched, maimed body, her
pitiful, torn heart, showing the good that she has done
and the pain which she suffered, will face the tribunal if
the Judge has only the leniency and kindness of an average fair man, he will absolve and welcome her.   Such is
my creed, although I am an unbeliever.
"Farewell, dear Laurent.   Have pity for my memory,
you who had no pity for me.   To iive within you is the
only after-life that I aspire to.   My dear friend, keep me
in you, with you.   You are the only thought that sustains
me in this ghastly solitude through which I trace my
ultimate steps towards oblivion.   Farewell!   I kiss you

with all my heart as though I were your wife. Do not
protest, you are already widowed of me, at the time that
you feel the faint rustle of this embrace. There is no
cause for jealousy in it, on your real wife's part.

"And also, remember, she will never, never love you
as I would have loved you . . . as I do love you, my
dearest, dearest!

"Camille."

III

In the moral agony through which Albine was
struggling, the sudden arrival of Berthe Lorande with
her tale of anguish, the impassioned consolation that she
had offered her, played the part of a fiery truce. But as
soon as the red taxicab which she watched rounding the
corner had disappeared, the concern over this trifling
incident faded, or rather if she thought of it at all it was
merely to say:

"Berthe thinks that this is suffering! Oh! would that
I had her heart, and that I were in her place!"

But during the very truce, as often happens in the
course of sleep, the mysterious mechanism of thought
had continued to evolve within her, less conscious but
none the less active. And the one possible issue, the
crack in the wall which the wretched woman had perceived in a flash just before Berthe's telephone call, now
appeared to her with the precision of a move on a chess
board. There existed one way of establishing this very
day between Roger and herself the final break without
disclosing to him what could not be disclosed. It existed;
it was evident; it seemed infallible. In order to set it
in motion, all one needed do was to lift the telephone
receiver hanging within hand's reach, name a certain
number, and as soon as a certain voice answered, to say:

"Come, I am waiting for you . . ." Then, when Roger came into this room which he had never entered, but where Albine wanted to receive him because the walls, the furnishings, the knicknacks, in the course of this lengthy, atrocious crisis which she had suffered, were so linked to her sorrow that they were the stone of her calvary and the wood of her cross and that she felt a sort of suggestion of sacrifice emanating from them; when Roger came face to face with her, it would only be necessary to utter certain words, and it would be Roger himself who would break the agreement and who would flee, not in despair, but filled with a disgust and indignation which would save him from despair.

There was the scheme. It appeared simple to Albine's mind, so lucid just now that it seemed to hang above her like a steady, bright lamp. One single, solitary secret must be kept at all price: at the price of the complete, detailed confession of all the other falterings in her life, at the price of everything that could destroy in Roger the purified picture that he had inwardly drawn of Albine, even at the price of ghastly lies. Roger must flee from this room and Albine's love, convinced that he was escaping something worse than death. He must rush away panting with fury and spitting his contempt in abusive terms. Then, doubtless, his very fury would save him from suicide. One does not kill oneself for the sort of creature Albine was going to reveal to him.

He would go away, live. Twenty-four! He was a child: he had so many years left in which to forget this incident which, after all, was but the outline of a plan over which hovered, from the very beginning, a sort of obscure and heavy constraint. A strange love this, which did not even inflame the surface of the flesh, which denied itself the zest of a kiss. Roger would forget. Albine knew by experience that the only tenacious memory of a broken, vanished love affair rests in the flesh. Roger's senses would recall nothing. He would forget. He would love other women. One woman more than the others. He would marry, have children and be happy. Albine, in a moment of hallucination, pictured herself sharing this happiness, looking at, touching, kissing children who, although born of another woman would be hers none the less, since they would be Roger's children.

Her heart melted; she sobbed. Ah! it was too much!

Was it not better, to tell the truth, to simply say to Roger: "Listen! You were not the son of the French governess. I am going to reveal to you who your mother is, your mother who not knowing you to be her son loved you as a son only, your mother who, loving you without knowing you, has slowly purified herself in this tender ardor, slowly cast off the past from her. Accept her. Forgive her. Love her!"

No. Impossible. At the mere thought, the wretched woman felt again the impenetrable wall looming up before her. To tell the truth would exact a greater price yet than everything which threatened her if she should keep the secret. If she did keep it—the shameful image which she would leave in Roger's memory would at least be that of a passer-by, a love adventuress. It would not be the memory of his mother. Would the unfortunate man survive this?

Thus, everything was driving the victim back to the solution which would bring the utmost suffering upon herself. And without delay: there was no more time left to defer or ponder. She made up her mind to do so, horrified, like a person jumping from a fourth story in order to escape a fire. She called Justine.

"I am feeling better, my girl. Will you telephone Mr. Vaugrenier that I will receive him here, immediately after luncheon, towards two o'clock?"

"Very well, madame . . ."

But when she saw Justine reach for the telephone, she flew into her dressing room shutting the door behind her. She was afraid of this far-away voice which she could not hear, but at which she could guess through the maid's answers. She was afraid that she would snatch the receiver from Justine's hands.

Through the door Justine said:

"Mr. Vaugrenier will come at two o'clock."

"Very well!"

"Does madame need me?"

"No. I will ring for you if I do."

And now, alone in the white tiled room, before her dressing table, placed so as to allow a dazzling, crude, brutal glare to light the figure reflected in the glass, Albine examines herself just as on the previous day Camille Englemann had done. It seems that a sneering fate is leading both of these lives through the same stages to ruin. But Albine has always observed the most merciless frankness in scanning her own beauty, contrary to so many women who compose their features instinctively, as soon as they see their reflection in a mirror. There she is, as forty hours of torture have left her. Very slightly, the morning's toilette had corrected a disorder which has now re-appeared. Her hair, which she no longer watched, has become disarranged. The negligée gapes carelessly, revealing the neck and the upper part of her breasts. Her arms are bare in the wide sleeves. Albine examines herself. Her impassioned wish of so many years when she was seated before her mirror, the wish that she may still find herself fit to arouse men's passion, still cause the ecstasy of desire, ah!

how far off it is now! The passion of men, the ecstasy of love—she despises it all. Didn't it cause her present state of despair? She looks at her face, her hair; she scrutinizes her neck, her breasts, her bare arms with a new anxiety. In the struggle which she will presently have with Roger, she would like to appear wounded, aged, definitely beyond the pale of passion and love!

Passion, love! . . . Horror seizes her at the thought that they may during that supreme interview burst forth from him who does not know, and reach to her who does. God grant that the forty hours of torture have mutilated her, aged her enough! She brings her eyes closer to the mirror, with minuter attention than in the days, when, light-hearted and eager for love, she thought: "I want to be more beautiful than I was yesterday." She examines herself. Berthe was right; the shade of her hair has altered, especially around the temples. In order to make sure of it, she tears out the tortoise shell pins that hold it in place; it falls loose now, concealing half the bare bosom beneath its fragrant warm thickness. Albine scrutinizes its roots. Yes; some seem white when seen at close range; but the chestnut reflection of adjoining roots absorbs this whiteness. The entire run of the shade has grown paler, there is no denying it. Albine senses that this pallor will grow, reabsorb little by little the amber colored pigment still imparting its brilliance to it; in a month perhaps, her hair will be gray. But to-day, this toning down of the amber luster, far from aging her makes her appear younger, like an imperceptible cloud of powder.

She remembers that once, having powdered her hair for a costume ball, she had noticed this youth-giving effect: the face, faintly colored, taking on, by contrast a more vivid glow. And precisely at this moment from the depths of her tortured heart an unusual onrush of blood

rises to the victim's face; the delicate cheeks seem art-
fully touched up; the lips shine with the glow of adolescence. To be sure, the big, dark eyes seem to sink deeper
beneath the arch of her dark brows, while the eyelids
spread purple shadows. But as the eyes themselves shine
with an intensified glow imparted by fever, as the features
of her face retain their pure outline, Albine is obliged to
admit that never, never, had she contemplated a more attractive, a more moving image of herself.

"Never, never!" she whispers, without daring to add:
"never have I been more beautiful!" And, for the first
time, this beauty seems abnormal and despicable to her.
Really, this Don Juane mask of love and passion clings too
closely to her. Neither time nor even suffering are able
to tear it off.

Of the forty hours of torture which fate had inflicted
upon Albine, Roger had spent the first few concentrated
upon himself, inwardly irritated at not having been
admitted to see Albine, moved at knowing her ill, yet not
in the least worried over the turn that things were taking.

At first no foreboding of an approaching crisis flashed
through his mind. Nothing in either his past, or what he
knew of Albine's past, contained this germ which Albine,
better schooled by life, knew how to feel in her own heart;
the germ which develops, isolated, secret, like the virus
of cancer, and which, like cancer, suddenly reveals itself
when it is too late to be cured. One fact only—and
Albine had foreseen it—could have aroused his
suspicions; if, upon his return to Paris, he had found no
word from Hobson whatever. But the letter was there,
awaiting him; it contained nothing abnormal, nor anything unlikely. Hobson, who was interested in Pasteur
researches, came to Paris several times a year, and like

most of his compatriots decided on his trips suddenly.
The letter was somewhat cold; but Hobson never was
"soft." Roger thought: "The old man is not pleased;
he still intends to force his little English girl upon me.
But he will not catch me." And he wrote at once to his
godfather an affectionate letter, confirming, however, his
plans of marrying Albine.

Thus, during the first two days, Roger felt neither foreboding nor anxiety. He did not insist on seeing Albine
and manifested his ill-nature only by his silence. He
neither wrote, nor telephoned. He confined himself to
replying with cold politeness to the spoken messages which
Justine conveyed to him. In the commonplace of these
messages—"Mme. la comtesse still has a headache. . . ."
"Mme. la comtesse feels somewhat better, but she is unable to see any one yet"—he felt neither lie nor defeat,
while a Guilloux would have at once suspected something
unforeseen, mysterious. To Roger, as to the majority of
impulsive, impassioned men who are fervent theorists as
well, woman remained the inexplicable enigma; especially
since he did not think her at all enigmatic and credited
himself with understanding her.

The prick of foreboding began to touch him only
on the morning of the third day. As though night had
brought him not counsel but clairvoyance, his memory
had gathered, linked together some trifling, recent incidents and dwelt upon them with a strange persistence.
Something jerky, feverish in Albine's attitude during the
last evening that he spent with her before going to Nancy.
Her wilful seclusion, the prolonged separation after his
return . . . the reticence of Justine's messages . . .
through these symptoms he almost perceived the working
of foreboding, he almost touched the spot that had
remained numb heretofore. But at this very moment

Justine telephoned to him to come. And his whole anguish was at once swept away by this imminent happiness: "I am going to see *her* again."

When at two o'clock the footman ushered him into Albine's library, anxiety once more gripped him. He asked himself: "But what is the matter with me?" He was struck with the absurd thought that Albine, having sent for him, would refuse to see him. Nervously he sauntered to the window, looked out on the deserted street, the lonely residence across the way, fenced off with foliage. He was already preparing his answer, should an attempt be made to really dismiss him. He was balking: "I have the right to see her even though she be sick, and I am going to." And facing the empty street, he was inwardly formulating these words, his fists clenched. He came to with a start when Justine's voice said softly behind him:

"Madame la comtesse asks monsieur to come to her room."

At once his undefined anguish shaped itself into concise anxiety.

"To her room? But then she is worse?"

"Oh, no, monsieur. On the contrary, madame la comtesse feels much better."

Albine was waiting for him, seated in an armchair near the window, against the light. A dark cloth dress, wide and soft, had replaced her dressing gown, as though she were ready to go out: but, with the gesture of a shivering patient, she was drawing a light fur rug about her lap. Between her armchair and the one where she would make Roger sit, she had placed an empire stand, small but heavy, littered with books. How pitifully childish was all this minute parading, in view of the tragic altercation to follow! She herself had entirely too clear a perception of the forces that were to clash, to imagine that they might be thwarted by the weight of a piece of furniture or the material of a dress. She only wanted to gain a few moments of security after the first look between her and him. And, too, she wanted to foresee the first words that would be spoken, the first attitudes that would have to be taken. She had tried to guess what would be the successive phases of this duel, not so as to protect herself, but in order not to stab her foe in the heart with a thoughtless twist.

"Albine!"

"My dear . . ."

He came in, and before she realized how it had happened he was already bending over her, his head against the hand which trailed on the fur rug; she felt the moisture of his eyes on her fingers. For a few seconds, perhaps one second only, there was absolute silence between them, without words, without gestures; a respite granted by compassionate fate. Had it lasted another moment Albine would have faltered in her set purpose; she was on the verge of helping him up, drawing close to her this restless child, renouncing lies, confessing her motherhood. But she had welded her resolution at entirely too vivid a flame to forget its burn. She came to, in a jolt of energy:

"Come, Roger. Be reasonable. We have serious things to say to each other."

The dry ring of these words contrasted so sharply with the tender, welcoming gesture that Roger sprang to his feet, sobered. The ill-nature of former days rose within him and his features set sulkily in what Albine called his "wicked face," he answered:

"Quite right. I beg your pardon for having forgotten that. We have to become acquainted once more. Six days without seeing one another! You have been ill?"

He had assumed a detached, impertinent air which became him badly and beneath which Albine felt his pain. She answered gently:

"Yes, I have had some unpleasant hours. Sit down here. Yes, here, opposite me and do not become my enemy. Had you seen me yesterday or the day before you would have pitied me. I am barely presentable to-day."

"You never have been more yourself," mumbled Roger.

And totally unaware of the fact that he was uttering the very opposite of words necessary to fortify Albine's ebbing courage, he added:

"To-day, you are too beautiful."

Then she perceived that her plan of offensive was upset, that she must burn her bridges.

With a motion of her hand she bade Roger to be seated, as he was coming toward her:

"Roger, I told you that we had serious things to say to each other."

He felt his jaws contract and mumbled with difficulty, still trying to turn his anguish into irony:

"Ah! I thought so! Something has happened."

"No, Roger, nothing has happened. Only during our six days' separation, I introspected carefully. I have finished for your benefit taking stock of my life. Do not protest. It was agreed upon between us."

She was forced to stop and moisten her parched tongue. He did not move; he had grown somewhat paler and in the ensuing pause his staccato breathing was distinctly audible. Albine lowered her eyes so as not to see that tortured face; she stared intently at his trembling, ungloved hands.

"So," she went on in a low voice, "I will tell you everything, as we agreed."

Roger's nerves exploded:

"I do not care in the least about what was agreed
upon. Is that the way to welcome me after six agonizing
days spent away from you? We take one another as
we are to-day. That is all!"

She insisted, uttering the words which she had prepared, and this, precisely, gave to her answer a somewhat
artificial, planned flavor, which Roger perceived as well
as she.

"Beware, Roger! You are now speaking in the heat
of anger, of impatience. And then, what you refuse to
hear to-day, you will some day torment me to find out.
I am certain, absolutely certain of it! I know you!
There must be nothing obscure between us. The whole
truth. Unless . . ." she felt intuitively that it must end
abruptly "unless we abandon our plans."

He sprang to his feet:

"What are you saying? What?"

She had not the strength to repeat it. She made a
dejected motion, signifying; "I have said what I said."

"Ah," burst out Roger backing away, "I understand,
you deliberated. You changed your mind."

The words which escaped Albine's lips this time were
totally unprepared:

"Yes," she said, "I did deliberate, alone, and quite
painfully. And since then you are dearer to me than
ever. When everything is broken between us, my life
will be but a shadow of its former self."

He stammered, no longer trying to hide his despair.

"So . . . so . . . you said . . . You were able to say
that it is broken! . . . You said that, you! You!"

She went to him and seized both his hands. Ah! to
hold him thus, submissive, weak! If she only could!
She spoke softly:

"Roger, I will not commit the crime of burdening
your life with me. In the first place one does not marry

Albine Anderny who is over forty years old when one is
in the prime of youth!"

He protested, in a wounded though vehement voice:

"No! No! You know very well that not a single
young woman can compare with you. And I am already
worn with life. You are younger than I am."

"For how long, careless one? Am I not forty-two
years old? Are you not twenty-four?"

He shook his head;

"I love you," he said.

She drew away from him, leaving him prostrated on
his chair. Walking backwards like a trainer watching
the beast which he has just subdued, she reached her
armchair, brought the fur rug over her lap, once more
became languid.

"Perhaps truly," she murmured, "I am the only one to
notice my age. I know exactly what is concealed beneath
my appearance. Such weariness, at times! Such re-
luctance at undertaking anything new! Such yearning
for quiet and rest! No, I have not the right to thrust
all this upon an almost childishly youthful life. Let me
speak. You are a child beside me. And do you know
what I understood in my solitude? That my love for
you has no right to be anything but that of an older
sister." She dared not say: a mother. "Besides, that
is exactly what it has been till now. Without our realizing it we underwent the effect of our difference in age.
And, thank the Lord, nothing material . . ."

She did not finish her sentence. But she had already
said too much. Her words humiliated Roger, irritated
him. He rose so abruptly that she feared an attack, and
instinctively folded her hands across her chest.

"Is that a reproach?" he questioned, coming close to
her. "Have I been too respectful?"

"No, Roger. But step back. Do not look as though you were threatening me. You have been absolute kindness and loyalty personified. Do not regret it. That is what allows me to free you of myself, to-day. Yes . . . a relief. I have made my decision. I will not inflict the burden of an old wife upon you. Especially an old wife with my past."

Her words carried such energy and such a convincing accent that Roger's impulsiveness broke. He receded a few steps with a characteristic motion. He stood there, his chin in his hand.

"Let us see. Let us see . . ." he stammered. "I am beginning to wonder whether I am dreaming. We took leave of each other six days ago in perfect accord. All the thoughts that you are voicing, you had ample time to ponder over already. You cannot convince me that a headache made a different person of you. I may be a child, as you say. At least I am an intelligent child. I see. I understand things. I do not allow myself to be deluded. Something new occurred within these six days, What is it?"

"Nothing happened."

"Go on! Speak! I want to know."

He was very close to her, still repressing the desire to brutalize her. But in that state he did not frighten her. And this anger, which she had foreseen, she faced, now, looking straight into his eyes.

"The only thing that happened," she said, completely self-possessed, "was that first your absence, then my illness, created a void about me on the eve of deciding my future. I saw the abyss, and I drew back. My life appeared to me as though I were called upon to judge a woman who had lived that life. Another woman, not I. Well! Roger, I forbid you to bind your life to such a life. That woman was what she was, it is her business. But you, so loyal, so straightforward, so pure . . . she is not for you."

Roger listened, very pale, but without interrupting her. Unfortunately Albine's nerves snapped. She burst into tears. At the sight of them Roger's pitying heart softened. What he mumbled did not at all answer Albine's words; with one leap he crossed all the obstacles that she had accummulated. And already he was imploring:

"I love you such as life made you. Do not send me away."

He was bending over her, their hands were clasped. Then she understood that the sacrifice must be accomplished. She said, very near to him:

"Roger, you do not know what my life has been. It seems to me that I did not know it myself until this final examination of my conscience. You do not know all of it. You were told of lasting affairs, which were almost public. But there are others which cannot be called love . . . ah! . . . Roger, you are hurting my hands!"

He loosened the vise-like grip of his fingers:

"Be still," he said, "I forbid you. Do not drive me insane. If you go on, I do not know . . . I do not know what. . . ."

"Very well," she said. "Let us not talk of this any more. Besides, I have no more strength left. But let go of my hands. You hurt me!"

He obeyed. He sat down opposite her, on the other side of the empire stand. It was an armistice of a few moments, assented to by the exhaustion of both foes. Albine thought that she had had the upper-hand enough to attempt the last blow.

"There is something else," she continued, "which I understood while meditating alone. I had told you in all sincerity that I was willingly renouncing my present mode of life, everything constituting its luxury, its beauty. Well! face to face with myself, I questioned myself. I understood that now, truly, I was ready to leave my home, to forsake society, to lead a mediocre existence, but I did not feel insured against regrets which might come to me later. As a young girl, or a young woman, one can thus change a life hardly begun. But a woman going on fifty, like myself . . ."

Albine had pondered at length over these sentences; she thought that they would have an unmistakable effect on Roger's highly sensitive self-respect. Was it not he who, from the start, had put forth as a cause for break, her wealth, her luxury, her social life? She felt surprised at seeing that he had not moved from his chair. He was thinking. And suddenly, he said half audibly:

"All this is not true."

Albine made a gesture of protest; he insisted:

"No. It is not true. I mean that you are not giving me the real reasons. You have determined to thrust me aside. You, therefore, seek . . . try to have me be the one who revolts . . . who goes away. Well! do not bank on it. You see, I am irritated. I am somewhat disgusted, because I feel some lies between us. But I am very calm . . . determined not to let myself be duped. Albine, you are going to tell me what the real reason is. Tell it to me because if you don't, I will know it just the same; and there . . . I believe I do know it."

A cry escaped Albine.

"You know it? But there is nothing! There is no reason . . ."

Instinctively she withdrew her hands, still numb, because he had again come very close to her. But he was very calm as he spoke; a strange, ferocious calm, the calm of an executioner.

"Yes. I know the reason. And I have only to see you upset as you are . . . I was well informed . . ."

"It is not true! There is nothing! There is only what I told you, and nothing else."

But her very agitation seemed a clew, a proof, to Roger.

He went on:

"I was told . . . first about your past, of course. Everything which you wanted to tell me now . . . everything, yes, everything . . . even the questionable trip, while a young girl, with Henriquette Dupont . . . even the clandestine confinement abroad, a few weeks before the meeting with Anderny. You will tell me nothing new. I did not seek to verify this; I had promised you that I would not. Your life, before you knew me, belongs to you. But . . ."

He hesitated, and it was the anguish on Albine's face that decided him.

"I was told—Guilloux assured me—a thing which I never wanted to believe . . . that there is someone in your life *now*. Yes, a lover! a lover! a lover!

"Ah! . . . that, Roger! No! . . . No! . . . It is not true."

For the moment she forgot her studied air of deject-ment, of physical misery; she rose before Roger and it was she who seized his wrists. She was panting:

"Who lied to you? Who told you this infamous thing? I don't want you to believe it. Search my life. Ran-sack my papers. Nothing, you will find nothing like it. When I saw you again, my heart was empty . . . and I have thought of nothing else since but you, of becom-

ing what you like, in spite of your airs of anarchy and
independence; a good woman. Roger, no man ever
touched me since. I even refused to see again those . . .
those who thought they had the right, as well as the ones
who hoped. I shut my door to every one, you saw it! I
reduced my social life to the barest necessity. Say you
believe me!"

"It is evident," he said, after a short silence, "that you
do not lie, now. Well . . . go on! Since this is not
the cause of our separation, tell me the real one."

She drew back. The outburst of sincerity had upset
the structure of lies.

She mumbled:

"The reason? I told you. A man of your age, a
man like you can not marry me. And I, on the other
hand, cannot at my age alter my existence, renounce . . ."

She stopped short, understanding that her words did
not sink in, that they broke, like flimsy arrows against
an armor of mistrust. Two eyes, staring at her motion-
lessly, were piercing her through. She saw in them a
thing which they rarely held; irony.

She remained silent, her energy entirely spent.

"Well," said the foe calmly. "Be it so . . ."

She understood that he was scoffing. She felt the
wind of disaster.

"Be it so," he repeated. "After all, perhaps you are
right. Why should I be especially privileged, I who do
not even measure up to Bellinconi, to Moreuil—Verdy,
the crown prince, all the others. Be it so! To hell with
marriage! All the same I am good enough to become
their successor!"

At the step which he took towards her, she drew
back so sharply that she hit the empire stand and it top-

pled over; the books scattered over the rug. Across the barricade formed by the small stand, thrown on the floor, she said, putting out her arms;

"Never! Never!"

At the same time, she kept on backing towards the door; for, in her painful premeditation, she had also considered the assault, the defensive, the flight.

But with one leap the agile foe was already at her side, and his black-clad figure, narrow-waisted and broad-shouldered, barred the way.

"I beseech you!" she implored.

She felt both her elbows imprisoned, imprisoned in the same iron vise which a while ago had bruised her hands. But in the intense pain it inflicted upon her she perceived salvation; for this time again she read only hatred in the eyes of her torturer. Face to face, he said to her:

"People were right. You are some sort of a monster. You made a fool of me. You cast a horrible spell on me only to drive me to despair afterwards. Really . . . there is no trying to understand you. You are simply a monster. And I think I am going to kill you."

She tried, with all her might, to free herself from the vise which gripped her. He reduced her to immobility, and they continued talking, without gestures, noiselessly, face to face, in bits of broken words.

"Do not kill me, Roger! For your sake . . . your sake . . ."

"Are you afraid?"

"Not for myself . . . for you. You can not . . . your life, afterwards, would be too horrible."

He answered, so close to her, that she felt the fire of his breath:

"Do you for a moment imagine that I would go on living?"

The shock of this sentence upon Albine's nerves was

so violent that she found the strength to free herself.

"You mean to say? You mean to say that you . . . that you would kill yourself?"

His reply fell, so careless that no clamor on earth could have been more tragic:

"Why, Albine! You know it very well!"

A second . . . this woman, languid, apathetic a moment ago, but now energetic—and now it is he who is overpowered, imprisoned in two arms strong with passion. He is going to resist, but his resistance suddenly breaks because Albine's burning cheek is against his; for the first time he feels Albine's lips on his temples, his hair, and there are kisses mingled with the words words she mumbles:

"No . . . I don't want you to . . . Roger . . . say you will not do this horrible thing! Answer! Why don't you answer me!"

And now that he has dropped into Albine's armchair, he sinks into a strange feeling of peace, as though the ominous fate weighing upon them had suddenly vanished. Never before had Albine held him in her arms, and now her arms are tightly clasped around his neck. Never before had he felt the touch of her lips, and now she devours him with kisses. What unexpected peace this embrace, these caresses bring him! He says, weak and beaten:

"Albine . . . How you speak to me! Never before did you hold me to you so. . . . Never before did you speak to me so. . . ."

It is she who, now, has recovered her strength, she who holds him, who restrains him. She fears him no longer.

"Do not ask anything! Give yourself up to peace! Let me heal you! Oh! you are crying, my little boy!" . . .

And now he is sobbing softly, beaten, overpowered. She rocks him. He does not know the secret of this profound accord, this absolute intimacy which established itself between them from their very first contact. But she who conceived him, who bore him in her womb and fed him with her blood, she does not wonder. No, it is not a poet's invention, it is the strongest of realities, this unity, divided but lasting, of two beings who were but one from conception till birth. What could be more logical, more consistent with nature than the submission of the flesh to it, than the deep wave surging from the bottom of the ages which breaks, in a similar case, the fugitive undercurrent of desire? Eternal humanity has always had this intuition. Instinctively, this child submits to it and, as soon as he has done so, he regains his balance. His relieved brain becomes more lucid. He does not understand yet; how could he? But he has dimly seen the light and he strains towards it. He feels confusedly that Albine possesses this light. He guesses, he is certain, by the way Albine embraces, clasps, calms and consoles him now, that she knows about him things which he himself does not know. Where did she acquire this knowledge during his few days' absence? A name rings through his memory.

He whispers:

"Hobson came to Paris."

And his eyes question Albine. Ah! hers no longer lie. They offer to his uncertain, troubled stare, resigned submission, the resolution to be truthful. Roger repeats:

"Hobson came to Paris?"

She inclines her head.

"You saw him?"

"Yes."

She puts her hands on his burning brow. She caresses him. She murmurs:

"Do not wear yourself out with seeking. I will tell you the entire, absolute truth."

He hardly listens to her. He follows his thought:

"That trip abroad . . . Guilloux told me . . ."

Albine implores him.

"I will tell you . . . I promise it . . . for the moment, calm yourself."

Unfortunate woman! The blood flows back to her heart, leaving her cheeks as white as a ghost. Roger, who has freed himself, looks at her and thinks, in spite of himself: "Oh! . . . now she shows her age." Like an electric current escaping when the switch is turned off, her luminous youth has vanished. . . .

They no longer speak, but their eyes remain fastened to each other. As much as she desired a while ago to defend her secret, she now wishes that words be spared her. She follows the progress of understanding in Roger's stare. She whispers:

"Hobson . . . I did not know it . . . knew me as a young girl . . . at South Croydon . . . during that trip . . . that trip in England."

She wants to clasp him, hold him again as she did just now, but she no longer dares. Yet this anguish between them cannot last: Albine feels that no human brain could withstand it; Roger has backed away, and, with the gesture of a hallucinated sufferer, he puts his hands to the bulging arteries of his temples. He staggers, as though he were going to crumple down. Ah! let her be lost, but let him be rescued! She is at his feet, she rolls her head against her victim's knees, her anxious hands touch him, clasp him; her words come, mad, breathless:

"Do not seek. Do not beat your head against the obstacle. I will tell you everything. Afterward, you will drive me away. I don't even ask you to forgive

me . . . I will disappear . . . I promise you . . . Tell
me that you will not despise me, my little boy . . . my
little child!"

And then . . . silence.

Two pitiful shreds of humanity become united; clinging to each other, they feel that if they were to separate,
their lives would immediately come to an end. No more
words of questioning, of explanation. He no longer
wants to speak or hear any. He does not know how
truth came to him. But he does know the truth. And,
in the complete downfall, this truth seems to him almost
kindly, at any rate beneficial. A moment ago he thought
that his life no longer had any purpose . . . well . . .
now . . . it has one. It is he now, who clasps
the wretched creature crouching at his feet; they mingle
the shy awkwardness of their embraces. . . . They
recognize each other, like people buried in a landslip trying to find each other.

She repeats obstinately:

"My little boy! . . . My little boy! . . ."

And as he too succumbs to the impulse of his whole
being, as he instinctively is going to utter the eternal
word, the appeal which all over the world the lips of the
son cry out to the mother, Albine, convulsed, puts her
hands over the burning mouth, silencing the feeble
articulation, the faint echo of the syllables, saying:

"Wait!"

EPILOGUE

The road leading from Bastia to the point of Cape Corse circles the winding coast, parallel with the sea, at times overlooking it. The villages crossed by this road are grouped in shallow valleys, faintly outlining the cliffs, and in spots bend down until they reach the little fishing ports called *'marines'* by the natives.

The highest peaks of this beautiful road are of course situated near the necks that join the eastern coast of the Cape with the western. Near Sassorosso the panorama stretches north to the French sea, east to the Tuscan sea, while west is a large, deep valley studded with a score of villages. The biggest of these villages, Valetta, gives its name to the valley.

A fairly good path, accessible to carriage, joins Valetta to the hamlet of Maorta, close to Sassorosso. Maorta is known for its Bernardine Convent, dating back to the XVIIIth century. The building looks like a huge barrack. The chapel, built at the time of the Empire in front of a clearing between the banks of the coast, opens on the most magnificent vista of the Italian ocean. About twenty nuns live in the convent. The laws of their order are lenient. They are not rigorously cloistered. Their mission being chiefly charity and education, they were able to cross without difficulty the period of secularization. From the valley of Valetta a few pupils of the best families come to them. They help the little neighboring communities when the harvest is poor and the peasants are in need. And because of their very isolation they enjoy a great deal of freedom.

It was in the chapel of Maorta that once upon a time, at that typically feminine season between summer and autumn, Berthe Lorande and the Countess Anderny, returning from a cruise in the Mediterranean had felt their hearts vibrate at the sight of two motionless nuns, absorbed in prayer before the Holy Sacrament, unveiled. On leaving the chapel, they spoke of their emotion. Their words were not swept into oblivion by the *libeccio* sea wind which had blown so violently all day.

Two and a half years had passed since the end of the world war.

The frenzied crisis which had shaken the whole world was subsiding everywhere, made itself felt only spasmodically; as after a fire in a powder mill here and there a cartridge explodes occasionally. Not that the desire to move, to be noisy, to feast and revel, had died out in this harassed generation; but something gloomy, dejected, an epidemic of renunciation was spreading little by little . . . and people once more began "waiting for the end," as they had waited during the war.

Only this time the end of what? They did not even know. And this is what gave to that tense expectancy the appearance of a neurasthenic nightmare.

However here and there society was readjusting itself as well as it could. Among the actors of the frenzied period some fell naturally once more into the routine of things. Maurice de Guilloux married the rich foreign heiress, long coveted, finally captured. Jean de Trévoux was winning his Captain's stripes at Ain-Tab. Albert Saulnois was lecturing beneath the cupola

of the Sorbonne. The Grand-Duchess Hilda was rein-
stated in Finsburg where her husband, incensed by the
latest scandal, was confining her permanently. As for
the shipwrecked of this storm, they had slowly joined
that obscure category doomed to be forgotten in war as
in peace: the vanished. Who still spoke of Camille
Englemann's discreet suicide? Very seldom one heard
the name of Berthe Lorande whose books were no longer
displayed in shop windows, who had ceased writing,
whom no one ever saw. And no one was concerned
with those others who had disappeared, Roger
Vaugrenier, Albine Anderny. In the anguish of the
morrow no one worried about the yesterday. It was
all one could do to defend one's own day, one's own
morrow. Selfishness lulled in each individual not only
peace but memory as well.

In May 1921, on a hot afternoon when the wind itself
seemed asleep, exhausted, a decrepit, open carriage
dragged by two mules and driven by a small, shriveled,
dark-skinned coachman was climbing through the brush-
wood up the road from Sassorosso to the convent of
Maorta. Albine and her son were in the carriage. Albine had kept the perfect beauty of her features beneath her white hair; the wrinkles under her eyes alone
bespoke her age. Roger's hair was completely gray
above his ravaged face.

They were coming from Valetta where they had settled seven months previously. Albine, with the re-
mainder of her fortune liquidated according to her son's
wishes, had bought there a moderately-sized house with
some grounds. Roger practiced his profession, and
while tending to his patients went on with his research
work.

They reached the convent a few minutes before four

o'clock. They were ushered into the parlor. They had announced their visit beforehand; Sister Monica, who used to be Berthe Lorande, had received permission to see them. They did not have to wait for her. As soon as they caught sight of her, a white figure which the polished parquet floor reflected as though she were walking on dark waters, they had the same thought: "She has not changed!" It was indeed, the old Berthe Lorande, dressed as a nun. Time no more than events had left any traces of age on her face. Yet the disappearance of the red halo of her hair, concealed beneath the veil and headband, had changed her completely.

If once upon a time, at the height of the crisis which shook them at the same moment, these two women had pictured a similar meeting, in a similar spot, after the catastrophe, they would have imagined it as something romantic, poignant, brilliant. Nothing could have been quieter nor in a way, more bourgeois; a country doctor living with his mother in a lost corner of the island, was paying a visit to one of their friends who had taken the veil; that was all.

It was not that Berthe's natural vivacity had disappeared; she remained eloquent as in former days, with an additional tendency toward babbling and laughter without cause, habits probably contracted in the company of her innocent comrades. But what surprised the two visitors was that Sister Monica gave the impression of complete forgetfulness, a real case of amnesia, concerning the events that had preceded her taking the veil. It was so obviously sincere and spontaneous that no allusion to that past could rise to the lips of the two visitors. "The witchery of the cloister has succeeded," they thought. However, with all the fire of former days Sister Monica was depicting convent life, the waking at nights for prayer, the fasting, the mortifications, the lengthy prayers.

"Ah!" she exclaimed, entranced, "to put all this into glowing words! I tried . . . but when Father Bonarmi, our chaplain, read my literary attempts he tore them up and forbade me to write another line."

And this confession, begun emotionally, ended in a gust of laughter.

But suddenly mother and son noticed that Berthe, having forgotten her own past, remembered that of others. Grown serious, she asked:

"And you?"

Albine and Roger exchanged a glance. Roger said:

"We came to seek peace in this mountain hollow where we live now. And it seems to us that we have found it."

He said no more; Albine remained silent. Berthe understood that like herself neither son nor mother wished to reopen the door which had closed on their past. Besides at that very moment other nuns entered the reception room; the Superior, Mother Sainte-Fine, two Italian novices, a Belgian refugee.

They had come not altogether devoid of curiosity to greet the visitors. They praised enthusiastically Sister Monica, her piety, her ardor, her endurance, her cheery kindliness:

"She has renewed the spirit of penitence within us," said Mother Sainte-Fine.

Sister Monica was smiling the same charming, modest smile of years ago, when they praised her novels.

At sunset the old coach returned towards Sassorosso. Mother and son were thinking. Perhaps they were comparing the bleak austerity of their joint lives where the guilty and the innocent were atoning together for the past to the ardent, impassioned penitence of Sister Monica, similar to the one which Don Juan Tenorio accomplished, so they say, in a Toledo cloister, enlightening the other monks by his saintliness.

"Roger?" murmured Albine.

"Mother?"

"Look at the crimson reflection of the setting sun on the chapel."

The mules were slowly walking up a short slope that cut across the downward path. The empire chapel appeared as though bathed in a pink glow, its stained glass windows ablaze. A reflection, perhaps, of this fire of heavenly love, that burned in the soul of the new convert, who, in that dull Corsican convent, always unsatiated, was striving to reach to God.

www.ingramcontent.com/pod-product-compliance
Lightning Source LLC
Chambersburg PA
CBHW030938260626
47169CB00002B/526